ACCOLADES

Ellen Mansoor Collier is back with her latest Jazz Age Mystery featuring Jasmine Cross.and it was superb. A fantastic and delightful read from page one until the very last page. I couldn't put VAMPS down, which is not surprising as I have loved the other books in this series. I love the characters and the trouble that they get themselves into. Nothing is ever simple for Jazz Cross and her friends and that is what makes this series so great. Set in 1920's in Galveston, Texas, this book is rich in historical detail and humor. I always find myself laughing at Jazz's antics and admire her gumption and determination to put wrongdoers to task.

I love this Jazz Age series because it is unique and different from other historical mysteries. This series is fun and sassy and always has me on my toes. If you haven't discovered this brilliant series, then you are missing out on a fun read. I simply cannot get enough. If you want a heroine who is smart, funny, and sassy, Jazz Cross is the one for you. I loved the ending to this book and it bodes well for the future of the series.
—*Kimberlee, "Girl Lost in a Book" Blog (2015)*

Jasmine Cross is back in all her feisty independence. Once again, Ellen Mansoor Collier does a great job of putting us in the Roaring 20's where we experience Vaudeville, Prohibition, fashion, and Galveston. If you're ever accused of murder, you want Jazz on your side! You'll find mystery, intrigue, and a lot of fun in VAMPS.
—*Amy Metz, A Blue Million Books Blog (2015)*
Author of the Goose Pimple Junction mystery series

I love this period in history and the storylines that Ellen Collier comes up with. Sammy finds himself in all sorts of situations and has to use his wits to get out of them. I love how Jazz stands up to some of the reporters in her office and doesn't sit back and just do the fluffy articles but really wants to be taken seriously as a reporter.

VAMPS was so captivating I couldn't put it down for one second! I really was looking forward to what happens next!
—*Paula Mitchell, Community Bookstop Blog (2015)*
(VAMPS named Book of The Month for August & September)

ACCOLADES

I discovered Ellen Mansoor Collier's Jazz Age Mystery series while doing historical research, and I feel like I struck gold, babies! GOLD! Collier's smart and classy writing style keeps the familiar cadence of a "whodunit" novel or film noir feature. With all the moxie of Lois Lane, Jasmine Cross is the kind of strong female character you will find yourself rooting for.

FLAPPERS is full of rich historical detail and colorful 1920s slang true to the era. Galveston, the "Ellis Island of the West," jumps off the pages. A fun and entertaining mystery drives the story along, but it was the story world that really won me over. Every aspect is fully realized and I couldn't have asked for better world-building. Hardcore History and Mystery Lovers alike will fall head over heels for this series, and readers will be enlightened and entertained.   *—Regina Vitola Mader, ME ReadALOT Blog (2015).*

Bathing Beauties' exciting and glamorous setting is hugely beneficial for this colourful and enjoyable novel.... With all its fun, chemistry, authenticity, plotting and ease in style and slang, this is very recommendable.
—ChristophFischerBooks.com (U.K., 2014), Top 500 Amazon Reviewer

I was totally taken with **Bathing Beauties**, the second in the Jazz Age series following the spunky, intrepid flapper-reporter, Jazz Cross. Collier combines historical trivia with a cozy mystery beautifully, and I'm falling in love with her 1920s Galveston. Jazz is wonderfully empathetic in a way that felt authentic, not modern. (She passes my I-want-her-to-be-my-friend test!) It was the perfect mix of historical detail and zippy plot to keep me happy... *Bathing Beauties* captures the dangerous allure of glamour, fame and easy fortune. *—Audra Friend, Unabridged Chick Blog (2013)*

GOLD DIGGERS is so much fun it should be illegal.
—Noreen Marcus, freelance reporter and editor (2014)

I loved this. Quite simply, it's a lady's version of the show *Boardwalk Empire*. GOLD DIGGERS is full of mobsters, shady deals and dirty policemen, and you never fully know who's trustworthy. Jazz is feisty, fearless and doesn't give a jot what the chauvinistic men around her think. She's great!

The author really seems to know her stuff, gently weaving in details without overwhelming or confusing an uninformed reader. The characters all have plenty of 'moxie' and are well thought-out and likeable. There's a constant sense of mystery that keeps you turning the pages, with a pace that's spot-on. *—Charlotte Foreman, BestChickLit.com Blog (U.K., 2014)*

VAMPS, VILLAINS AND VAUDEVILLE

A Jazz Age Mystery (#4)

Ellen Mansoor Collier

Text Copyright © 2016 by Ellen Mansoor Collier

Cover Design: Ellen Mansoor Collier
Copyright ©2015 (Ellen Mansoor Collier)

Interior Page Design: Ellen Mansoor Collier and Gary E. Collier

Cover Artwork: Vintage Photographs (c. 1920s)

Illustrated Cover: George Barbier "Pantomime Stage" (c. 1924)

DECODAME PRESS

All rights reserved. Published in the United States by DecoDame Press
www.flapperfinds.com

ISBN: 978-0-9894170-8-2

Second Edition

The text of this book is Garamond 12-point

CONTENTS

Enjoy the Complete Jazz Age Series by Ellen Mansoor Collier:

FLAPPERS, FLASKS And FOUL PLAY
A Jazz Age Mystery #1 (2012)

BATHING BEAUTIES, BOOZE And BULLETS
A Jazz Age Mystery #2 (2013)

GOLD DIGGERS, GAMBLERS And GUNS
A Jazz Age Mystery #3 (2014)

PREFACE

By: Ellen Mansoor Collier

Before Las Vegas, Galveston, Texas reigned as the "Sin City of the Southwest"—a magnet for vamps, villains and vice. Inspired by real people and places, the Jazz Age Mystery series is set during Prohibition in 1927 Galveston, where businessmen rubbed elbows with bootleggers and real-life rival gangs ruled the Island with greed and graft. **VAMPS, VILLAINS AND VAUDEVILLE** incorporates a fictitious vaudeville troupe with actual Galveston gangsters to create a make-believe series of events and murders.

Starting in the 1880s, vaudeville remained popular for decades, originating as a burlesque show and evolving into more of a variety show with animals acts, comedy routines and different types of entertainment, much like the traveling carnivals of that time.

With the advent of the movies, and especially the talkies in 1927, vaudeville quickly fell out of favor and by 1932, had all but disappeared. **VAMPS, VILLAINS AND VAUDEVILLE** attempts to capture the fading glory days of traveling vaudeville shows and describes a fictitious director's desperate efforts to keep the production alive.

During Prohibition, the Beach and Downtown gangs fought constant turf wars for control over booze, gambling, slot machines, clubs and prostitution. To keep the peace, the gangs tried to compromise by dividing the Island into two halves: Bootleggers Ollie Quinn and Dutch Voight headed the Beach Gang, south of Broadway and on the Seawall, along with the notorious Maceo brothers, Big Sam and Papa Rose.

Colorful crime boss Johnny Jack Nounes ran the Downtown Gang, the area north of Broadway, and partnered with a dangerous Syrian thug, George Musey. According to Gary Cartwright's book **GALVESTON**, second-hand man George Musey only had one arm, and **VAMPS** fabricates a possible scenario in which Musey loses his right arm. I've only seen one actual photo of Musey—with both arms intact—so the accident may have happened in the late 1920s-30s.

The infamous but long-gone Hollywood Dinner Club on 61st Street was located in the Beach Gang's territory, near West Beach. Mario's Italian restaurant is an invented Downtown Gang headquarters off Broadway, not connected to the current pizza place in Galveston. However, Martini Theatre (the current location was built in 1937) and most places mentioned in the novel are actual locales still in existence.

Originally from Sicily, the Maceo brothers, Rosario and Sam (Papa Rose and Big Sam), immigrated to Louisiana with their family in 1901. After moving to Galveston, they eventually took control of the Island, known as the "Free State of Galveston" for its vice and laissez-faire attitude, for roughly 25 years, from late 1927 on until their deaths. The Maceo empire faded when Sam Maceo died in 1951 of cancer, and Rose Maceo passed on due to heart disease in 1954.

VAMPS, VILLAINS AND VAUDEVILLE is loosely based on real and fabricated events leading to the Maceos' gradual take-over of both gangs in the late 1920s and early 1930s. The vaudeville troupe storyline was my own creation, not based on actual events.

The *Galveston Gazette* is a fictitious newspaper but the headlines in the novel are based on actual stories that appeared in national newspapers and *The Galveston Daily News,* the first and oldest newspaper in Texas, founded in 1842 and still in publication. Since many of the gangland crimes and activities went largely unreported and/or under-reported, the main characters and circumstances in the novel are invented and not intended to malign or distort actual persons, places or cases, but are purely the author's imagined version of possible events.

CHAPTER ONE

Friday

"Please take your seats. The Villains, Vixens and Varmints Vaudeville Show is about to begin." The master of ceremonies' mellifluous voice boomed across Martini Theatre, and lights dimmed as a uniformed usher escorted us to our front-row seats.

Disoriented, I tried not to trip in the dark while the orchestra broke into a classic overture. Agent James Burton and I squeezed in the cramped seats, our elbows and knees bumping, his long legs stretched out in front. Always a gentleman, he rarely took my hand in public though we'd dated steadily for four months now.

You'd think I still lived in my old University of Texas dorm with its strict code of conduct: No ODA—over-display of affection.

To ward off the nippy November air, I'd gotten decked out in a black burnt-velvet frock and a snug velvet cloche with a rhinestone hat pin. The society editor—my boss, Mrs. Harper—had snagged two front-and-center seats to Friday night's opening performance. No doubt the traveling troupe expected the *Galveston Gazette* (rather, me) to give them a rave review.

Well, we'd see if this dog-and-pony show lived up to its billing, literally. The MC gave a short introduction and a chubby clown paraded onstage with a spotted pony, a small terrier-mix perched atop its back. When the clown tried to coax the pup to stand on its hind legs, the spunky mutt refused to cooperate, while the audience laughed with glee.

Next Farmer Brown came onstage with Polly, a "talking pig" that oinked and grunted to *Old McDonald*. Luckily the pig drowned out Burton's groans of, "You call this entertainment?"

"Relax and enjoy the show. You've got to admit, it's funny."

"I'd rather catch crooks than endure this nonsense."

"Hogwash! Personally, I think the pig is cute." I felt sorry for the poor farmer who beamed proudly at his porky pig. "You do your job, and I'll do mine."

Burton could be so stubborn and yes, pig-headed at times.

After the animal acts came a beautiful ballerina, a French mime, a boyish barbershop quartet, and a short scene from Gilbert and Sullivan's *H. M. S. Pinafore*. A chorus line of long-limbed hoofers clad in sparkly sequined tap pants and tops danced to lively Cole Porter tunes, reminding me of the bathing beauties.

When Vera, a burlesque dancer, appeared in a Gay '90s costume and feather boa, Burton perked up, saying, "This is more like it!"

"Hush!" I nudged him.

Fortunately she only strutted around the stage twirling her boa, not disrobing, while the men clapped and whistled. What a relief! Overall, the performers seemed more polished than the local yokels who competed in talent shows, hoping to be the next Fanny Brice, Buster Keaton or Theda Bara.

Still, I couldn't concentrate, I was so excited about going to Houston on Saturday. My best friend Amanda and I planned our first weekend visit there since my half-brother Sammy had relocated to Houston. Our pal Nathan agreed to chauffeur us in his Model T because he couldn't wait to see his "Miss Houston" bathing beauty, Holly. Could they rekindle their summer romance?

I'd tried to beg off this assignment to prepare for our trip, but my boss always found a way to make me work until the last minute.

"Vaudeville is so old hat," I protested. "Wouldn't *you* rather attend? It's right up your alley."

"What do you mean by that, young lady?" Mrs. Harper eyed me under her wide-brimmed floral Edwardian bonnet. "Are you implying that I'm an old-fashioned fuddy-duddy, not as modern as you young flappers?"

Yes, that's exactly what I meant. "Not at all. I thought you'd enjoy the show more since I prefer moving pictures. I can't wait to see *The Jazz Singer!*"

"Hold your horses, Jasmine. After you write your review, then you can go on your jaunt to Houston. You need to turn it in to the copy desk by morning." She softened her tone. "Take your young man and have a good time. I think you'll be pleasantly surprised."

My young man? She made Burton sound like a pet Scottie. Sure, I was sweet on him, despite my mixed feelings: Did I really want to date a Federal officer with such a dangerous occupation? As the lone Prohibition agent in the "Free State of Galveston"—where mobsters mingled with police and politicians—I worried his days might be numbered. The Treasury Department could ship Burton off to a new town on an even riskier assignment. Worse, Galveston gangsters could gun him down any moment, just for doing his job.

During intermission, the MC announced a last-minute replacement for Dick Dastardly in the final act. So far, the routines seemed accomplished yet rather outdated, a point I'd make in my review. No need to be rude or demeaning, but a little constructive criticism never hurt, right?

"Now we can make our escape," Burton half-joked.

"The show's almost over. Besides, I can't give my honest opinion without seeing the whole production. What kind of critic would I be?"

"A happy one?"

After the break, Burton stayed seated, stoically suffering through two corny comedy acts. He sat up after a sword-swallower appeared, and applauded a knife thrower who narrowly missed his victim, a beautiful showgirl in a silky gown. I yelped when he aimed an arrow at his brave target—and struck an apple on her head.

"These are my type of acts," Burton said with a grin, while I clutched his arm, trembling.

Next "Milo the Magician" took the stage, elegant in a tux, top hat and white gloves, and performed his requisite card tricks and rabbit in the hat act. Millie, his pretty redheaded assistant, flitted around in satin tap pants and top, diverting the audience's attention.

I cringed when Milo sawed his willing sidekick in two halves while Millie smiled sweetly at the audience. Then he made her disappear in a large painted box—and reappear again in a gypsy outfit. Voila'!

Last but not least, Milo invited a volunteer to participate while he distracted the audience with his sleight-of-hand, deftly stealing the man's wristwatch. "Do you have the time?" Milo asked the flustered fella, who fumbled for his missing watch. The crowd gasped in astonishment when Milo pulled it out of his top hat.

The final act highlighted a short scene from *The Perils of Pauline*, featuring a dastardly villain wearing a black mask and cape trying to kidnap helpless, hapless Pauline. Twirling his handlebar moustache, the evil masked man tied poor Pauline to a tree while the Tom Mix character managed to chase off the villain, and rescue his beloved damsel-in-distress. Yes, the act was so corny and hammy that it was comical, but I enjoyed the melodrama of it all.

I knew Amanda, an aspiring actress, would love the show. Too bad the troupe stayed in town for only a week.

After the show, the performers gathered on stage, and as each act stepped forward to take their separate bows, the applause grew louder. When the *Perils of Pauline* actors appeared, the audience stood up, clapping wildly and cheering as the performers grinned and waved. Seems I was wrong about vaudeville: The appreciative audience gave all the actors a standing ovation.

Strange, I noticed the villain smiling at me from his vantage point onstage—or was he? Surely I imagined it...until he took off his top hat and held it out to me like a rose, or a bribe. Then he gave me a bold wink—right in front of Agent Burton. Blushing, I did a double-take: Was the villain *flirting* with me? Or did he know I worked for the *Gazette*?

"Looks like the mystery man has his eye on you," Burton teased. "Should I be jealous?"

"Dick Dastardly?" I laughed it off. "He must want a mention in the *Gazette*. You know actors and their egos."

"No, I don't. Do you?"

"Only Amanda." My best pal reminded me of a bottle of Champagne: sparkly, bubbly and ready to pop. "Say, we need to shake a leg. I have to write my review tonight, and start packing. Why not come to Houston with us?"

"Some other time. Give my regards to Sammy. I don't want word to get out that I'm consorting with criminals."

"You're a riot." I knew he meant it as a joke—sort of. Sammy, my black-sheep half-brother, owned the Oasis speakeasy on the Downtown Gang's turf, and their rivalry with the Beach Gang provided a constant source of trouble and turmoil.

As we left, I glanced at the stage and saw the villain watching us, his arms crossed, looking puzzled.

What did he expect—an interview? A bouquet of flowers? My phone number?

"What are you going to do in Houston?" Burton asked during the drive to my aunt Eva's boarding house.

"See the sights, visit Sammy, go to his new bar...excuse me, restaurant."

"What sights? A bunch of oil wells and cows? I hear Houston is a cesspool," Burton cracked.

"Why were you so eager to take Sammy there?"

"We needed to make a quick get-away. And it's not exactly a resort so I thought he'd be safe. Only wildcatters and wild women show their mugs in Houston. Not worth a trip for local lawmen." He snorted. "I doubt the water is even clean enough to drink. Full of germs and gunk, like oil and chemicals."

"Gee, thanks," I pouted, sinking in my seat. "Now I'm really excited to visit Sammy."

"Sorry, Jazz, I'm just razzing you. Guess it's my way of trying to talk you out of going."

"You had me fooled, mister. Glad to know you care." At the boarding house, we lingered on the porch, enjoying the crisp fall air. "I wish you'd take the weekend off and come with us." I smiled and squeezed his arm. "You can stay with Sammy or share a hotel room with Nathan."

"They're not my first choice of a roommate..." He gave me a wink. "Sorry, Jazz. Weekends are my busiest time. That's when all the rats and racketeers come out at night."

Despite the gangs' control, Burton still believed he could make a difference in Galveston. I admired his conviction, his willingness to confront local mobsters and bootleggers. Since he knew he couldn't single-handedly stop the constant flow of alcohol, at least he wanted to create a few detours.

We sat on the porch swing, saying our good-nights. But before he could even give me a peck on the cheek, my aunt Eva rushed out, exclaiming, "Jazz, you've got a telephone call. The same fella who called ten minutes ago."

"What fella?" I asked Eva. "Nathan?"

"He wouldn't give his name, just said it's important."

My heart skipped a beat as I raced to the phone.

"Jasmine? It's Frank. We've had some trouble here and we can't reach Sammy."

"What's wrong?" I held my breath. Frank and Dino had run the Oasis ever since Sammy escaped to Houston, and they'd never once called me, though I stopped in each week to check on the bar.

"It's an emergency. Can you come by right away?"

I heard panic in his voice.

"What kind of emergency? Is anyone hurt?"

"I'd rather not say over the phone."

"I can ask Agent Burton to drive me—he's here now."

"Sure, as long as he keeps his mouth shut."

"Shut about what?" My hand gripped the candlestick phone.

The line went dead.

CHAPTER TWO

"Frank said there's an emergency at the Oasis!" I rushed over to Eva and Burton, waiting in the hall. "We've got to go there. Now."

"What else did he say?" Burton frowned.

"He didn't explain. Can you drive me?"

"Ready when you are."

"Please be careful." Eva turned to me. "Before you go, Jazz, don't you have work to do?"

"My review can wait." I sighed, worried about my deadline *and* my trip to Houston. "Don't stay up. May be a long night." I raced out the door with Burton, telling him what little I knew. "Frank sounded panicked, said he couldn't reach Sammy. He's never called me before so it must be serious."

"Does he know I'm coming?" Burton asked.

"He said it's fine as long as you don't spill the beans."

At the Oasis, the door opened automatically. What, no password? Frank motioned us inside, his face dripping with sweat despite the cool fall climate. He bolted the heavy wooden door behind us, hands shaking. What was wrong? Cigarette smoke mingled with a sweet smell I think was marijuana or hashish—not that I had any experience with the stuff. Reefer madness failed to reel me into its clutches.

Frank sat down on Dino's usual bar stool as if to steady himself. "Thanks for coming."

"Where's Dino?" I looked around for the baby grand.

"He's out back." Frank swallowed, then studied Burton. "I know you're a good egg and all, so I hope you don't blab to your cop buddies. Believe me, we had nothing to do with this mess."

Burton crossed his arms. "What happened?"

A knock sounded on the door, and Frank slid open the slot. "We're closed for the night. Come back tomorrow." Since when did he turn away business on a Friday night?

"I'll make it quick." Frank started rubbing his hands back and forth on his pants, a nervous habit. "Two jokers had a few drinks, and started shouting and shoving each other. I called Dino and asked him to break up the fight. 'Take it outside,' he told them, but they didn't listen. So he grabbed each one by the collar and gave them the bum's rush out the back door."

"Were the Beach and Downtown gangs fighting again?" A familiar scenario.

Frank shook his head. "No one I recognized."

"Sounds like you took care of them." Burton raised his brows. "So what's the matter?"

"I'd better show you." Frank stood up unsteadily, and held onto my arm as we walked upstairs. Outside, the November night felt chilly, and I wrapped my velvet coat tighter. A half-moon cast a pale light on the narrow alley.

My breath caught when I saw Dino leaning over a figure sprawled at an awkward angle. Oh no.

I held back, not wanting to believe anything was wrong, especially with Sammy so far away in Houston.

Slowly I edged closer and stopped, staring in shock: A handsome young man lay in the alley, clutching his stomach and gasping for breath, dark blood staining his shirt and trousers. His delicate features looked ghostly, even angelic, in the faint moonlight.

"What were you saps thinking, leaving a man half-dead behind your bar?" Burton demanded. "For God's sakes, why didn't you call an ambulance?"

I wanted to reach out and comfort the poor fella, ease his suffering. "How is he?"

"Barely alive." Burton knelt by the victim and examined his wound. "Seems he was stabbed in the abdomen and lost a lot of blood. Any idea who did this?"

"Beats me," Dino said. Frank looked around, as if lost.

"Where's the knife?" Burton asked. They both shrugged in reply. "What were you going to do, let him bleed out in the alley? We're taking him to the hospital." He searched the victim for ID, patting down his pockets.

"I'll carry the guy, but that's as far as I go," Dino grumbled. "Count me out."

"What a sport," Burton snapped. "Can you bring a blanket to cover him up? His body's getting cold. Besides, there's a lady present."

"Don't worry about me. Just help him." I stood there, transfixed, studying the stranger's face in the faint light.

"I'll drive," Frank offered. "My car is parked here in the alley. It's the least I can do."

"I'll say." Burton frowned. "I'll follow behind."

Dino returned, holding out a blanket like a dirty diaper. Down the alley, a door opened and a cook came out with a trash bag, stopping to stare with obvious interest. I grabbed the blanket from Dino, shaking it like a matador, to block the view. Finally he retreated to his bar. What a Nosy Ned!

"You have no idea who he is or what he was doing here?" Burton repeated as he attempted to pick up the victim, waiting for Frank and Dino to help.

"We didn't exactly exchange pleasantries before Dino gave them the boot," Frank said. "Friday nights are always full. Pay day, you know." As usual, Dino remained mute.

I spread out the blanket on the back seat, glad that Frank didn't care about appearances or even ruining his car. Or did he? Sammy might think twice before he risked getting his pricey Roadster bloody, even to save a life.

Reluctantly, Dino lifted the man under his arms, Frank held his middle and Burton picked up his legs. Slowly the trio carried him out to Frank's car while I held the door open. "Careful," Burton warned. "Let's sit him up so he won't lose any more blood."

Drops of blood left a trail of bright red splotches in the alley. "You'll need to wash that off right away." I cringed. "Don't make Buzz clean it up."

"Why don't you do it?" Dino scowled at me.

"Fix your own mess." I glared right back.

After they placed the victim upright in the car, I tucked the blanket around him, careful not to touch his open wound. "I'm coming, too," I said, my eyes misting.

"You don't need to go," Frank said. "I can take care of things." His voice was husky with emotion.

"Look what happened last time," I reminded Frank. "I never saw Horace again."

Burton patted the seat by him. "You can ride with me."

I stuck my head in Frank's car to make sure the victim was still breathing. Suddenly his hand shot out, clasping my wrist, blue eyes popping open for a brief moment.

"Viola," he whispered before drifting off. "Viola."

CHAPTER THREE

"Viola?" I squeezed the young man's arm. "Who's Viola?" Did he mistake me for her? But he'd already slumped over in the back seat, apparently unconscious.

I shook Burton's shoulder. "Did you hear? The guy said 'Viola' before he passed out. Think it's his girlfriend? He's not wearing a wedding ring, so I doubt he's married."

"Viola? Who knows? At least it gives us a lead." Burton started the car as I got in, not bothering to open the door for me, signaling for Frank to go ahead. "What else did those knuckleheads tell you, if anything?"

"Not much. Frank said the victim got into an argument with a fella so Dino kicked them out. Maybe Buzz or Bernie saw what happened. Want me to ask?"

"Later, after I file a report. Let's see if this poor sap even makes it to the hospital."

I sucked in my breath. "Was it that bad?"

"I'm no doctor, but he's lost a lot of blood. His youth could be his saving grace."

"I hope so. What if he dies?" I voiced my worst fears. "Will you have to involve Dino or Frank—or Sammy?"

"Depends. The cops need to investigate either way." Burton slowed to a stop in front of John Sealy Hospital. "Sorry, Jazz, I'm afraid you'll have to cancel your trip to Houston."

Peachy. How would I tell Sammy? Or break the news to Amanda? One more lousy problem, one more helpless victim to rescue. Of course I felt for the fella, but why'd this happen now?

Burton raced into the hospital entrance. "We need a stretcher. Hurry, it's an emergency!"

Two orderlies followed Burton outside to Frank's car and gently placed the man on the stretcher and took him in. Frank waited two whole minutes before he raced off, tires squealing.

As the orderlies carried the dying man out of the room, a stout nurse appeared with a clipboard, her pencil poised. "You brought in the stabbing victim? We'll need to take down his information. Are you a friend or family member?"

"Neither." Burton avoided her piercing gaze.

The nurse gave me the once-over. "How about you, miss? Girlfriend? Sister?"

"Neither," I repeated, looking away.

She let out an impatient snort. "Well, what's his name? Address? Doesn't he have a place of residence?"

"I don't know him. We...I...found him in an alley on Market Street," Burton admitted.

"Oh, really? And what were you two high-steppers doing slumming on Market Street?"

Why was it any of her beeswax? I held my breath, hoping Burton wouldn't mention the Oasis or anyone by name. He squared his shoulders, and pulled out his badge. "Raiding the gin joints. Doing my job. What else?"

"You don't say." She acted as if he'd pulled out a ten-cent tin sheriff's badge from Woolworth's five-and-dime.

Didn't she recognize Agent Burton from the papers? Where had she been living, under a sand dune?

She placed her hands on her ample hips, clipboard and all. "And I suppose you picked up this tart while you were making the rounds."

"Excuse me?" My cheeks flamed, and I faced her, crossing my arms. "Who are you calling a tart? We're being good Samaritans, trying to save a stranger's life, and you're giving us the third-degree? This is a police matter and frankly, it's none of your business."

The nurse blushed and her mouth opened like a gaping fish, then clamped shut.

Burton's face reddened. Did my outburst embarrass him?

"I'm afraid he's a John Doe for now. I'll try to question him in the morning. Our detectives may stop by later."

I glowered at the nurse, glancing at her name tag. "What's your name? Mrs. O'Hara?"

Her face softened, just a tad. "Yes. Let me know if I can be of further assistance."

So far she'd been a hindrance without giving any assistance. To be polite, Burton tipped his hat. "Try to take good care of this young man. Good night, ma'am. We'll be in touch soon."

Ma'am? She didn't deserve to be called ma'am. In Burton's Roadster, I snapped, "Boy, what a bossy old biddy she was."

"True, but you don't want to antagonize her," he said. "We may need her help later."

"Antagonize *her*? She acted like *we* were the suspects."

"Gotta admit, our story sounds a bit fishy. A well-heeled couple comes in out of the blue with an unidentified bloody body? I don't blame her for being suspicious."

A couple? I was momentarily distracted by how easily that rolled off his tongue.

"Thanks for not mentioning the Oasis," I told Burton with gratitude. "I don't want to get Frank or Dino in any hot water."

"Do you believe their story?" He studied me in the dark. "Those two jokers have been known to panic before, act on impulse."

I mulled it over, thinking about a few unfortunate incidents. "Right, but why'd they call if they were guilty?"

"They didn't know I'd come along tonight. And it was easier to call you than spill the beans to Sammy. *If* they even tried to call him. Do they know you're his half-sister?"

I shook my head. "They may suspect that we're related or have a past history, that's all. I doubt they'd try to stab the poor guy 'cause of a ruckus in the bar. They're used to gang fights by now."

"Let's hope you're right." Burton stared straight ahead. "I'd hate to shut down the Oasis while Sammy is away."

CHAPTER FOUR

Not the same old tune. "You must be kidding," I told Agent Burton. "Why punish Sammy? I thought you were friends, especially after all you've done to help him..."

"Hey, this isn't my department. But if word gets out there was a stabbing at the Oasis..."

"A couple of drunks got into a fight in an alley, *not* at the Oasis," I pointed out. "There's no proof that Frank or Dino were involved. Why drag Sammy into this?"

"Sorry, Jazz." Burton pulled up to the boarding house, shifting to face me, acting apologetic. "I'm trying to be fair. I can't give you or Sammy special treatment."

"Special treatment? I only want you to do what's right. Please don't jump to conclusions until we get all the facts straight, OK?"

"Facts? Isn't that your area of expertise?" He grinned at me in the dark, his teeth glowing under the Victorian street lamps. "I'll go see the victim tomorrow and try to get a few answers. I advise you to stay in town and postpone your trip to Houston."

"Yes, sir." I jumped out of the car, and leaned over the window. "Don't bother walking me to the door, Agent Burton. I don't need any *special* treatment."

With that, I tossed my curls and stormed off down the walkway, resisting the urge to look over my shoulder. Sure, I realized I was being immature, but he knew how much I cared about my only brother. Sammy certainly didn't needed more cops sniffing around his bar, especially while he was away in Houston.

Amanda and Eva rushed out of the parlor. "What happened?"

I gave them the short-hand version. "Sad to say, a young fella was stabbed outside the Oasis so we drove him to the hospital. I'll find out more after Burton interviews the victim tomorrow."

Eva looked relieved. "At least he's still alive."

"Unfortunately, Burton told me to stay in town for now." I gave Amanda a sad smile. "He actually threatened to shut down the Oasis, if necessary."

"Oh no!" Her face fell. "We can't go see Sammy in Houston?"

I hated to disappoint her. Still, we couldn't do much to help Sammy if we left town.

"Looks that way. Maybe we can visit Sammy over the holidays?"

Amanda brightened a moment, considering that idea. "That'd be swell. As long as he's safe."

I stifled a yawn. "It's been a long day. I have to get up early to write my review. Good night, girls."

But I couldn't fall asleep, worried about the handsome victim, wondering about Sammy. Would our John Doe make it overnight? Worse, if he died, who would be blamed—Sammy?

Saturday

Saturday morning, I tiptoed out the door before eight, hoping to get my review into the *Galveston Gazette* in time to make the Sunday paper. Half-asleep, I boarded the trolley to work, the cool breeze and clanging noise jolting me awake. Who needed coffee when a bouncing, jerky, squeaky trolley car did the trick?

Only a handful of reporters peppered the newsroom, hunched over their typewriters, in worse shape than I felt. I stifled a smile when I heard Mack, our senior star reporter, snoring over his Smith-Corona. My boss rarely made an appearance on weekends, saying she needed her sanity—and her beauty sleep. Still, she promised to look over my review in time for the deadline.

I pulled out my notes from last night's performance, glad for the diversion. No, the show wasn't for everyone, especially the highbrow, high-hat crowd, but I enjoyed the humor, the variety, the parodies.

I'd especially laughed out loud at a few amusing animal acts and their antics. And finally there was the dastardly villain who seemed more sincere than sinister. Why had he stared at me so intently?

I was pounding out a rough draft on my noisy Noiseless Remington Rand typewriter when Nathan stopped by my desk, carrying his trusty camera.

"Hey, toots, I thought you'd be home packing now. Ready for our grand adventure?"

Ratz! I'd forgotten to mention the delay to Nathan, who was eager to see Holly, Miss Houston, his fizzled flame from the International Pageant of Pulchritude this past summer.

"Sorry to say, we need to postpone our trip to Houston."

His face fell. "Why? What's wrong?"

"Change of plans." I stalled, clamming up in front of the nosy news hawks. A stabbing would make their day—and the front page.

"Did Amanda and Sammy break up—again?"

"Not this time." Tell the truth, I suspected Sammy already had a squeeze or two in Houston. Whenever we caught him flirting, he'd say: "Can I help it if the dames throw themselves at me?" No joke: Sammy's dark good looks attracted women like winos to a speakeasy.

Our cub reporters swiveled around in their banker chairs, alert as guard dogs. Even Mack perked up, pretending not to eavesdrop, but I saw his fingers tapping the desk, hoping for a scoop.

I motioned for Nathan to meet me in the break room, littered with coffee cups, cigarettes and newspapers, and reeking of smoke. The news hounds expected us gals to keep it clean, but I refused to be their—or anyone's—personal maid.

Inside, I told Nathan, "Frank called me about an emergency at the Oasis last night. Burton and I went down there after the show, and..." Nervous, I stuck my head out, before I continued..."we found a young man stabbed in the alley."

"Was he dead?" Nathan's eyes grew big as plates. "Did Dino or Frank kill him?"

"No! Besides, the victim is still alive." Why did everyone suspect those two? Didn't they have Sammy's best interests at heart?

After I described the situation in more detail, he shook his head. "Poor Sammy. I always thought his place was jinxed."

"I'm beginning to wonder," I agreed. "You're not disappointed about cancelling our trip to Houston? You can still go see Holly without me and Amanda tagging along. Less baggage."

Nathan stared at the worn wood floor. "To be honest, I'm relieved. I wasn't sure if my old Tin Lizzie would make the round-trip. Between us, I doubt Holly cares if I visit her or not. I don't want to be her umbrella, an old stand-by she takes for granted. A looker like Holly probably has men vying for her affections all the time."

I hated to admit, he was probably right. Nathan was cute in a Tom Sawyer kind of way, but perhaps a bit home-grown for such an adventurous, worldly gal like Holly.

"Give her time, Nate. She's not the type to settle down and get married—not yet. Keep in touch and see what happens. Why not play the field yourself?"

Once again, I felt compelled to offer unasked-for advice to my friends when I was in no position to dish out suggestions for the lovelorn. Who did I think I was—an agony columnist?

The minute Burton and I got closer, I always managed to sabotage our relationship. Two steps forward, four steps back.

I expected Nathan to tell me to jump in the lake, but instead he seemed grateful. "Thanks, Jazz. Maybe we can postpone the trip a few weeks. I'll tell Holly that I got tied up, make her think I'm too busy to see her. Let's hope absence *does* make the heart grow fonder."

"Attaboy. I'll bet Holly comes around, sooner or later."

I'd started polishing off my piece when Mrs. Harper's phone rang. "There you are," Burton's clipped baritone came over the line. "We need to talk. Why don't I come by and give you a lift after work? How soon can you leave?"

No hint of irritation in his voice. I bit my lip, angry at myself for acting in such a childish way last night.

"I'll be ready in a jiffy. Give me half an hour, tops." I revised my review to sound more positive and dropped my clean manuscript on Mrs. Harper's desk. Just in time.

Agent Burton strode through the *Gazette* entrance like a good-old-Southern boy in his new Stetson and boots. Even Mack looked up with interest, but I simply smiled and didn't say a word until we were safely outside, ensconced in Burton's Roadster.

"So what brings you here, stranger? New in town?" Fluffing up my hair, I smiled at Burton, hoping he'd forgotten about my little temper tantrum.

"Part business, part pleasure." He started the car and punched the gas. "I called Big Red this morning about our John Doe and fortunately, they said he made it safely out of surgery."

"That's great!" Now I could stop worrying about him *and* Sammy, at least for a while.

"Why don't we drop by now and ask him a few questions? He seemed to trust you so I hoped you'd do the honors—with me in the room, of course."

In a way, I felt flattered, but also a bit disappointed. I thought Burton wanted to kiss and make up—instead he wanted to recruit me on a fact-finding mission. Naturally I had a personal and professional interest in this case, but why did he always want to discuss business first, not pleasure?

"At your service." I saluted him. "Want me to ask anything special? I can't just blurt out: 'Who stabbed you and why?'"

"Why not? Find out who he is and what he was doing in the area, then lead up to the stabbing. Watch his reactions to your questions, to determine if he's lying or telling the truth."

"Are you trying to tell me how to do my job?" I flashed a coy smile. "Leave it to me, James, but please feel free to ask your own questions. Your way."

"You know I will. I just thought this case needed a woman's touch. Your touch."

"Why, thank you, kind sir." I smiled, hoping I could pull it off.

At the hospital, we parked and entered, looking for Mrs. O'Hara. A few nurses bustled down the halls, carrying pans, trays and clipboards so Burton approached an older nurse, flashing his badge.

"I'm Agent Burton, and we brought in a John Doe last night, a young man around twenty-five, suffering from a stab wound. They told me he's recovering from emergency surgery today. I'd like to ask him a few questions, if he's better."

"A John Doe? Last night?" The matronly nurse looked puzzled. "Let me check."

Worried, we watched her question a few nurses and the front desk clerk, pointing in our direction, then she scurried down the hall.

"Wonder what's wrong?" I whispered.

Burton frowned. "I thought his surgery was successful. Maybe he's had a setback?"

Ten minutes later, the harried nurse returned, a hand on her cheek, her face beet-red. "Agent Burton, I'm sorry to tell you this, but...uh...we can't find our John Doe," she gulped. "He's not in his room, and to my knowledge he wasn't formally discharged. To be honest...he seems to have disappeared."

CHAPTER FIVE

"Disappeared? How can a grown man just disappear?" I stared at the nurse in disbelief.

"A patient can't vanish in thin air." Burton looked astounded. "What kind of rinky-dink operation do you run around here?"

"I beg your pardon?" The nurse threw back her shoulders. "I'll have you know that John Sealy Hospital is one of the finest institutions in Texas, if not the United States. We only employ the best doctors and nurses..."

"Are you sure he didn't...pass away?" I interrupted her tour guide speech, fearing the worst. "Since he wasn't identified, perhaps they put him in a new room, or listed him under a different name?" Yes, I was grasping at straws, but there had to be a logical explanation.

"I realize how it sounds, but we don't *misplace* people," the nurse huffed. "Perhaps the man escaped...I mean *left*. If so, obviously he had some help."

"Obviously." Burton frowned. "Who's in charge? I'd like to speak to him. Now."

"Or her," I added.

"I'm sorry, sir, but *he's* off duty. You can return Monday and talk to Mr. Stanley Smith."

"Fine. I'll do that, Miss..." Burton studied her badge. "Miss Klondike."

"*Mrs.* Klondike," the nurse corrected him. "I'll contact you if the man turns up."

"Please do." He handed her his card. "I'm Agent James Burton. Ask for me by name."

She glanced at his card. "You're the new Prohibition agent? Why are you investigating a stabbing? "

Ignoring her, Burton turned on his heel, ushering me out the door, breathing hard. "Can you believe this place? Losing a patient right out from under their noses? Very unprofessional."

"I'll say." No doubt Burton believed Galvestonians were a bunch of hicks compared to the first-rate hospitals in New York—or were they all as disorganized? "I wonder how he got away, without any ID or cash. Suppose he couldn't pay his medical expenses."

"In any case, the story seems fishy. I wonder if they're covering up something?"

"You mean like a botched operation?" I mulled it over. "Still, how could he leave without anyone noticing, like she said? What if someone tracked him down and tried to finish the job?"

"You may be right." Burton nodded. "Given the location we found him, I'd say it's gang-related. Maybe he's a snitch for Sammy's old pal Johnny Jack. Say a Beach Gang thug found out and knifed him on the Downtown Gang's turf—to send a message."

"Sounds familiar. But he didn't seem like a gangster. Too clean-cut, too attractive. And he didn't exactly dress like a goon with his bow tie and tweed jacket—more like a College Joe type."

I admit, I'd been fooled before—by cutie pie thug Colin Ferris.

"So why is this frat rat hanging around bars on Market Street? Looking for some action on the side?"

"James!" I blushed, recalling our visit to Mrs. Templeton's brothel. "We both know he can go to Post Office Street if he wanted female company. Don't you remember, he whispered "*Viola*" to me before he passed out? She must be his sweetheart or friend, someone important to him. Maybe he contacted her from the hospital and they ran away together."

"Always the romantic." He reached over and tugged on my curls. "Too bad he won't get very far in his condition."

"Shouldn't we try to locate him? We can go back to the Oasis and ask the regulars if they saw anything last night."

"Maybe later, when the sun goes down and the drinks go bottom up," he cracked. "Other than that, I'm out of ideas. Without a name or occupation, we don't have much to go on. And we can't file a missing person report when we have no idea who's missing."

"Don't worry." I patted his hand. "We'll think of something."

Suddenly a young ice cream vendor on a bike veered in front of Burton's Roadster. "Watch out!" I stuck out my arm across his chest as he gripped the steering wheel tight. Luckily he swerved in time to avoid hitting the youth, cursing under his breath. Jeepers!

As we neared the boarding house, I spied a male figure on the front porch. But I couldn't make him out so far away. "Slow down," I told Burton. "Do you see that fella?"

"Is that Sheriff Sanders?" He said with a start. "Looks like he's lost some weight."

"Aunt Eva's beau? I thought he was still on a special assignment in Houston."

My poor aunt was heartbroken after her new-found sweetheart got transferred out of town a month ago. Apparently the sheriff did such a good job of uncovering corruption in Galveston, he was in demand all over Texas. Luckily, Sanders kept in close touch—he called Eva at least once a week, usually on Sundays—so their long-distance romance still had a chance.

"That's not Sheriff Sanders," I told Burton as we got out of the Roadster. We both stared at the stranger, our jaws falling open like mechanical banks. "That's Dick Dastardly."

The vaudeville villain sat on our front porch swing, in full make-up and costume, complete with a glossy black cape, top hat and fake handlebar moustache.

CHAPTER SIX

What in the world was Dick Dastardly, the vaudeville villain, doing here—still in costume? Was this a prank? Was he trying to influence my review or snag an interview for the society section?

Slowly I approached the stranger, casting wary glances at Agent Burton as I trudged up the walk. Thank goodness he was here with me if I needed any help.

"Jasmine, how are you? I thought that was you on the front row." The villain barely gave Burton a glance. "It's been a long time."

I did a double-take. How did he know my name? "Sorry, sir, but I don't recognize you. Who are you? What do you want?"

"Jazz, has it been that long? Have I changed that much?"

Jazz? Only my friends called me Jazz.

The villain's voice sounded familiar, with a slight Texas twang. Then it hit me: my old high-school sweetheart. "Derek?" Dumbfounded, I stared at him a full minute before I saw past the heavy make-up and dramatic costume. "How could I recognize you with that face paint on? What are you doing here, in that get-up?"

"Oh, this?" He fingered his cape. "I'm on my way back from a dress rehearsal. The director wants to iron out any kinks in the show. When I saw you last night in the audience, I was shocked...I had to see you again."

Long-lost Derek, the wandering ex-beau bound for Hollywood, back in town. We didn't formally call it quits since nothing kept us together—we just wanted different things, at different times. Never mind the fact he barely kept in touch these past two years, an eternity now. He didn't so much break my heart as put it on ice for a while.

"I didn't see your name on the program," I stammered. "I had no idea it was you."

"The lead never showed up so I had to fill in at the last minute," he explained. "I'm the understudy for several acts. So how'd you like the show?"

"Very entertaining. Lots more fun than I expected."

"Glad we passed the test." His gaze lingered on me, looking me up and down like a man just released from prison. "I've gotta say, Jazz, you're a sight for sore eyes."

My face flushed and I wondered if Burton overheard. Clearly he had excellent hearing because he crossed his arms and challenged Derek like a linebacker.

With his Stetson on, Burton resembled the sheriff facing off against the villain in a scene straight out of a Western: good vs. evil, the villain vs. the hero, *mano a mano*. Except they weren't acting and this scenario was playing out on our front lawn. What now? Who was *I* supposed to be—Pauline in peril? I'll bet the neighbors enjoyed watching this melodrama as they hid behind their lace curtains.

"I didn't know villains made house calls." Burton glared at Derek, stepping forward, inches from his face. "Jazz, just say the word, and I'll toss this lollygagger out on his can."

The villain—I mean, Derek—blinked with pleading brown puppy-dog eyes. "Give us a minute, James." Holding up my index finger, I led Derek to the side of the house, away from the street. Not that I wanted to be alone with him, but I *was* curious.

His face lit up and he gave Burton a triumphant smile as he waltzed past.

"How have you been? Do you work in vaudeville full-time now?" I asked casually, trying to ease the tension we all felt.

"Part-time. Work comes and goes, so I jumped at the chance to travel with a vaudeville troupe. Gives me some great experience, but it's hard to compete with silly animal acts." Derek shrugged and let out a frustrated sigh.

I noticed he didn't mention me in that sentence, as if our relationship never mattered. Did I have any feelings left over for this fickle fella? So what if I did? He'd made his choice and I'd made mine, for now.

Derek held his cape across his face and wriggled his eyebrows, more like Groucho Marx than the Phantom of the Opera. "So what did you think of my act?"

"You were swell. You're a natural." I grinned, enjoying his puzzled expression.

"Is that a compliment? Or are you pulling my leg?"

"I just turned in my review, so you'll have to wait for my full report," I teased him.

"I'm holding my breath." He puffed out his cheeks like a blowfish, pretending to swim underwater.

I couldn't help but smile. Derek always acted like a clown, making me laugh, quickly changing the subject when our talks became too heavy.

"Be serious for once. Why'd you come here, today?"

"I want a chance to talk, to explain why I moved to California so suddenly." Derek looked away, acting sheepish. "To be honest, Jazz, I thought you'd refuse to see me if you knew who I was. Figured you considered me as a real-life villain, so I dressed the part."

"Frankly, I don't know what to think. So much has changed." He studied me as I tried to hide my pent-up feelings, much the same way he'd disguised his identity. "Tell the truth. Why didn't you ask for my opinion before you took off for Los Angeles?"

"Your opinion—or your *permission*?" He raised his brows. "Honestly? I was afraid I'd chicken out if I told you my plans first."

"Permission? I don't own you and vice-versa. Never did." Damn, all the things I wanted to say to Derek, all the anger and resentment I'd built up after he left town two years ago without warning. True, we were too young to get serious, and neither of us wanted to get married. Still, didn't I deserve an explanation—if not an apology? Even now, I felt wary, hurt, betrayed, all in one.

A cool breeze ruffled his cape and I laughed nervously, realizing how comical we must look, standing outside in broad daylight. "Derek, sorry I brought it up. Now isn't the time or the place to discuss our past, especially not here, not in front of Burton."

"Why not? They'll assume we're rehearsing a play—the villain and the vamp."

"Vamp? You think I look like a vamp?"

"A sexy vamp with dark hair and pale skin, just like Clara Bow."

Clara Bow? The "It" Girl? I perked up. Derek moved closer and reached for me, but I turned away, flustered.

"Sorry, I don't want to lead you on. As you can see, I'm dating Agent Burton."

"Story of my life. Always the understudy, never the lead." He backed off, hands up like goalposts. "Say, why don't we have lunch this week? Catch up on the past two years. I'll be busy at night with the show, but I'm free during the day."

"Lunch?" I hedged. "I doubt I can squeeze it in. I'm a full-time reporter now."

"Look at you, the big-shot." He razzed me, flashing a dazzling smile. "Don't they allow you to eat?"

"What do you really want, Derek?"

"Can't we still be friends?"

"What kind of friends?" Sure, he seemed sincere, but I couldn't tell if it was all an act. I stalled, curious, afraid to give in to him. Yet he could be so persuasive...

"Good friends." Derek stole a glance at Burton, who was waiting on the walkway, rocking on his heels. "Seems like a stand-up Joe. Lucky fella."

"He's a great guy." I smiled at Burton, grateful for his patience. So why risk ruining our relationship just for a *friendly* lunch?

Burton ambled up, thrusting his chest at Derek. "Your minute's up, sport. I believe this is your cue to exit."

Derek looked startled, then squeezed my arm in a too-familiar gesture before he dashed down the walkway. "Let me know if you want tickets to the show. I'll call you later."

"What was that all about?" Burton worked his jaw.

Was he jealous? "He's an old friend."

"A *friend*? What did he want?"

That's what I'd like to know. "It's a long story. Let's just say we have some unfinished business."

He narrowed his eyes. "Do you plan on finishing your *business*?"

CHAPTER SEVEN

I tried to keep my face blank so Burton couldn't see me struggle with my emotions. Which emotions? All I felt now was confusion.

When I didn't answer, Burton shrugged. "I'm just surprised, that's all. He doesn't seem like your type. Never seen a man wearing so much make-up in broad daylight. I thought vampires only came out at night."

"He's an actor," I replied, a tad defensive. "Goes with the job."

"Well, don't let me get in your way."

Burton started to walk off, but I tugged on his arm. "Believe me, there's nothing between us. What about tonight?"

"What *about* tonight?" he repeated, stone-faced.

"Don't you still want to go to the Oasis and look around, talk to the customers? We might find a witness or two."

"Wouldn't you rather watch your actor boyfriend perform?"

Annoyed, I shook my head. "He's not my boyfriend."

"The way he made googly eyes at you....seems he has some regrets." He paused, staring down at his boots. "How about you?"

"Regrets? We dated in high school, before I met you." I ran my fingers through my curls. Was Burton teasing or testing me? "Forget about Derek. Aren't we going back to the Oasis? I want to search the alley before dark, and ask Frank and Dino some questions. Though I doubt we'll find out much from Amos and Andy."

Burton gave me a hint of a smile. "Yes, ma'am. See you in an hour." He mock-saluted, then drove away without looking back. I entered the boarding house, hurt that Burton hadn't even walked me to the door.

Amanda and Aunt Eva sat inside the parlor, their chatter subsiding when I sat down.

"Was that who I think it was?" Amanda folded her arms. "Your missing beau, Derek? Excuse me, ex-beau. Why's he back in Galveston?"

"You won't believe this. He played the villain in the vaudeville show we saw last night," I stalled, not wanting to go into great detail.

"The villain? How fitting," Eva added. "As I recall, he broke your heart." Did she have to rub it in?

"Applesauce! Of course I was disappointed when he left town. Who wouldn't be?"

"Disappointed?" Amanda snorted. "I'd say more like devastated. What did he want?"

"Good question." I heaved a sigh. "I'll let you know if I ever find out."

Later that day, Burton showed up around five, giving us time to look around the Oasis before the regulars took their places. The air was getting cool, and I'd slipped on my gold and burgundy brocade coat with the black velvet collar, hoping to disarm him with my sparkly new outfit.

Burton let out a wolf-whistle when I came downstairs. "You look like the tiger's stripes! What's the occasion?"

I struck a vampy pose. "I wanted to get all gussied up for my fella. Do I need an excuse?"

"Sure you wouldn't rather stop by the theatre first, show off for your old beau?"

I rolled my eyes at him, ignoring his jab. After we got into his Roadster, I asked, "Did you go by the police station? Any news on the victim?"

"No dead bodies so far, and he still hasn't turned up at the hospital, dead or alive."

"Did you say anything to the cops?"

"Not yet. I checked the police reports, and no sign of him so far." Burton frowned. "How does a dying man sneak out of a hospital without a trace?"

"Someone who doesn't want to be found." I mulled over the few facts I knew. "I wonder what they were fighting about? Was the assailant trying to kill him or scare him to death?"

"Maybe both. Luckily the wound must be shallow if the victim managed to walk away."

"If he did walk out on his own. He sure lost a lot of blood," I sighed. "Let's hope he's still alive, for everyone's sake."

"Sorry to tell you, if there's an investigation, Sammy may be forced to return to Galveston."

"I bet he'd rather face the cops than Johnny Jack. Nounes isn't one to forgive or forget."

On Market Street, Burton parked behind the Oasis and helped me out, holding me up when my heel caught on his running board. In my glad rags, I wasn't exactly dressed for snooping in an alley.

I stepped gingerly onto the uneven pavement, littered with broken bottles, wood crates, cardboard boxes and debris from the weekend's revelry. The sun glowed a peachy-pink, still light enough to search the alley for any remnants of last night's crime.

Burton stomped around in his cowboy boots, kicking away some bottles and cans. Even as a temporary Texan, he'd taken to wearing a new Stetson and boots all the time. Yet he retained the proper mannerisms of a civilized Yankee, difficult for him to blend in with the rough-and-tumble Texas crowd.

"Seems they washed off most of the blood." I pointed to his boots. "Careful. You might destroy some evidence."

Burton began looking along the building's edges, moving a few boxes. As a Prohibition agent, Burton wasn't used to scouring crime scenes—but then again, neither was I. "I'll bet the men had a fight before the victim got stabbed. Maybe we'll find some clues?"

"All I see is a bunch of garbage," he complained. "No signs of a struggle. Nothing out of the ordinary."

I walked further down the alley, checking the grounds, looking around the trash cans. I glanced behind a tin Coca-Cola sign, only to see a scrawny orange tabby cat cry and scamper away. Poor stray, searching for scraps, like Golliwog. Did Bernie, the cook, have any left-over catfish in the kitchen?

A sparkling object caught my eye, and I crouched down to examine it: a marcasite button, engraved and enameled in such fine detail that it had to be Victorian. Not your usual bum's clothing.

"What do you make of this?" I showed Burton the glass button.

"Looks old, like it came off a gentleman's coat." Burton shrugged, unimpressed. "But that doesn't mean anything. Could belong to anyone. May have been lost weeks ago."

"But why is such a fancy button still here? Surely someone else would have picked it up. Say, why not ask Dino or Frank what the other man wore last night?"

Burton looked skeptical. "I doubt they pay any attention to men's clothing."

"It's worth a try."

Dino sat rooted in his usual spot by the door. "What's the word?" His dark eyes darted back and forth, not too happy to see me or Agent Burton.

Was he joking? "She sells seashells by the seashore." Thanks to Frank, I came prepared.

"You here to shut us down, Fed?"

"We're trying to help." Agent Burton bristled. "Whether you like it or not."

Boy, everyone seemed testy tonight. "Break it up, you two lugs." I put my arms out, trying to run interference like a boxing referee.

Inside the Oasis, I asked Dino, "Any news about last night? Did you find out anything?"

Dino shook his boxy head. "Nope, working too hard. Had to spill the beans to Sammy. He got mad, said he couldn't trust us no more." Glad I wasn't the one to break the bad news. With his hot temper, I imagined Sammy was livid, ready to point fingers.

"How's the poor sap? Is he OK?" Dino asked. "Frank said he didn't stick around long at Big Red."

Burton shrugged. "Who knows? The guy's gone. Vanished."

"He's alive?" Dino sat up. "That's a good sign."

"Hope so. Hey, did you notice if his friend wore fancy clothes, a nice coat or jacket?" I held up the button. "I just found this out in the alley."

"They looked like a couple of cake-eaters to me, not from around here." He smirked. "I was too busy to notice their buttons."

Burton gave me an *I-told-you-so* look. "What *did* you notice? Anything?"

"Ask Frank," Dino said. "He was tending bar. I was up here, doing my job."

"Mind if we talk to some people?" I asked, then headed downstairs, not waiting for an answer.

"Go ahead," Dino barked. "Try not to scare off the customers."

At the bar, it was still early, nice and quiet. Frank glanced at me and Burton nervously, and started wiping down the long oak counter, all but ignoring us. I motioned him over, trying a new approach.

"Say, does this button look familiar? Maybe the assailant lost it off his jacket? It's made with real marcasites, not tin." I held out the button in my palm.

"How would I know?" Frank examined the button and shook his head. "Doesn't ring a bell."

"Did you notice how the friend was dressed?" I asked.

While Frank fidgeted, Burton and I exchanged glances. What was he trying to hide? "Just answer the lady." Burton frowned. "She's asking a simple question."

"OK, the guy looked like a sissy, all decked out like a billboard."

"I wonder if they're dandies or perhaps performers?" Frowning, I recalled the outlandish outfits in the vaudeville show. "What time were they here?"

"Around six or so. They hung around half an hour before they started arguing." Frank smoothed out his shirt. "Maybe they were waiting for someone."

"Did they mention a gal named Viola?"

"I doubt they were fighting over a dame," Frank snorted. "Maybe it was a lovers' quarrel. You know, those fancy-pants boys."

So who was Viola? "Any idea why they were fighting?"

"Who knows?" Frank shrugged. "Dino kicked them out around seven. We didn't notice the body until later, say about ten or so. That's when we called you."

"You mean the victim had been lying out in the alley a few hours?" I grimaced.

"Who found him?" Burton asked.

"Buzz. He was taking out the trash and stumbled over the body. We told Buzz the rummy was sleeping off his liquor, and he didn't ask any questions. Luckily it was too dark to see the blood."

"Poor kid." Again I wondered about the unhealthy environment Buzz was exposed to on a nightly basis. Who else could take in the orphan boy? I thought of Finn, the newsie, who spent most of his time on the streets, trying to help his mother and her brood of children. "Well, you did a good job cleaning up the alley. I don't see a drop of...anything."

"Gotta hand it to Buzz. He does as he's told. A good kid. Sure misses Sammy."

"Sammy misses him too." I lowered my voice. "So you never found a weapon?"

Frank shook his head and shrugged. "Sorry, can't help you."

Burton pushed back from the bar. "Told you this was a waste of time," he muttered.

"Don't you want to question the customers?"

"Why bother? They won't talk, especially in front of me. These guys can spot a lawman a mile away."

"Well, let's find out if Buzz saw anything." I waved to the boy, sweeping up in the corner.

His toothy grin widened as we got near. "Hiya Jazz, hiya Burt. Can you butt me?"

"Burt?" Burton smiled at his new nickname. "Butt you? Where'd you hear that, son?"

"You're too young to smoke, Buzz." I shook my finger playfully in his freckled face. "Hey, I was impressed with your clean-up job outside. The alley looks nice and clear."

"Thanks, Jazz. Bernie spilled a bunch of tomato sauce out back. Real sticky stuff."

I shuddered, wondering if Buzz really believed their tomato sauce story or was playing along. "Say, sport, did you notice anything else unusual outside? Maybe a wallet, scarf, hat?"

Buzz crinkled his button nose, looked around, then pulled out a kitchen knife from his apron pocket, caked with a dried, rust-colored substance...like blood.

"Were you looking for this?"

CHAPTER EIGHT

I sucked in my breath. A kitchen knife? "Where'd you find that? Out in the alley?"

Buzz nodded, and jutted out his chin. "Finders keepers."

"Let me see it, sport." Burton wriggled his fingers.

"Wait. There may be prints on the knife handle," I pointed out.

"You don't wanna touch it. Feels sticky." Buzz made a face and wiped his palms on his baggy jeans. "Am I in t-t-trouble?"

"Not at all. Is it OK if we borrow this, Buzz?" I asked. "Can you get us a clean cloth?"

Buzz nodded and scampered to the kitchen. Burton whispered, "You know what this means? The attacker could be anyone who was here that night, including Dino or Frank."

I glanced at Frank with a pang of guilt. He frowned, probably wondering what we'd said to Buzz. "But why stab a total stranger? What's their motive? Besides, why would Frank and Dino call *me* afterwards if they were guilty?"

"Who knows what really happened? So far we've only heard their version," Burton said.

I had to admit, he had a point. "True, Dino has gone off half-cocked in a crisis. With Sammy away, they're left to their own devices. If so, maybe it was just an accident?"

Burton looked doubtful. "Did you know half of most killings are accidents, not intentional murders—attempted murders perhaps. Crimes of passion."

"Passion? Murder seems more like hate."

"I'm no shrink, but they say love and hate are closely related. Don't forget, I work with Homicide cops all day."

Buzz returned with a clean towel and placed the knife on top. Burton gingerly wrapped up the knife, careful not to touch the blade, and slipped the bundle in his jacket.

"See you later, Buzz. Thanks, Frank." I waved as we headed for the stairs.

"What was that all about?" He frowned, looking suspicious. "Try not to involve Buzz, OK? He's just a kid, for Christ's sakes."

"Don't worry, we were just shooting the breeze. Let me know if you hear from Sammy."

In the car, I told Burton, "Close call. Frank wouldn't be thrilled if he knew Buzz just handed over their bloody kitchen knife. Let's skedaddle before he finds out we waltzed out with the weapon, right under his nose."

"The alleged weapon," Burton corrected me, starting his Roadster. "We need to match blood type to the victim's wounds first. Kinda hard to do when there's no body."

"Can't forensics test it for fingerprints?"

"Sure, if the prints are already on file. I have a feeling this case isn't so simple."

"Let's hope the victim is on the mend, not lying in a ditch somewhere."

"You said it." Burton turned toward the Seawall, driving by the beach. "Hey, I'm getting hungry. Are you in the mood for some Italian food, say at Mario's? You look too nice to call it a night."

"Mario's?" A nice Italian restaurant rumored to be frequented by the Downtown Gang. "Sounds good, but that bloody knife made me lose my appetite."

"Maybe we can share a meal? Besides, we need to talk."

Burton looked at me sideways as he drove along the Seawall. The November breeze felt crisp and cool, not humid for a change.

"We do?" My stomach clenched as I braced for our "talk."

"How well do you know that vampire? I mean, fella?"

"Derek? Like I said, he's an old friend." I stammered, fingering my bead necklace.

"How long were you together? Don't give me that *old pals* routine."

I avoided his gaze. "We dated in high school off and on for two years, the usual song and dance."

"Is that all? Was he trying to get fresh today?" Burton worked his jaw.

"He's just being friendly." Had Derek purposely tried to provoke Burton—or me?

"Too friendly. He was slobbering all over you."

I blushed, wondering how much he saw. "You're all wet."

"So what's the story with you two?"

"There's not much to tell." I tried to edit myself before I blurted everything out. "Derek was a senior, I was a junior at Ball High. After he graduated, he hung around Galveston for a while, working odd jobs, restless as hell. Then I moved to Austin to attend college at UT, and we sort of lost touch. Later he decided to try his luck in L.A. and left town. We were too young to get serious."

I left out the tearful good-byes, the homesickness, the late-night phone calls. Sadly I had to drop out of college when my father died, so my dreams of being a journalist like Nellie Bly were dashed—until I got the job at the *Gazette*. Still, writing blurbs about weddings, debutantes, and society matrons wouldn't win me any prizes.

Burton seemed skeptical. "Lots of people get married right out of high school."

"That wasn't in the cards for me." I stared out at the pale beach contrasting with the dark waves, white foam like creamy icing. "I want to be a real reporter, like Nellie Bly."

"That crazy female reporter who got committed to a New York insane asylum?"

"Bly only *pretended* to be crazy to expose their inhumane treatment. Turned out most of the women were perfectly sane. Several were foreigners who couldn't speak English. Wish I was half as brave." I sighed, knowing I could never pull off that stunt. Ten days of abuse and torture in a madhouse? No, thanks. "Still, I'm not cut out for domestic life. Not now, not yet." Probably never.

"You and me both." Finally he cracked a smile, patting my leg. "I like a gal with moxie."

"Thanks." Did that mean he was a confirmed bachelor? "What about you, James?"

He didn't answer as he drove along the Seawall, then parked facing the beach. For a few moments he sat in the dark, staring at the waves crashing on the shore, not talking. The night seemed still, peaceful, save for the seagulls squawking as they glided over the ocean, white wings furled like flags.

Now I was really curious. "Come on, James. I told you mine, now you tell me yours. Do you have a secret past?"

"Don't we all?" He started the Roadster and headed for Broadway. "You might as well know...I was almost engaged once. A long time ago."

CHAPTER NINE

"Engaged? You?" Why was I so surprised? Burton was a young, good-looking fella with a steady job—not the safest job in the world, but honorable, and I assumed the pay was decent. At 28, Burton was what Mrs. Harper called an "eligible bachelor, ripe for picking." Still, I didn't consider Prohibition agents *family* men—their jobs were too dangerous, too unpredictable.

"Why *not* me? I've been known to catch a few ladies' eyes." He sounded smug as he parked at Mario's, off Broadway, and helped me out of the car.

"I'll bet." I wondered about the lucky lady who actually tried to pin down Burton—was she the one who got away? Or had he disentangled himself by choice?

"What happened?"

"Let's just say it didn't work out." He avoided my eyes and opened the restaurant door, handing his Stetson and coat to the hat check gal. I kept my cloche and new coat on to stay warm—frankly, I'd splurged too much on this particular ensemble to let anything out of my sight.

The maitre d' looked at us approvingly, probably since we were overdressed for a casual eatery, only a few notches above Sammy's speakeasy. Guess they had no idea Burton was a Prohibition agent. "A table for two? Right this way."

He seated us at a cozy table by the window and pulled out my chair. I pretended to peruse the menu, but I was dying of curiosity. "So why did you call it off?"

"Bad timing. Wrong place, wrong dame." Burton pretended to mop his brow. "Luckily I escaped before we got handcuffed."

Funny choice of words. "You didn't give her a ring? Did you actually propose to her? Or was it her idea?" I tried to contain my nosiness, but I wasn't succeeding.

"We sort of fell into it. Nothing that formal." Burton seemed amused as he looked over the menu. "What would you like to eat?"

I got the hint. Now I was really curious—and how! How could we discuss trout vs. salmon, or lasagna vs. chicken marsala or anything when all I could think about was his ex-fiancée? So many questions I wanted to ask, but perhaps she should remain a mystery.

After the waiter took our order—mixed grill and seafood—I had a chance to glance around Mario's. Candles flickered in the dim lights and a violinist strolled around the restaurant, stopping at each table to accept a request or more likely, a tip. Personally I preferred jazz, yet I enjoyed listening to classical music for a change.

During dinner, we made small talk, careful not to bring up the bloody knife or missing man or even Derek in case of eavesdroppers. I literally had to bite my lips *and* tongue to keep from blurting out nosy, none-of-my-business questions. Still, it seemed forced, when all I wanted to do was ask about his ex: What was she like? Was she pretty? Why did you *really* call it quits?

Finally when I couldn't stand it, I asked, "Why did you move to Galveston—because of your break-up?"

He nodded. "Partly. I needed to get out of upstate New York. I felt suffocated, stagnant, living and working in the same town where I grew up."

"Why Galveston, so far away? I imagine it's very different than what you're used to."

"That's exactly why I accepted this assignment." He grinned. "I thought an island atmosphere might seem more like a tropical vacation. Lucky for me, I got to meet you, and enjoy the company of a beautiful woman."

What a line! "Boy, you're a smooth talker." I batted my lashes. "Keep it up, handsome."

Without warning, a menacing man knocked into our table and stood there, as if daring Burton to fight. The table wobbled and I reached out to steady the candles, worried the tablecloth might catch on fire. I looked up to see a thug glaring at Burton, a smirk on his strong features.

The waiter arrived with our dinners, took one look and scurried away to the kitchen. The restaurant buzz died down to a whisper while the diners waited for Burton's reaction. Slowly he removed his napkin and stood up, facing the bully, not afraid to back down.

"Excuse me, but I believe you bumped our table," Burton said evenly, working his jaw. "If you have anything to say to me, we can go outside. Now."

The goon patted his tailored jacket pocket, indicating a gun. He moved inches away from Burton, chest puffed out like a rooster.

"I'll say it to your face, Fed. Johnny Jack has a message for you and your good pal, Sammy: Keep off the Downtown Gang's turf—or else."

My stomach knotted. How did this thug know Burton and Sammy were friends?

"Oh yeah?" Burton leaned in, blue eyes narrowed. "Is that a threat?"

"I'd call it a warning." The hood glared at Burton, his eyes dark as coals. "You'll know when it's a threat."

Then he tipped his hat, leaning over so close I smelled whiskey on his breath. "Sorry to spoil your dinner, little lady. But if you know what's good for you, I'd suggest you find another fella."

What? Why was he threatening both of us—in public? Was he gunning for both Burton and Sammy? I held my breath, placing my hands in my lap so no one could see them shaking. If he really wanted to harm Burton, he could have shot at him, at us, outside. A scary thought.

The goon left as suddenly as he'd appeared while the diners stared at Burton, perhaps hoping for a real showdown. He seemed unfazed—or else he was a better actor than Derek.

"Who was that bully?" I asked when I could breathe.

Burton pressed his mouth tight. "George Musey. He runs the Downtown Gang when Johnny Jack Nounes is gone or occupied."

"That's George Musey?" I shivered. "Sammy says he's dangerous, worse than Nounes."

The hard-boiled gangsters knew how to keep their ugly mugs out of the papers and the public eye. Safer for them, not for their rivals. In contrast, Sam Maceo reveled in the spotlight, always eager to spread his goodwill and retain his good name.

"We haven't crossed paths before, but I've heard rumors." Burton patted my hand, as if comforting a frightened child. "Sorry about that interruption. Where were we?" He signaled for the waiter, who stood by the kitchen door, eyes wide.

"Is everything jake?" the young waiter asked warily, and set down our plates.

"Just a misunderstanding," Burton said, picking up a fork. "Looks good."

"James, how can we eat when that gangster just threatened us— in front of everyone?" I tried to keep the fear out of my voice. "Is he just bluffing?"

"You know how Rose Maceo watches out for Big Sam, Ollie Quinn and the Beach Gang?"

"Of course. He's Sam Maceo's big brother, the protector and the punisher." Everyone in Galveston knew Rose Maceo's penchant for guns and fists.

"Right. George Musey plays the same role in the Downtown Gang. He's Johnny Jack's right-hand man, known for his violence and hot temper. He acts first, thinks later—as mean and cold as a rattlesnake."

Burton put down his fork, his voice low. "Sorry to say, we'd better not be seen together for a while, until this incident dies down."

"*Dies* down?" Poor choice of words. "What about Sammy? Think they'll find him?" I gulped, worried they might track him down in Houston.

"That goes double for Sammy." Burton stared out the window, watching the fog slowly envelop the night. "No one escapes the Downtown Gang and gets away. Not from Nounes or Musey. Not for long."

CHAPTER TEN

Here we go again...I shuddered, afraid of Musey's threats, worried about both Burton and Sammy. Thank goodness Sammy was safe in Houston—60 miles away from Galveston.

I waited for the violinist to start playing, to drown out our conversation before I badgered Burton for more information. "What I want to know is, why did Musey show up out of the blue? Do you think he followed us? Or did some snitch call him the moment we arrived?"

"Possible," Burton nodded. "Musey and Johnny Jack obviously have friends here, or they get a piece of the take. For all we know, the gang controls this place. I wouldn't be surprised if Mario's was a front for mob activity, an easy way to launder money."

"Makes sense. But why did he threaten you like that? He's taking a big risk, confronting you in public. I thought mobsters worked in the shadows, behind the scenes."

"Musey thinks he's the head honcho while Johnny Jack is gone." Burton rearranged his silverware as he spoke. "Nounes must still be out of town, maybe looking for new suppliers and outlets for his booze, or perhaps new business partners. So Musey sees a chance to take over his pal's operation, when he's not looking."

"While the big cat is away, the rats come out to play." Suspicious, I glanced at the diners, who tried to avert their eyes. "They seem innocent enough. Still, I wonder if anyone here is also involved in the Downtown Gang? In any case, I'm getting the willies. Why don't we shake a leg?"

"You mean do the Charleston? Here?" Burton cracked.

I smiled at his joke. "You're a riot."

"What about dessert? No ice cream?" Burton teased, knowing my cravings for sweets.

"You said the magic word. I'm not ready to go home."

After we paid, Burton helped me with my coat and we began heading for the hat check stand. That's when I heard a woman cry out, "My beaded bag! Help! Somebody stole my purse!"

Burton rushed over to the attractive young woman, and diners gawked while the maitre d' and staff gathered round. I stood near her table, craning my neck to listen.

"Madam, are you sure there hasn't been a mistake?" The maitre d' looked upset as he tried to calm the crowd. "Perhaps it was misplaced during dinner. Why don't we help you look for it? We can search the premises at once."

"Of course I'm sure." The flapper's short curls bobbed, and she threw down her white napkin, indignant. "I always carry an evening purse to dine out. One minute my bag was on the table, the next moment it was gone."

"When did you first notice it was missing?" Burton asked her.

Nervously, the young woman clutched her throat, gasping, "Say, you're the man involved in the tussle with that bully. My purse disappeared right after he left. I've looked everywhere, in my coat pocket, even under the table. I'm so worried! I kept my valuables in there."

"Were you seated here all night or did you go to the powder room?" Burton asked.

"We've been right here the whole time," her dapper date confirmed, squeezing her trembling hand. "She never left my side. Some scoundrel lifted it right off the table!"

"If you give me your information, we can investigate further," Burton offered.

She frowned, her blue eyes anxious. "Say, who are you? A cop?"

"I work with the police department, yes." Burton smiled to console her. Thank goodness he didn't announce that he was a Prohibition agent to the unsuspecting guests. We'd had enough drama for one evening.

"Before I give out any private information, you should search your entire staff!" The flapper pointed at the workers standing by, singling out our waiter. "Start with him! He hovered over me all night, admiring my jewelry. Probably trying to find a way to steal my purse!"

The poor young waiter's face turned beet-red as he turned his pockets inside out and the maitre d' patted him down. "Nothing, madam," the maitre d' said with relief.

"Well, then I want *all* of your workers searched, including the kitchen help. At once!"

Nodding, the maitre d' clapped his hands and asked our waiter to get the remaining kitchen staff. Clutching my mesh bag, I motioned for Burton to come over. Of course I empathized with the victim—getting robbed was my least favorite activity—but this could take all night.

Who was this rich gal anyway, and why did everyone kowtow to her demands? She seemed familiar, yet in her low-cut shimmery beaded gown and jeweled choker, she looked more like a vamp or a gangster's moll, not a society princess. Were those real gems or rhinestones?

"Does every person here need to be searched and interrogated?" I sighed to Burton. "Robbery isn't even your department. What if it takes all night?"

"Just being a good Samaritan. But you're right. I can think of better things to do with our time. I'll get her information so we can leave."

While Burton wrote down the victim's name and phone number, I surveyed the dining room, wondering about the timing of the theft. Had the thief used our confrontation with Musey as a chance to steal the bag—or would Musey's men be that stupid and greedy?

Outside, stars covered the night sky, twinkling like white Christmas lights. "Glad Musey's gone. He gave me the creeps." I shuddered.

"Musey is a creepy fella." Burton smiled. "Sure it's not too nippy for you?"

"I like the cool night air. Such a pleasant change from the muggy summers."

"You said it. Galveston is almost tolerable in the fall."

"Say, why don't we get ice cream cones at Tootsies? Then we can take a walk on the Seawall," I suggested.

"Sounds swell." Burton helped me get into his Roadster and we headed to the beach.

As we strolled along the Seawall, he took my hand, and I snuggled against his shoulder, glad for a change of scene. Now the unease and awkwardness I'd felt earlier after Derek's surprise visit was gone, almost forgotten. The waves curled and unfurled as we listened to the ocean sounds, the screeching seagulls, the roar of Model Ts and Cadillacs and Studebakers driving down Beach Boulevard.

Still, the ugly confrontation with Musey stuck in my mind, and I couldn't help but bring it up again: "Do you think it's just a coincidence that the woman's purse was stolen after Musey appeared? Think he may be connected?"

Burton shook his head. "Frankly, petty theft is beneath a hard-boiled hood like Musey. He's in the big leagues, not a common criminal. I doubt he or his men would stoop so low as to swipe a handbag. That's like taking penny candy from the five-and-dime—an easy mark."

I held onto Burton's arm as we watched the waves crash onshore. "Maybe Musey thinks *we're* easy marks. He has some nerve, threatening a Fed agent in such a busy restaurant. What does he want with you?"

"Musey's just testing me while Nounes is gone." Burton shrugged. "He wants money, power, control, like any typical gang leader."

Great—that's all Galveston needed: more cut-throat gangsters vying to be top gun, literally.

CHAPTER ELEVEN

Agent Burton and I stopped for some chocolate chip ice cream at Tootsie's, and for once it didn't drip all over my glad rags. As we walked along the Seawall, the soft breeze turned into chilly gusts of wind. Burton noticed me shivering, and placed his jacket over my coat, gallant as usual. Afterwards he drove me home and we lingered on the porch saying our good-byes, but he didn't come inside.

Too much had happened that day, too many unpleasant surprises. Burton brushed my cheeks with a light kiss and waved as he drove off.

Disappointed in his *let's-be-friends* parting peck, I went inside, wondering if he was still angry about Derek. After making small talk with Amanda and Eva, I crept upstairs and turned on my Egyptian maiden perfume lamp, hoping the fresh citrus scent would lull me to sleep. Instead of sleeping, I tossed and turned, replaying the day's events, anxious about Burton and Sammy—again.

By the time I finally nodded off, I dreamed that Musey and Derek were villains in the vaudeville show, complete with black top hats and capes. Burton and Sammy played the heroes, of course, and wore cream-colored Stetsons and badges on their lapels.

The lawmen circled the evil villains, guns drawn like an old silent Western, when a shot rang out and a body fell to the ground. The dream seemed so real that I awoke in a cold sweat, frightened to death, not knowing if the good guys or bad guys had won.

Sunday

Sunday morning, I got up early and dressed for work, hoping to get a sneak peek at my review. From past experience, I expected it to be edited beyond recognition, and wanted to be prepared for any changes. Since I now knew Derek acted in the show, I wondered what he'd think of my critique—not that his stereotypic villain performance rated much of a mention.

The trolley squeaked and creaked as it bounced along, keeping me from falling asleep. Outside the *Gazette* building, Finn hawked the Sunday paper, giving me a bright smile. Figured newsies and news hawks never got Sundays off. "Hiya, Jazz. What'cha know?"

"Whatever I read in the paper." I grinned and handed him a few coins. Noticing his threadbare outfit and worn-out shoes, I made a mental note to find him some suitable clothing. Still, Finn was too proud to accept charity, so I'd have to invent a reason to give him a new change of clothes. Maybe a job as a copy boy?

"Sold many papers today, Finn?"

His face fell. "Waiting for folks to get out of church."

He made it sound like they were locked up in prison. "I'm sure you can find a few sinners on the sidewalks." All he had to do was find the nearest speakeasy. "Hey, did you see my review in today's entertainment section?"

"You don't say. Attagirl, Jazz!" Finn beamed at me as I pointed out my review, doubtful he could even read.

Luckily the newsroom was quiet and I sat down at my desk for a quick look. The vaudeville troupe had provided stock photos of the show and actors, naturally highlighting their best features. Derek's handsome face was positioned right next to my piece, as if he headlined the show.

To be honest, seeing him again stirred up feelings that I didn't even remember, or didn't want to acknowledge. Had Burton noticed?

I skimmed the review, comparing it to my original version. So far, so good. But near the end, I stopped to re-read the part about the villain. Apparently the director or someone contacted the paper to make sure Derek's name was included as a last-minute replacement, stating that the original lead actor had dropped out at the last minute without mentioning why. The review implied that Derek had not only saved the day, but the entire show, with his professional performance.

What? I didn't write that!

A short sidebar with Derek's bio listed his credits and high school accomplishments with a bold 24-point headline: **HOMETOWN ACTOR HEADED FOR HOLLYWOOD** and a smaller subhead: **A STAR IS BORN IN GALVESTON.**

"Damn!" I muttered out loud. What hogwash! The article seemed to gush over Derek and his talents, highlighting his meager roles in local plays and regional productions as if he were the next Douglas Fairbanks or Lionel Barrymore.

Worse, since the bio wasn't by-lined, folks might assume *I* did the gushing. Oh, brother—this publicity stunt was beyond humiliation.

Who planted this piece of claptrap—the director? Derek's high-school drama teacher? What would Derek and Burton think when they read this puff piece? No doubt they'd assume I still had a crush on my ex-beau. Who had the gall to publish this junk—my boss?

Of course I was no Dorothy Parker and the *Gazette* didn't compare to *The New Yorker*, but this scheme seemed totally unethical, not to mention unprofessional. Did Dottie ever have to endure such a disgrace?

My short-lived career as a theatre critic had ended before it began. Fawning and gushing didn't qualify as an actual critique. Could I ever undo this damage?

Furious, I crumpled up the paper and threw it in the trash— where it belonged.

A couple of newsmen stumbled in, reeking of booze and cigarettes, and barely gave me a glance. I covered my face in shame, wishing I'd never let Mrs. Harper rope me into reviewing that stupid show, and wasting my time with amateurs. Worse, the sugar-coated, purple prose undermined any credibility I'd earned as a journalist.

I couldn't stay here and risk getting razzed by the reporters, so I made a mad dash for the door, cheeks flushed with embarrassment.

Outside, Finn stared at me with concern. "What's wrong, Jazz? Why the long face?"

"My career as a journalist is over," I told the little tyke. "Not to mention my love life is ruined." True, I was being a bit melodramatic, but that summed up exactly how I felt.

"Aw, gee. Is it as bad as all that?" Finn frowned.

I nodded. "Sorry I can't watch your papers today. Some other time, sport?"

"Sure, Jazz. Don't worry about me."

"Hope you sell out!" I patted his scrawny shoulder and forced a smile. Sell out? How ironic—after reading that rosy review, readers would assume *I* was the sell-out.

I searched in the alley for Golliwogg, my semi-adopted stray black cat, but sadly she wasn't around to lift my spirits. Hanging my head, I trudged home, bypassing the trolley, not wanting to see anyone. Even walking by the corner bakery and sweets shop failed to entice me inside.

As I turned down our street, I noticed a spiffy Roadster parked in front of the boarding house. Could it be? I raced down the sidewalk to the front door and opened it wide: my big brother stood in the hallway.

"Sammy! You're here!" I stared at him as if he were a mirage. He grinned and enveloped me in a warm bear hug. If anyone could cheer me up, it was Sammy, my wild, wayward half-brother.

CHAPTER TWELVE

"Sammy! What are you doing here?" I smiled so widely my cheeks hurt. Amanda stood by his side, holding onto his arm. "How long have you been here?" I gave her a cross look, meaning: *Why didn't you tell me?*

"Came down to see my two favorite ladies. I had the day off and thought I'd surprise you. Just got into town."

"Isn't it swell?" Amanda grinned. "Here I was, moping around, depressed, because our trip got cancelled."

"And I wasted time at some silly show." I nodded, not mentioning the stabbing victim. Surely he knew by now?

Sammy looked around conspiratorially. "Eva's still at church, right? No one's here?"

"Don't worry. She'll be gone all day. Most of the boarders are out of town or in church."

In the parlor, we made ourselves as comfortable as possible on the old worn horsehair furniture. I sat on the sofa across from Amanda and Sammy, who snuggled on the loveseat. Sammy looked ruggedly handsome, dressed in a sports jacket and slacks and rumpled white shirt. He'd grown out his dark wavy hair, tinged with new touches of silver—already, at 32?

I couldn't help but notice that his smooth olive complexion seemed pale and sallow, and dark circles ringed his olive eyes. "You look tired," I blurted out. "Were you driving all night?"

Sammy nodded and rubbed his blood-shot eyes. "Houston is a hopping boom town. I wanted to get here early, before folks got out of church."

"Glad you finally took a day off." I recalled Musey's threat from last night, but decided not to bring it up now. Not yet, maybe later. "What about Nounes? Sure it's safe to be here?"

Sammy shrugged. "I'm just in town for the day, then I'll be on my way."

Inwardly, I sighed with relief. "So how do you like Houston?" I'd asked him on the phone a few times, but he'd always said, "It's OK," and evaded my questions. "How does it compare to Galveston?"

"I like it fine. Lots of new money. Folks coming to town to make a quick buck." He leaned forward, clasping his hands. "Did you know Houston is hosting the Democratic National Convention next year? Business will really be booming then. People are piling into the city daily, building the Albert Thomas Convention Hall, getting the city ready for all those muckety-mucks. Lucky for me, politicians sure like to drink."

"Those hypocrites," I fumed. "They vote to poison their own citizens while they hire private bootleggers for their fancy shindigs. I'll bet they drink their rich friends under the table."

Sammy nodded with a grin. "I'd rather give them a drink than my vote any day."

"You said it, Sammy." Amanda beamed at him, blue eyes sparkling, clearly smitten.

"Say, I wonder if they're going to discuss repealing Prohibition?" I added. "Everyone knows the Volstead Act is a farce. The public doesn't pay attention, and neither do the police."

I thought of Agent Burton, who tried so hard to uphold a law that no one took seriously, a useless amendment that even he questioned.

"I hope so. The sooner they vote down that stupid law, the better." Sammy's face clouded with emotion. "I hate paying these crooks top dollar for booze on the sly. I just want to run a legit restaurant and bar—a high-class joint like the Hollywood Dinner Club or the Turf Club—and not have to kowtow to these greedy rum-runners. They get rich off the backs of poor working-class stiffs who only want a rum and Coca-Cola to help relax after a hard day."

"Bravo!" Amanda gave Sammy a hug. "Well-spoken. Wish you could run for Congress."

"And join the enemy? No, thanks." Sammy frowned but his face flushed, pleased.

I took the cue to give them some privacy. "Why don't you catch up and I'll get us some snacks." Retreating to the kitchen, I asked, "What would you like?"

"Hot coffee for me," Sammy said. "It was a long, hard drive in the dark."

"Your poor thing," Amanda cooed, twirling her blonde curls. "Make mine hot chocolate, please?"

"Coming right up." I tried to eavesdrop while I bustled around the kitchen, making sandwiches and drinks, wondering if Sammy and Amanda were still an item.

After Sammy's sudden departure to Houston, she hadn't brought up the painful subject. So far they seemed to be getting along quite well, though I knew Sammy's roving eye didn't settle on any one gal for too long.

A bona-fide bachelor, he had no trouble juggling vivacious vamps or daring dames. Truth was, he liked to stretch his sea legs, as he admitted.

I handed them ham and cheese sandwiches and their hot drinks, and we made small talk while we munched on lunch. For a while, it seemed as if Sammy had never left. How things had changed in such a short period of time.

"What's your bar like in Houston?" I asked, sipping my hot tea.

"A hole in the wall in Market Square, by Downtown. Not a bad location, but it's not the same without Doria hanging over the bar," he told us. "I miss you two gals stopping by."

"Do you mean it?" Amanda's face lit up like a Chinese lantern. "Music to my ears."

"Why naturally, sugar plum."

Oh, boy, all this sweet talk was giving me a toothache *and* a headache.

Sammy put down his sandwich. "So how's Agent Burton? I hear he was with you Friday night when you came by the Oasis. Everything copacetic?"

I knew he really meant the stabbing, not our relationship. "Sure, we're fine. In fact, last night we ate out at Mario's." I gulped down my sandwich, trying not to mention Musey.

"Mario's?" Sammy frowned. "That's a major mob hang-out for the Downtown Gang. Burton knows that, doesn't he?"

"Really? Looked like a nice place to me." I tried to act nonchalant, but my heart started thudding harder in my chest. "Maybe he likes the food."

Sammy's olive eyes flashed. "You know I'm grateful to the guy, but he's just asking for trouble. Anything happen while you were there?"

"Matter of fact, a lady's purse was stolen off her table. Still, purse-snatchers are all over Galveston," I said, to change the subject. "You remember I got robbed last summer. Luckily, Finn saved the day and tripped him just in time. Never found out who took my bag, but I suspect it was some Beach Gang flunky."

"Probably." I knew Sammy's loyalties were torn between both gangs. He finished his sandwich and stood up, wiping his hands and mouth with a napkin. "Hate to eat and run, gals, but I'd better go check on the Oasis. It was closed when I drove by this morning. No telling what those two goofballs did last night."

"Can we come with you, Sammy?" Amanda jumped up. "I'll be ready in a jiffy."

Sammy grinned. "Sure, if you don't mind hanging around a stinky old gin joint."

After she went upstairs, he pulled me aside. "Any news about that stabbing? I can't believe the guy just vanished."

"I'll say. Without a body, there's no evidence, no crime. Seems like he walked straight out of Sealy hospital."

"Thank God." His eyes narrowed. "What about Burton? Has he told his cop buddies?"

"Buddies? You have more friends on the force than he does. But no, I don't think so. And I doubt the staff wants to advertise the fact they *lost* a patient, even a John Doe."

Sammy seemed relieved, his shoulders relaxing. "Bet he wanted to skip out on his bill."

"I wouldn't be surprised."

We clammed up when Amanda returned, smelling like a perfume factory. Before we left, I wrote a note for Aunt Eva, and we all piled in Sammy's car, chattering while he drove us to the Oasis. On a Sunday, Market Street didn't seem half as menacing or dangerous, the sun basking the whole street in a warm haze.

Frank swung open the door as we approached, giving us a worried glance.

"It's about time you lounge lizards showed up for work," Sammy cracked. "So what's new? Made us a bundle of jack?"

"You had a visitor last night." Frank fingered his spectacles, surveying the street before slamming the door.

"Who?" Sammy moved toward Frank and I distinctly heard him whisper, "A dame?"

"I wish it was that easy." Frank looked like he was chewing on nails. "Your old pal, George Musey."

CHAPTER THIRTEEN

"Musey? That old trouble-maker?" Sammy blanched, and glared at Frank. "How in hell did George know I was coming to town?"

"Don't look at me, boss. I didn't tell a soul." Frank shrugged. "Maybe a customer overheard me talking to you on the phone."

"A *customer?* Next time keep your mouth shut and your eyes open. What do I pay you for?" Sammy scowled at Frank as he paced the empty bar, waving his hands around, cursing under his breath. "That's all I need, Nounes and Musey breathing down my neck."

So Musey's threats to Burton weren't just for show. After Mario's, he must have intended to pay Sammy a visit that very night, and was gauging Burton's reaction. So how did Musey find out Sammy planned a trip to Galveston? Did Sammy's partner in Houston tip him off?

Finally Sammy sat down, pulled out a Camel and blew smoke rings at Doria, our wooden masthead and mascot. Ever stoic, Doria stared straight ahead with a worried look on her chiseled face. "Next thing I know, Johnny Jack will show up asking me for back rent. I'm paid up, right?"

"No problems there. We've got it all covered."

"Prove it," Sammy demanded. "Show me the receipts."

"Now?" Frank's eyes darted back and forth, alarmed. "How about some beverages first?"

Sammy draped his arms over our shoulders. "Sorry, girls, I'm not being hospitable. You want anything to drink—a soda pop?"

"I get soda pop all day at Star Drugstore," Amanda said. "How about some giggle water?"

Sammy motioned to Frank. "Make it a Mary Pickford—a sweet drink for my sweet gal."

Amanda smiled. "I like the sound of that."

"Which one—my gal or the drink?" I teased her.

"Both." Her blue eyes twinkled.

Frank handed Amanda her cocktail, and a Moxie for me, giving us the eye. Then he gestured for Sammy to go to the back office.

While we waited, Amanda and I sipped our drinks, feeling uncomfortable. "Wonder what's wrong?" she said. "I get the distinct impression Frank wants us to leave."

"Don't mind Frank. He's such a worrywart, always expecting the worst."

"The worst?" She frowned. "Say, what do you know about this George Musey?"

"Only rumors." I buried my face in my drink.

Trying to change the subject, I told her about my butchered review in the *Gazette*. "The whole article sounded more like a press release advertising Derek's acting services than a real critique. What happened to objective journalism?" I griped. "James will think I'm madly in love with Derek. And Derek will think I've been pining away for him all these years."

"Can't you do anything? Write a disclaimer or letter of protest to the editor?"

"Once it's printed, I can't do much of anything. Worse, people will believe it's all true."

"I'm sorry, Jazz," Amanda consoled me. "I always thought your job was so exciting."

"More like nerve-wracking." I let out a sigh. "Too many ups and downs. Maybe I should work at the P.O."

"Try working as a waitress or a telephone operator. Talk about a big, fat headache!"

When Sammy reappeared, he looked as disappointed as we did. "Maybe you ladies shouldn't be here now. Frank can give you a ride back to the boarding house."

"And leave you here alone?" I said to Sammy.

"Thanks, Jazz. I can take care of myself."

What had Frank told him about Musey? I felt guilty for not warning him about the gangster earlier, but I didn't want to spoil his good mood.

After Frank hurried off to the office, I tapped Sammy's arm. "Say, I forgot to mention something..."

Amanda read my signals and, without a word, headed to the powder room. No reason to blab about Musey's sudden appearance and not-so-subtle threat.

I took a deep breath. "Last night at Mario's, Musey purposely bumped our table, and tried to pick a fight with Agent Burton."

"No shit? Musey was there? What was he doing, threatening Burton?"

I nodded. "He gave him a message, for you both: Keep off the Downtown Gang's turf."

"What in hell? Musey expects me to pay him back, but stay out of my own bar? He'd better not be planning to take over the Oasis."

Sammy shook his head in frustration. "Why didn't you say anything sooner?"

"I was so happy to see you...I didn't want to ruin the day. What does Musey want?"

"Cash, what else? He's still sore about the lost rum shipment. How in hell will I ever find enough dough to satisfy him?"

My heart seized, knowing Burton's raid on the Downtown Gang's booze drop caused this predicament—though to his credit, he *had* tried to help Sammy escape.

"Are you sure that's all he wants? Even if you pay up, will he keep asking you for more dough?"

"I don't have a choice, do I?" His expression softened. "Jazz, don't worry. I know how to handle Musey. I just wonder if he's going out on his own, or if he's got Johnny Jack's blessing?"

"Sure you'll be OK?" I asked. "If Nounes knows you're here, he may come after you."

"That's my problem." He frowned. "Not yours."

"Of course it's my problem. You're family." Sammy could be so stubborn sometimes. "Hey, why don't you drop by the boarding house later? Eva will be happy to see you."

"Eva? Happy?" He seemed skeptical.

"Believe it or not, she's changed since she met Sheriff Sanders," I assured him. "Not so judgemental."

"Oh yeah? OK, I'll try to stop by." Sammy shrugged. "Before you gals leave, why don't you show me where you found the...uh...man? Did you take a good look around? See anything interesting?"

"Only a fancy button." I lowered my voice. "But Buzz found a kitchen knife smeared with dried blood and something sticky."

"A kitchen knife? One of ours?" His head snapped toward the kitchen. "Where is it?"

"Burton's got it now, in case something, or someone, turns up."

Sammy's eyes flashed. "What does he plan to do with it? Turn it over to the cops?"

"Bunk. He wants to keep it safe. Better than letting Buzz hide it here."

"Ready to go, girls?" Frank handed Sammy the box and ledger, and he placed it behind the bar.

"So you think it was just an argument gone wrong?" Sammy asked Frank as we filed upstairs. "Nothing planned or premeditated, like a murder?"

Frank shrugged. "Seems that way."

As we stepped into the alley, I saw the sky had turned a golden-coral, dark palm trees framed by the evening light, reminding me of silhouette pictures.

"Where was he?" Sammy wanted to know, too preoccupied to notice sunsets.

Glancing around, I let out a scream and pointed at the ground.

A woman's body lay near the area where we found the first victim, her kohl-rimmed eyes open in surprise.

CHAPTER FOURTEEN

"Oh my God." Frank stared at the body in shock. "Not again."

Like a duet, Amanda joined me in screaming our heads off as we ogled the poor woman, transfixed.

Frank hissed, "Pipe down, you two!"

Sammy seemed dazed, blinking in surprise, his normally tan olive skin pale as paper.

"What in hell?" he muttered, looking up at the sky. "Why here? Why me? Why now?"

A portly shopkeeper stuck his head out the door, calling out, "What's all the ruckus?"

"Just a rat hiding in the garbage," Frank replied. "A fat scary one."

"Well, keep it down, will ya? We can hear you big cry babies ten miles away."

Sammy blocked the body from view, and we backed off, averting our eyes. No one said anything for a few moments as we studied the poor young woman. In her mid-twenties, the victim wore a snug cloche, heavy make-up and ill-fitting clothes, a top and flimsy skirt outfit, under a simple wool sweater. Not exactly a fashion plate.

"Any idea who she is? I don't see a purse," I gulped. "Now we have a Jane Doe to go along with our missing John Doe."

"Great," Sammy groaned. "This is all I need. Why do bodies keep showing up here?"

"Sure you don't know who she is?" Frank asked.

"I don't recognize her." Sammy patted down the woman's sides. "Unfortunately, she doesn't seem to have any ID. But I'd bet my bar Musey is involved."

"No surprise," Frank scowled. "He wants payback. Revenge. But I have no idea how this dead dame figures into his plan."

I piped up. "Could she be a prostitute?"

"She's too ugly to be a whore," Frank muttered. "Look at her, piling on the face paint, wearing those crummy, second-hand clothes."

"Show some respect," I snapped. "Hasn't this poor gal suffered enough without you insulting her in death?"

"What's it to you?" Frank said.

"Have you seen the homely hookers by the docks?" Sammy interrupted Frank, making a face. "Those are some ugly mugs."

Amanda snapped out of her stupor. "How would *you* know about hookers on the docks? Or anywhere else for that matter?"

"I've seen some broads there while I was out doing business." Sammy avoided her gaze. "Don't worry, doll face. I wouldn't touch those bug-eyed Betties with a ten-foot pole."

While they bickered, I wailed, "What should we do? We can't leave her here."

Sammy stood over the body, examining the victim without actually touching her. "Come take a look." He waved us over, pointing to the red marks on her neck. "Seems she was cut and strangled with some kind of sharp wire or cord."

Curious, I edged closer, noting the thin bloody creases across the woman's throat—the fine lines like red slices—trying not to upchuck. Sure, I've tagged along to a couple of crime scenes, yet I couldn't stomach a woman's murder. Too close to home.

Despite the different circumstances, her death reminded me of the recent bathing beauties' tragedy. Still shaky, I forced myself to scrutinize her from head to toe, taking in her heavy-handed make-up to her chunky shoes. Something about her seemed familiar, but I couldn't figure out what or why. "She doesn't look like a streetwalker to me," I said. "Ever seen her before?"

Frank shook his head. "I'd remember a flour lover like her. Plus she seems awfully tall and big-boned to entice anyone. Sorry, lady."

Could she be Viola, the victim's girlfriend? What were they involved in that got her killed? I kept my thoughts private, not wanting to speculate without any facts.

I walked over to console Amanda, who watched the scene in silence. Street-smart as she was, I knew seeing a murder victim upset her to no end.

"Let's not stand around here making small talk." Sammy told Frank. "Get a blanket or rug from my office. And call Dino to help. I'm not leaving her here all night."

After Frank left, I asked, "Where will you take her—to the morgue?"

"Hell, no. Guess who'd be the first one accused of murder?" Sammy's eyes held a defiant gleam. "I feel like dumping her off at the Kit Kat Club, in case George and Johnny Jack are setting me up. Hate to think they killed this gal just to ruin my business. I'd like to see them try."

My heart sank. "You're going to drop her off there like a sack of potatoes? Sammy, that's not a good idea. You can't leave a body behind a bar. It's still twilight. Someone will see you."

"They left her behind *my* bar." He frowned. "Don't worry, we'll wait till after hours when no one is around."

"So where are you going?" I bit my lip, exchanging worried glances with Amanda. She stood next to me, covering her mouth, shaking in fright. Ditto for me.

"We don't know yet and you don't wanna know. Better keep you gals out of this mess."

"Anything I can do?" I asked.

"Keep this under your hat. Don't tell anyone, especially your nosy newshounds."

"Why would I blab to them? They don't pay attention to a society reporter anyway." Then I added, "What about Burton? He might be able to help."

"By turning me in?" Sammy shook a finger at me. "Sorry, but that includes your boyfriend. In fact, better not even tell him I'm in town."

"After all he's done for you? Fine way to treat a pal. OK, mum's the word." I walked away in a huff, trying to shake off my irritation. "I'll see what I can find."

"I'll help, too," Amanda said. "Better than standing here, staring at a sad corpse. What kind of evidence are we looking for exactly?"

"Signs of a fight or struggle, anything out of the ordinary, bloody clothing, a purse or wallet," I explained as we scoured the area. "I feel sorry for Sammy. He comes to town for a visit and finds a corpse behind his bar?"

"I wish they'd take her away—and fast," Amanda said. "I'm getting the heebie-jeebies with that dead dame so close, her eyes wide open, like she's watching us."

"I'll say. I'm sick to my stomach," I agreed. "This whole thing seems fishy to me. First a strange guy gets stabbed here, then a woman turns up dead in almost the same spot? The attacks must be related."

"You mean the same person committed both crimes?"

"Maybe. Or the Downtown Gang is sending Sammy a warning: Get out of town—and stay out. I wonder if we can find any evidence linking the two victims?"

My mind raced with wild ideas: If she was Viola, maybe John Doe escaped Big Red just to find her? What if he caught her with a fella, and strangled her in a fit of jealousy? Or maybe she hired a hit man to kill her beau, and the assailant tried to stab him to death—not realizing he survived the attack. So John Doe confronted Viola and forced her to tell him the truth.

Talk about a crime of passion! I'd be better off writing pulp fiction or dime novels with my vivid imagination.

While I scanned the area, I saw the usual debris—crates, rotting food, bottles, broken glass—and stepped carefully to avoid soiling my shoes.

"Some fun reunion this turned out to be," Amanda whined. "I thought Sammy and I would have a romantic date alone, not spend our time sniffing out garbage."

Indeed the alley smelled like rotting fruit and vegetables mixed with bad booze. The whole area needed a shot of Chanel No. 5 or some cheap Woolworth's *eau de toilette*.

Holding my breath, I looked behind the trash cans, shook some boxes, moved a couple of crates. Big mistake: A huge gray rat ran by me, along the fence. I squealed and jumped out of the way. Yikes! Where were the stray cats when you needed them?

Frank and Dino shushed me saying, "Keep quiet!"

"Get me out of here!" I griped. "Ain't we got fun?"

"You said it, sister." Amanda made a face.

By the fence, I saw something shiny by a trash can, and bent down to pick it up with my hanky—a thin wire. "Looks like some sort of metal string or cord." I showed it to Amanda. "Think this could be the murder weapon?"

"Why not give it to Sammy? He'll know what to do."

"I'd better hold onto it for now. Too incriminating."

I wrapped the wire in my hanky and stuffed the bundle in my purse to consider later.

"Why cause more trouble for Sammy?" She agreed.

"What if he's right? Say, Johnny Jack planted the body here to frame him, get the cops to shut down his bar?"

"That's a lousy way to treat one of your own."

Yet until we found out the victim's identity, we'd never know the connection, if any, to Sammy or the Oasis.

Now I watched as the three men wrapped the poor woman in a worn-out blanket, stumbling when they tried to pick her up. As Frank struggled to carry the body, he complained, "Damn, this dame weighs a ton."

"Watch out!" Sammy snapped when Frank almost dropped the victim by her shoulders. Her skirt flew up, revealing a sight we weren't supposed to see: A faded pair of boxer shorts, and a rather well-endowed part of the victim's anatomy. We all gaped in unison at the unveiling.

"Well, I'll be damned." Sammy stopped in his tracks, staring in shock. "She is a he."

CHAPTER FIFTEEN

"Oh my goodness!" Amanda gasped, blue eyes wide. "Would you look at that!"

That was exactly what I was trying hard to avoid. I did a double-take, too stunned for words, trying not to ogle the woman—I mean, man.

"Well, I'll be a monkey's uncle!" Frank slapped his forehead.

Sammy worked his jaw. "Now I have a dead fairy on my hands."

"Why would a man dress like a woman—unless he had a good reason?" Amanda pointed out. "Maybe he's an actor, or performer? That may explain the face paint and cast-off clothes."

"Sure, the back-alley kind," Frank cracked. "But how could he *perform* in that outfit?"

"You slay me." I rolled my eyes at Frank. "I'm sure there's a logical explanation."

"Logical?" Frank replied. "Some john probably found out that *she* wasn't quite what he expected, and he didn't like the surprise."

"Why don't you and Dino ever check the alley?" Sammy snapped. "Keep it clear of vagrants and drunks."

I moved closer to the he-woman, examining his face, wondering why he looked so familiar. The way the moonlight cast a glow across his delicate features...then it hit me. "Frank, take a closer look. Could he be the same John Doe? Can you check his torso—for a stab wound?"

"I'd really rather not touch him...I mean, her." Frank backed off. "Not my type."

"Fine. I'll do it." I put on a brave face, averting my eyes from his private parts and gingerly lifted his skirt. "Oh, my god. That's got to be him!" I gasped when I saw the stitches in his side, wondering what the victim did that was so terrible, he deserved to die. "It's our John Doe. Poor guy."

"You don't say." Frank leaned over, studying his face.

"Now I know how he left the hospital without anyone noticing. He must have been desperate to leave, disguising himself that way."

"Fairies enjoy wearing women's frocks," Frank snorted.

"Come on, cut the crap." Impatient, Sammy started to pick up the victim's torso. "Let's go before anyone gets suspicious. We've wasted enough time gabbing out here."

I watched as the men stuffed the body in Frank's car, trying to rearrange his long limbs, finally shutting the door. "What next, boss?" Frank asked. "I don't want to drive around town with this stiff in my car."

"I'd like to dump him on Johnny Jack's playground, but that's too close. They may suspect the Beach Gang or the Maceos. I don't want to start another gang war. Better find neutral ground 'till I can skip town."   Despite being in rival gangs, Sammy valued his friendship with the Maceo brothers too much.

"What a pal." Frank frowned. "You get away while we clean up this god-awful mess."

Sammy's scowl silenced Frank. "Let's hope they never connect the dots."

"Sure you're doing the right thing, Sammy?" I asked. "Shouldn't you call the cops?"

"And be accused of murder? I'm already in hot water." He looked apologetic. "Sorry we can't give you gals a ride home, but as you see, we've got our hands and car full."

Wish I could change his mind, but I didn't have any bright ideas. "Don't worry about us. Just be careful and stay out of sight."

Sammy put a finger to his lips. "We were never here."

The evening faded fast. Amanda and I decided to walk home and forego the trolley. How could we discuss a murder on a streetcar full of people?

As we walked and talked, I heard a few dogs barking in the distance, their yelps urgent, frantic. I imagined John and Jane Doe crying out for help during the attack, their pleas ignored.

"I wonder if the killer was the same person who stabbed this poor fella?" I said to Amanda. "The first method didn't work, so he strangled him with a wire."

"Someone must have really wanted him dead to try to kill him twice," she said. "But why return to the same crime scene and risk getting caught?"

"Maybe they were looking for something," I suggested. "Or the killer dropped some evidence and wanted to confiscate it?"

"Like what? Money? Booze? Weed? I didn't see anything out there, just a bunch of crap."

"Who knows?" I let out a sigh. "Whatever the reason, I hope it was worth dying for."

Monday

When I walked into work Monday morning, a few reporters started jeering, "Where's your new beau, Jazz? Did you ditch the Fed Agent for a villain in a cape?"

Hank called out, "Never thought you went for sissies. Sure he likes dames?"

"Do you share make-up tips and borrow each others' clothes?" cracked Pete.

"Take a hike." I glared at the jokers. "Here's a tip: Don't give up your day jobs. For your information, I never wrote that puff piece. Someone added the sidebar without my knowledge."

"Oh, yeah? But your name's on top," Hank retorted.

"I only wrote the review. Well, most of it anyway. Do you believe everything you read in the paper?" I stomped off, refusing to give Hank the last word.

At my desk, I debated confronting Mrs. Harper, and decided to wait until I cooled off. I tried to proof a few stories, but the victim's carefully made-up face floated across the pages. Who was he trying to fool—and why? And what had Sammy done with the body?

Finally I focused on work, avoiding eye contact with Mrs. Harper and even Nathan, afraid I'd spill the beans. I'd never make it as a poker player—at least not a good one.

Luckily Mrs. Harper seemed too absorbed in her gossip column to notice me. Must have been some juicy scandals or events over the weekend that I wasn't privy to. Thank goodness she didn't ask about my trip to Houston, yet.

Nathan came by at lunch, but I brushed him off, saying I had a deadline. Truth was, I wanted to stick around in case the newsmen heard about the victim.

The dreaded call came by mid-afternoon—to Mack, of course. For some reason, the police respected him—or else they were afraid of him—so he always got the first scoop.

"You don't say. Late last night? Wearing ladies' clothes?" He chuckled into the phone. "Sounds interesting. Thanks for the tip."

Mack stood up and gathered his notepad and satchel, brimming with papers. I tried to act nonchalant. "What's new, Mack? Anything exciting?"

"Nothing that concerns you, toots." He gave me a blank stare. "If you see Nathan, tell him to meet me at Martini Theatre— pronto."

"Martini Theatre?" Oh no, not there. Why in the world did they pick that place to deposit the body? "I went to see the vaudeville show there Friday night. Did you read my review?" Sure, I wanted to distract him, but why did I have to bring up that drivel?

"Seemed more like a love letter than a critique." He smirked at me under his safari hat. "You got a thing for villains in face paint?"

"Like I told you, I didn't write that claptrap!" I fumed, frowning. "I don't know who did, but when I find out, I'll give them a piece of my mind."

"Talk to your boss." Mack gave me a condescending smile. "Sorry I can't chit-chat all day. Some of us have work to do."

Aha! I suspected Mrs. Harper had taken "poetic license" with my copy, making up gushy statements about Derek's talent and attributing them to me. I couldn't let her get away with such a blatant tactic as adding my name to an "article" I didn't write. Did she think I wouldn't mind her putting such sappy words in my mouth—rather, on paper? Why would she humiliate me in print?

Now murder took precedence over mayhem. I tapped on the darkroom door and Nathan came out, looking like a sleepy cub bear hibernating for the winter.

"Nate, Mack wants you to take photos at the Martini Theatre. Some big story."

I played dumb, as Sammy suggested. Boy, was it hard keeping secrets from Nathan.

"Isn't that where the vaudeville show is playing? What kind of story? A murder?" He perked up and grabbed his camera gear.

"Mack sure left in a hurry. Mind if I tag along?"

I didn't wait for his OK. Grabbing my bag, I followed him out the door, not bothering to ask Mrs. Harper for permission. She certainly didn't ask *me* for permission to print that PR piece about Derek and his "rare talent."

Nathan raced to Martini Theatre like an erratic ambulance driver. A few reporters and cops stood around in a circle, taking notes, staring down at the he-she figure lying sprawled in the alley. I held back to watch the scene unfold. What were they waiting for? Why didn't they take the body away, show some respect for the deceased?

A rumpus sounded and I turned to see two burly cops coming out of Martini Theatre, flanking a familiar young actor wearing a black top hat and cape, his head down, his wrists trapped in handcuffs.

Derek?

CHAPTER SIXTEEN

Why in the world had the cops arrested Derek? Did he have anything to do with the murder—or was he being charged with a different crime?

Standing here with my mouth open wasn't going to get me any answers. I resisted the impulse to follow Derek to the squad car lest I wanted more razzing from the reporters or worse, an interrogation from the police.

I made my way over to Mack. "What happened?"

"What does it look like?" He motioned toward the cops, who shoved Derek into their car. "Your boyfriend was arrested for the murder of Patrick Mulligan."

Finally the victim had a name. "Murder? Derek? He wouldn't hurt a fly."

Eyebrows shot up and a few newshounds crowded around me. "The suspect is your beau? What's he like? Is he violent? Are you his alibi?"

"What?" I stepped back, out of their line of fire. "No, I'm not his alibi or his girlfriend. We're old pals from high school, that's all."

Two reporters in derby hats sidled up to me, probably from the *Daily News*, the big fish looking down at us *Gazette* guppies. "How does it feel to see your sweetheart arrested for murder? Ever notice any homicidal tendencies?"

"Bunk! Derek's not a killer. And he's not my beau."

A thin guy with curly brown hair thrust his face in mine. "Oh yeah? Did you witness the murder?"

"Hogwash!" I raised my hands like two stop signs. "Hold your horses, fellas. How do you know he's guilty? Where's the proof? I'm sure this is all a big mistake."

Pulling my floppy hat over my face, I backed away from the group, took a last look at the poor corpse, and rushed off. I wanted to find a side entrance into the theatre and get past these vultures, so I could figure out what really happened.

Then it occurred to me: Wasn't I aspiring to be one of them? Were all news reporters so pushy? Boy, I'd try to use more tact when questioning innocent people, not these interrogation tactics.

No one noticed me as I slipped into a back door. Inside, the theatre smelled like paint and cigarette smoke. I looked around for a troupe member to question and noticed a young ballerina in a pale pink costume walk down the hallway. "Excuse me..." I began, smiling at her.

"Who are you?" She frowned and pushed back her light brown hair. "You're not supposed to be backstage."

"I'm a friend of Derek's," I said. "What happened? Why'd they arrest him for murder?"

"It's horrible, isn't it?" She lowered her voice. "Don't you know? Derek replaced Patrick in the show. Patrick was the original Dick Dastardly."

"You don't say." I drew back as if she'd slapped me. "Frankly, that small part isn't worth murdering someone over. I've known Derek for a long time. He's not a killer."

"Says you. See, Derek was Patrick's understudy in different productions. They never really got along because Patrick assumed Derek wanted to take over his roles."

Her dainty fingers fluttered as she spoke. "You know, the classic case...the understudy becomes the star."

Was she pulling my leg? "So why blame Derek? He's just doing his job."

"Apparently he did his job *too* well. The director talked to Derek about replacing Patrick permanently." She turned around in a half-circle, practically pirouetting in place, glancing over both shoulders. "When Patrick found out, he was furious. He accused Derek of back-stabbing, and trying to undermine his performance. So when Patrick showed up with stab wounds...well, you can imagine what we thought, that Derek was being quite literal. Too literal."

"Stab wounds?" I played dumb, realizing Patrick must have come here after he left the hospital. Who helped him escape, disguising him as a female? "Come on, Derek's not that stupid or vicious. He wouldn't resort to killing his so-called rival, even if they do play villains."

"Maybe they took their feud too far." She raised her brows. "They had a big fight in front of the whole crew. Patrick was so upset, he left and ended up missing his act."

"You mean last Friday—opening night?"

She looked surprised, then narrowed her eyes. "How did you know?"

"I was there Friday night, when Derek filled in for Patrick at the last minute. By the way, I'm with the *Gazette*."

She flung out her hands and scurried away. "Oh, no! You're a nosy newspaper reporter, trying to dig up dirt!"

"Applesauce! I'm trying to help Derek. I was only there to review the show." I followed her, as persistent as the male newshounds. "Say, is your name Viola?"

Her face colored and she ducked inside a room marked Bella on the door. Her own dressing room?

"Can't you read? I'm Bella, the lead ballerina in Swan Lake." She stretched out her arms like a swan. "I fill in now and then, if they need a fresh act."

"Good for you." I smiled and stuck my foot out when she tried to close the door. "Wait, one last question. Is there anyone in the show named Viola?"

"No....why do you want to know?"

"I just want to help Derek," I said, wringing my hands.

"Then go down to the police station," she snapped. "Prove he's innocent. Don't waste time talking to me."

With a bow, she shut the door in my face. Deflated, I poked my nose in a couple of rooms but didn't see anyone else to question. I tried to stop a stagehand carrying a wooden tree, but he kept going. So I snuck out the side entrance and joined the dwindling group of gawkers, trying to make myself inconspicuous.

By now, an ambulance had arrived and I watched the coroner examine the victim, studying the strangulation marks on his neck. I moved closer, listening to Mack and several newshawks belt out questions: "Can you pinpoint the time of death? Murder weapon? Was he cut by a knife or razor blades? Did he die instantly or later? Approximate age? Anything else unusual?"

Normally, I'd jump into the fray, but I already knew too much. So I kept my mouth shut, worried I'd blurt out some private information.

"Looks like he was strangled with a type of wire," the medical examiner said. "Perhaps fishing wire or string." He took off his gloves and touched the victim's pale neck, sliced with thin red lines. "His neck feels sticky, like some sort of residue."

"You mean rosin?" A handsome blond young man spoke up. "We use rosin to make our instrument strings smooth, easier to play." I made a note to ask him a few questions, wondering if he knew Derek.

"Yes, that must be it," the coroner nodded, giving the guy a grateful smile. "Thank you, son. Could be from the strings of a musical instrument, maybe a cello or violin."

A violin? With a jolt, I recalled Patrick's last words to me the night he was stabbed: Viola. What was he trying to tell me—that the guy who stabbed him was a viola player? Perhaps one of the musicians in the orchestra—or someone with access to a string instrument?

Anxious thoughts swirled as I tried to analyze the situation, glad I'd left the wire I'd pocketed from the alley at home. Even if I turned it over to the cops later, wouldn't that seem suspicious? I hated to involve Sammy, but I couldn't hide potential evidence in a murder investigation, could I? Why bother now? The M.E. already figured it out without my help.

I walked over to the young musician, who stood by the curvy burlesque dancer and magician's assistant, still in costume. Teary-eyed, they gaped at the victim, arms linked, staring as if in shock. Touched by their reaction, I realized the troupe must be like a close-knit family who'd lost one of their own.

"Excuse me, are you a violinist?" I asked the young man. "What's your name?"

"Mike. Actually I'm a bassist." He beamed with pride. "My first year as a pro. Just graduated from high school. Needed to make enough money for Julliard..." His voice faded. "But I doubt my parents will let me travel with the troupe now if they hear about this murder."

"I'm sorry, but maybe it's for the best." I felt for the kid, yet doubted a life on the road provided a safe environment for a budding musician, considering the circumstances. "By the way, has a violinist or viola player joined the orchestra recently? Or anyone who plays a string instrument?"

"Not officially." Mike shrugged. "We often have extra people play with us for side gigs—private parties, hotels, nightclubs. The director likes to rotate musicians and actors, mix things up, try out new songs and acts."

"Interesting. Sounds like fun." How did he keep track of everyone, I wondered?

"Fun? Tell that to the poor folks losing their jobs."

"Must be tough." I nodded, considering his words. Was that a possible motive for murder? "Thanks for your help, Mike. Good luck with everything."

Stepping back, I watched Nathan busy snapping photos, and observed the crowd of performers, police and potential suspects. Was the real killer here, watching the scene, trying to blend in? In this colorful cast of characters—jugglers, clowns, acrobats, actors, musicians—anyone could be a killer in disguise.

I felt a tap on my shoulder and looked up to see Agent Burton staring at me, his eyes cold. "Thought I'd find you here." He waved his hand at the commotion. "Looks like your fella is in a real jam."

CHAPTER SEVENTEEN

My face turned crimson. "Derek may be in a jam, but he's certainly not my fella. Where'd you get that big idea?"

"I read your rave review of his performance in Sunday's paper," Burton said. "He makes a fine villain, but I wouldn't call him the next Rudolph Valentino."

So he *had* seen those silly articles, unfortunately. How long would I have to explain away that tripe? "Believe me, I didn't write those puff pieces. I only wrote the review, but not the gushy part. I'm positive Mrs. Harper planted the stories, along with his flattering bio. How she snuck them past Mr. Thomas, I don't know."

"You don't say." He looked skeptical. "Tell me, why would the society editor do that for some low-rent actor?"

"Beats me. I plan to confront her later."

"I'd be interested to hear her side of the story."

We watched the squad car driving off with Derek inside, sirens blaring. "Fitting end for a real-life villain," Burton cracked.

"Derek may be arrogant, even high-hat, but I assure you, he's no killer."

"You know him better than I do, obviously." Was that a jab? Burton glanced over at the victim, still sprawled out in the alley. "What have we here?"

"Meet Jane Doe." I gestured toward the body, glad for a change of subject, however gruesome. "Looks like our John Doe disguised himself as Jane, maybe to hide from his killer. Too bad his costume didn't work."

"What? *She* is the same person, the stabbing victim?" He blinked. "Are you sure?"

"See for yourself. Let's just say I uncovered the evidence. Don't ask me how."

"I think I can guess." Burton tried to hide his smile. "So that's how he slipped out from John Sealy without anyone noticing."

"Seems Patrick went in as a John and waltzed out as a Jane. He became a temporary she. Sadly, he wasn't very successful."

"Patrick? Glad the victim has a name."

"Patrick Mulligan, a creative jack of all trades."

"Any idea what happened?" Burton asked. "Did your reporters dig up any details?"

"As a matter of fact, I talked to Bella, a ballerina in the theatre." I lowered my voice to a whisper. "Turns out Derek and Patrick had a professional rivalry. Patrick was the lead and Derek was his understudy."

"This is getting interesting. So your pal Derek does have a motive. No doubt he had the means and opportunity as well." Burton looked up at the overcast skies as if searching for answers. "Think Derek also stabbed him Friday night?"

"How could he?" My face felt hot. "As you recall, he performed in the show we saw that night."

"Yes, just in time to play the villain." Burton scowled. "There you go, rushing to his rescue again. How do you know he's innocent?"

"Murder isn't his style." I placed my hands on my hips, trying not to act upset. "Say, since when do you investigate murders, Agent Burton? Shouldn't you be on Market Street, busting up bars?"

Burton seemed so eager to pin the blame on Derek that I couldn't bring myself to tell him about finding the instrument string in the alley behind the Oasis. I didn't want to get Sammy involved in this case—if I could help it.

"I'm just playing devil's advocate. As a reporter, you need to consider all the angles."

"If Derek really did the deed, would he dump off the body here, where they both work?"

"Good point." Burton nodded. "My pals in Homicide tell me the victim was probably killed elsewhere and the body moved here later."

"Oh yeah?" I gulped. "And how did they figure that out?"

"Forensics has all sorts of ways to determine the who, what, where, how—and time of death. Lividity for one."

"What's that?" Did I really want to know?

"I'm no doctor, so bear with me," he said. "Lividity refers to blood supply in relation to gravity. An M.E. can usually determine if a body's been moved, or left in any position too long, by dark bruises and skin discoloration. That helps pinpoint the time of death."

"Thanks, Dr. Burton." To me, he sounded exactly like a smug, know-it-all doctor. "Speaking of blood, whatever happened to the knife?"

"Unfortunately they couldn't get a clear set of fingerprints." Burton looked disappointed.

"That's too bad," I replied, secretly relieved. What if Frank or Dino *were* involved?

"Forensics also discovered that in addition to blood, the knife handle was covered in a sticky residue."

"A residue?" Like rosin, I wondered? "Did the cops ask where the knife was found?"

"I just told them it was by the body, out in the alley." Burton shrugged. "I didn't specify which alley."

"I appreciate it, James." I gave him a smile, grateful that he didn't mention Sammy or Buzz or the Oasis. "Did they find out anything else?"

He nodded, watching my reaction. "I heard that a witness saw two men leaving these premises early this morning. Perhaps the killer wanted to finger Derek or someone else at the theatre?"

"A witness?" I blanched. Did he mean Sammy and Frank—or was he testing me? "You don't say. Who's the witness—and what was he or she doing here that early?"

"Who knows? It's all speculation at this point. Better leave the investigation to the experts."

"Of course." I agreed. "Maybe the murder has nothing to do with acting or the theatre. For all we know, Patrick got mixed up in something else." I let out a sigh. "Such a shame."

"Don't worry, we'll find his killer. I think we're on the right track." Burton raised his brows. "By the way, Jazz, how's Sammy doing? I hear he's back in town. What else are you not telling me?"

CHAPTER EIGHTEEN

I froze, staring at Agent Burton in surprise. "What do you mean? I'm not hiding anything from you..."

"Sure?" Burton said. "For one thing, you're looking away. Did you realize your left eye twitches when you're not telling the truth?"

Was I so transparent, so easy to read? "I've never lied to you. Are you calling me a liar?"

"Not at all. Let me reword that. We'll call it withholding information."

My face flushed, and I tried to ignore his penetrating blue gaze. Maybe he was right about avoiding eye contact. "If I am, it's for a good reason."

"Sammy?"

I turned around, my face blank. "Guess I'd better head back to work. See you later."

Before Burton could stop me, I rushed off, as far away as possible. I found Nathan by his Model T, fiddling with his camera. "Haven't you taken enough shots? I'm getting the jitters waiting while everyone ogles the dead body."

"Hell, no. A fella dressed up as a female winds up dead behind Martini Theatre? The public will eat it up."

"You sound like Mack," I groaned, rolling my eyes.

"What's wrong with that?" Mack came up behind us, grinning like a hyena. "This story is gold. I can see it lasting for a week or more, while the police try to apprehend the killer. Was it a lovers' quarrel? A tale of vengeance? Professional jealousy? Revenge? Cain versus Abel? Or a simple case of mistaken identity?" Mack rubbed his meaty hands together, his dark eyes gleaming. "The possibilities are endless."

Mack reminded me of a late-night radio serial, and just as corny. Still, I wondered why the victim was at the Oasis that night, and why did he return? And why did the killer use violin strings—or was it a viola?—to choke his victim? Was he a musician or was the wire simply a handy tool? Did the killer want to send a message—to Patrick, or someone else?

Most of all, why in hell did Sammy pick *this* spot to deposit the victim? He must have wanted to take the heat off himself and the Oasis. Did Amanda give him the idea with her talk of performers? Or did Sammy know more about the murder than he was letting on?

Burton must have noticed I was impatient to leave, since he walked up, asking, "Need a lift back to the office?"

Our quarrel was forgotten for now. "Sure. I've had enough forensics for one day." Grateful, I excused myself to Nathan and Mack, who didn't mind one bit.

After we got settled in his car, Burton turned to face me. "You never answered my question."

"Which one?" I started rambling, though I knew what he meant. "Sammy's fine. He just came down for a quick visit and plans to leave as soon as possible. I meant to tell you, but he asked me not to say anything to anyone."

"I'm not just anyone." Burton cut me off. "Jazz, tell me why you're protecting Sammy—not that he needs any protection, especially from you."

How to begin? "Remember our pal at Mario's? Musey stopped by the Oasis later that night, demanding money. Seems he and Johnny Jack still feel cheated after the booze drop got mucked up, so he's expecting a big pay-off."

"Where's Sammy going to get the cash?" Burton asked.

"Good question. I'm afraid of what they might do to Sammy if he doesn't pay up."

"Sammy should be doubly afraid. Johnny Jack may be a blowhard, but George Musey doesn't make threats lightly."

"Can you help Sammy?" I pleaded.

"I'll do what I can, but I'm not exactly rich." Burton looked upset as he turned the corner toward the *Gazette*.

"I didn't mean for you to loan him money. Can you find a reason to lock up Musey?"

"Again? Musey's got a lot of pull with the cops. I can't make any promises."

Burton parked in front of the *Gazette* building. "Jazz, your left eye is twitching again. Is that all? Anything else you want to tell me?"

I tried to act nonchalant, but guilt overpowered my resolve. Not to mention my left eye gave me away.

"Please don't say anything to the cops yet." I paused. "I may have found the murder weapon that killed the victim. The M.E. was right—it's an instrument string. That's what Patrick meant when he whispered, *Viola.*"

"You don't say." Burton looked surprised. "Where was it—at the Martini Theatre?"

"No..." I had second thoughts: Was I incriminating Sammy if I told Burton the truth? "If I tell you, I'd be putting you in an awkward position."

Burton gave me a wry smile. "I put myself at risk when I got involved with you."

"Gee, thanks." I took a deep breath. "I found it in the alley behind the Oasis, near the victim. The same spot we saw him before."

Burton stared at me without speaking. Finally he said, "That's odd. Why was the victim first stabbed, then killed at the Oasis? How in hell did he end up at the Martini Theatre?" His eyes widened. "Are you saying *Sammy* dumped him off? But why there?"

"Amanda saw his outfit and make-up, and guessed he was a performer—she probably gave Sammy the idea. He wanted a neutral place that wouldn't start a gang war."

"Sure that's the whole story?"

"I know it may sound like a cover-up, but you know Sammy is honest. He only tried to protect his bar and his staff. Can you blame him?"

Burton scratched his chin. "Doesn't it seem rather coincidental that Sammy showed up the same weekend that this actor was murdered? Then he moved the body away from the Oasis to avert suspicion, and perhaps point fingers at the vaudeville troupe?" He avoided my eyes. "I hate to even bring it up, Jazz, but...what if Sammy *is* involved?"

CHAPTER NINETEEN

"Sammy just panicked, that's all." I tried to convince Agent Burton. "See, that's why I didn't tell you earlier. I knew you'd assume the worst." Annoyed, I almost bolted out of the car, but he gripped my wrist, tight.

"Jazz, bear with me. I can't figure out why the victim was stabbed, then later killed, at the Oasis. Like you said, it may have nothing to do with Sammy. Do you have the violin string with you?"

"No, it's at home." I bit my lip, wishing I'd kept my mouth shut.

"You know we should turn it over to Homicide. Want to swing by the station later, and show it to them?"

"Not now. Give me time to think it over." I let out a sigh. "I'm so worried about Sammy. How can I keep his name out of this murder investigation?"

"What difference does it make if he's innocent?"

"*If* he's innocent? Of course he's innocent! I know he may seem guilty..."

"Calm down, Jazz. We'll figure it out." Burton held open my door, giving me the eye. "How about a ride home after work? Then you can turn over the wire to the cops."

I stalled, debating what to say—definitely a "damned if I do or don't" dilemma.

Finally I nodded, giving in. Wouldn't it be worse for everyone if I withheld potential evidence?

"OK, see you around five o'clock. Say, can you do me a favor? Tell me what the cops and the M.E. find out."

"Same goes for your reporters," he said, driving away.

When I entered the newsroom, I heard a chorus of voices—naturally Hank's jeer was the loudest: "I heard your new beau is in the slammer. Too bad your Fed friend can't bail him out."

"Sorry you fell for a *lady* killer," Chuck cracked. The guys burst into laughter.

"You slay me." I held my tongue, wishing I could tell them what I *really* thought.

Bracing myself, I made a beeline for Mrs. Harper's desk. "Did you hear the news? Derek got arrested for the murder of Patrick Mulligan, a vaudeville troupe actor."

"Murder? Derek?" Mrs. Harper blanched. "Why in the world would they arrest poor Derek?"

"I heard he and Patrick were rivals in the troupe, and competed for the best parts."

She looked wary. "But Derek is such a fine actor. No need to kill a rival for attention."

My boss gave me just the cue I needed. "Say, do you know who wrote those glowing reports on Derek? I was shocked when I saw them, right next to my review."

Flustered, Mrs. Harper raised her chin. "Why, I did, of course. You see, I'm old friends with his mother. We were classmates in school, and both of us served on the Ball High student newspaper." She shrugged, as if the matter seemed irrelevant. "I was only trying to give his acting career a little boost."

Clearly she didn't care about boosting *my* career.

"What about the other performers and musicians in the troupe? People will accuse me of playing favorites, singling him out for praise."

"I didn't think you'd mind, given your *history*..." She bristled, acting offended.

"Our history?" So Derek's mother squealed about our past romance. "Sure, we dated while in high school, but that's old news." I motioned to the bullpen. "Now the fellas think I'm sweet on him."

"Oh, is that what all the noise was about?" This time my boss looked genuinely perplexed. "I'm sure a handsome young actor like Derek has lots of admirers."

She refused to see the point. "Isn't the purpose of a review to give your unbiased, critical opinion?" I argued. "Aren't newspapers supposed to be fair and objective?"

"Why would they assume *you* wrote the other articles? They're not even by-lined." Mrs. Harper dismissed me with a flippant wave. "Well, no harm done."

No harm done? Only my reputation was at stake. "What about the rave review of Derek's performance under my name? I may lose my credibility as a journalist."

"Who will notice or even care about those articles besides the vaudeville troupe?" Mrs. Harper huffed. "After all, this is only entertainment. Not life and death."

"Since Derek was accused of murder, it *is* a matter of life and death." Exasperated, I turned to go, knowing she'd never understand.

"Wait, Jasmine, you gave me an idea," my boss called out. "Why don't you pay Derek a visit in jail? Interview him, get his side of the story. Was there any evidence that puts him at the crime scene? A motive? He may not talk to Mack or the boys, but I know he'll open up to *you*."

What? Was this an actual assignment or another favor for her friend? Or just a sneaky publicity stunt?

I could see the headlines now: HOMETOWN HERO WRONGLY ACCUSED OF MURDER. With a subhead: BETRAYED ACTOR BEATS THE RAP AND PROVES JUSTICE PREVAILS!

"As far as I know, he's still down at the police station. Is this for the news department or the society section?"

"Depends on what you dig up." Mrs. Harper gave me an encouraging smile. "Good luck."

I was wary. "What if it hurts Derek's reputation?"

"Even bad publicity is good for an actor's career. Especially for a villain. After all, I doubt he really is the killer. You can help prove his innocence."

I knew it—she *admitted* it was a PR ploy. "Can I get off early? I'll try to interview him behind bars."

She nodded her approval. Was she trying to pacify me or hoping I'd get a scoop for her society pages—or both? In any case, now I had two solid reasons to visit the police station today. If she only knew why.

CHAPTER TWENTY

After work, Agent Burton picked me up as planned, noticing my mood had changed from sour to sunny. "Why are you suddenly so eager to talk to the cops?"

"Not the cops—Derek."

"Trying to spring your fella from jail?"

I rolled my eyes. "Mrs. Harper asked me to interview Derek for a story. Is he still in custody?"

"They're holding him indefinitely," Burton told me, "hoping the real killer will trip up."

"The cops should be investigating the orchestra musicians, not poor Derek. What if it's a frame-up? The whole troupe had access to the instruments," I pointed out.

"If we knew the real motive, we might make more progress," Burton admitted.

Briefly we stopped by the boarding house, and I told Eva I was dining out with James that evening—easier than explaining the whole Derek-is-in-jail fiasco. I tiptoed upstairs and took out the hanky holding the wire, stuffing the bundle inside my leather clutch bag.

Inside the car, I showed the steel wire to Burton, hoping it might clear both Derek and Sammy.

"Looks like it came from a string instrument, all right."

With a sigh, I handed him the bunched-up hanky containing the wire. "Can you give it to the cops while I interview Derek? Then will they let him go?"

"This isn't definitive proof," Burton said. "We can't rely on circumstantial evidence and speculation."

"I found it at the crime scene, by the body. What more proof do you need?" I softened my tone. "Please don't mention Sammy or the Oasis, OK?"

"I'll do my best. Thanks for giving me the wire."

Did I have a choice?

At the police station, all heads turned as Burton and I walked in. My heart sank when I spied Derek sitting in the jail cell behind bars, slumped over against the dirty, stained brick walls. Derek perked up when he saw me, and waved for me to come over. A few cops sat huddled together in a corner, smoking cigarettes, and a joker wolf-whistled at me, calling out, "Over here, doll. Come sit on my lap."

Of all the nerve! "No, thanks," I snapped at the sap.

Burton approached the cops, eyes blazing, and they dried up, fast. The police chief gestured for Burton to come into his office, craning his neck to stare. Did he think I was a new suspect? Without waiting for an invite, I made my way to Derek's cell, ignoring the chorus of catcalls. Guess they didn't get a lot of ladies inside the station—at least not nice gals.

Though he'd only been in custody a few hours, Derek already had that washed-out, sickly pallor of a convicted criminal—like the jailbirds I'd seen in the papers and news reels. I felt a stab of sympathy seeing him look so desperate, clinging to the bars, pacing his eight-by-eight jail cell like an inmate on Death Row. Then again, he tended to be melodramatic even in real life.

"What are you doing here, Jazz? I hate for you to see me this way." His face fell, then instantly brightened, reminding me of the happy/sad drama masks on theatre programs. "Say, thanks for the great write-up. You made my day! I didn't know you still felt that way about me, considering you have a new beau and all." Derek pressed himself against the bars, his voice soft.

"You're all wet!" My cheeks flamed beet-red. "Don't flatter yourself. I only wrote the actual review. Those puff pieces were my boss's bird-brained idea."

Derek's sad drama face fell into place. "OK, I got the telegram. Frankly, I *was* surprised. Figured you were still mad at me for taking off that way. Now I feel like a fool."

"Blame my boss, Mrs. Harper. Remember her? She's friends with your mother."

Derek made a face. "That old blue-nose? They used to gossip like two clucking hens."

"No wonder she became a society editor. In fact, she suggested I do a story on your arrest. She said any publicity is good publicity."

"Yeah? What if some so-called critic says our show stinks?" He raised his brows. "Gotta admit, the troupe wasn't thrilled with your lukewarm review, or the spotlight on my budding career."

"Mrs. Harper never breathed a word to me about those stupid stories," I said, feeling guilty for no reason. "I only said some acts seemed old hat—I didn't say they were terrible. Say, do you want me to help you or not?"

"I'm the one stuck behind bars. What do you think?"

"OK, first I need to ask you one question." I studied him, watching his reaction. "Did you kill Patrick?"

"Of course not!" He drew back, looking betrayed. "Now why would I go and do a fool thing like that, and possibly close down the show? It's the first good gig I've had in months."

I crossed my arms, wondering how much to trust him. After all, he did make his living as an actor, pretending to be other people.

"As I recall, you don't like playing second fiddle. Speaking of, do you play any string instruments? A viola, perhaps?"

Derek seemed crestfallen. "Have you already forgotten? I only play saxophone."

That let him off the hook, for now. "So why did they arrest you? They don't really think you did it, do they?"

He looked around the station. "Who knows? Someone must have fed the cops a bunch of hooey. They're spreading lies, rumors, saying Patrick and I were big rivals, that I had an ax to grind. What bullshit! Patrick and I were friends, good friends."

"Friends?" I was taken aback. "That's not what I heard. You think you're being framed?"

He nodded. "I think the troupe ganged up on me, set me up as revenge."

"Because they're *jealous*?"

"Actors can be extremely competitive, especially for star roles," Derek said. "Reviews can make or break a career—and a show."

Sure, I knew about the power of the pen, but I had no idea Derek might land in jail due to some positive press. Clearly Mrs. Harper's good intentions had backfired.

"I suppose you're right. Any idea who may be behind this scheme?" I asked.

Before he could reply, Burton returned and gave Derek the once-over. Then he motioned for me to follow him to a back office.

"The captain wants to see you, Jasmine. Now."

CHAPTER TWENTY-ONE

"Me? Now? Why?" I played dumb. Hadn't Burton taken care of the instrument string?

Burton firmly gripped my elbow, guiding me down a long, dimly-lit hall, as if I were a ward of the state. "He just wants to ask you a few questions."

Yikes! I glanced back at Derek, afraid I might be in the jail cell next to him soon. "What did you tell him?"

"I only said you uncovered some evidence at the crime scene." His tone softened. "Don't worry, I'll be in the room with you."

Small comfort. Burton led me into a large, orderly office where the captain sat behind a long mahogany table that doubled as a desk. Was this his headquarters or the interrogation room?

A few framed certificates and awards covered the walls, including a college diploma from Sam Houston State University in Huntsville. So he wasn't just some local yokel who'd done well, he was a degreed professional who could easily outsmart a society reporter into spilling her guts—if I had any left after this fiasco.

I'd never formally met Captain Johnson before, much less been grilled by him. Tall and thin, with spectacles and balding hair, he reminded me more of a mild-mannered accountant than a police captain. How should I behave? Shy and meek, like a shrinking violet, or as my usual Nosy Nellie self? My hands started to shake and I took a few deep breaths to calm down.

Great—now I really looked guilty.

Captain Johnson stood and smiled, followed by a firm handshake. "Nice to meet you, Miss Cross. Agent Burton here speaks highly of you."

"He does?" I shot Burton a wary look. "So why am I here?" What a tactful opening line.

The captain's face broke into a grin. "You have the wrong idea, Miss Cross. You're not here as a suspect. Agent Burton tells me you have some information in this case that might prove useful." He sat down behind his desk and indicated the banker's chairs across the table.

"First, I'd like to know your relationship with the suspect, Derek Hammond. After reading your glowing *Gazette* report, I take it you two are close friends?"

My face flushed and Burton turned toward me, waiting for my reply. Oh, boy, was I going to wring Mrs. Harper's honking goose neck when I got to the office—after I broke out of jail!

"I only wrote the review. I didn't write the glowing part." Johnson seemed confused, so I started blabbering: "Yes, we were good friends in high school, but that was a long time ago. I mean, it wasn't *that* long ago, I'm only twenty-one..." I took a breath. "We simply lost touch."

"Obviously you've renewed your friendship since then?"

Was it so obvious? "No, I wouldn't call it that...I mean, we're friendly, but I've hardly seen him." I cleared my throat. "Ask Agent Burton. I didn't even recognize him at the vaudeville show."

"I understand Hammond is an actor and from all accounts, he plays a believable villain. Does he have a hot temper? Is he hostile or violent, capable of killing someone? Could he be guilty of...murder?"

"Of course not." I shook my head. "The Derek I knew isn't a killer. He claims he's being framed."

"Is that so? Did you consider the fact he might be lying? Perhaps he was in character, as they say, and got carried away?" Johnson's brown eyes glinted. "I hear he and the victim were rivals?"

"Not at all. Derek isn't a vindictive or vicious person. He's as decent as they come."

"I know you want to help your friend, but so far he seems to be our main suspect." The captain's eyes drilled through mine. "Any other information you can provide?"

"Derek told me he and Patrick were good friends, not enemies. He thinks the troupe may be jealous about my...the stories in the paper. The *Gazette*."

Burton shifted in his chair, signaling an end to this line of questioning. Thank goodness. "Jasmine found some evidence at the crime scene," he spoke up, nudging my arm. He placed my wadded-up hanky on the captain's desk, and revealed the steel wire.

"I think it's from a violin or viola," I stammered. "My fingerprints are probably all over the string, but I'm not guilty, promise."

"I doubt we can remove fingerprints from a thin steel string." The captain chuckled. "Sure would make our jobs a lot easier. So tell me, where'd you find it? By the body?"

"Not far. You know, in the alley." I looked away, not meeting his curious gaze.

"The alley?" Johnson studied the string in the light. "Appears to have some blood residue which confirms our suspicions. Why didn't you give it to the coroner at the crime scene? He determined the murder weapon most likely was a violin string—and this proves his theory."

Was he trying to trick me? "I wanted to, but I..I..didn't have it with me."

Captain Johnson tilted his head, alert, like a dog perking up at a fire engine. "But I thought you found it at the crime scene? The alley behind Martini Theatre, right?"

"I found it in an alley, yes." I squirmed in my chair, my face starting to perspire. Now I knew why they called it the hot seat. "Near Market Street."

"And pray tell, what were you doing on Market Street, digging around in a back alley?" His once-warm brown eyes turned dull as dirt.

"I was just...helping someone. A friend lost something, and I was looking for it."

"It? What's it? Which friend? The suspect?" Johnson's brows shot up. "Tell the truth, Miss Cross: Did you witness the crime? Did you see the killer's face? If so, why are you protecting him? Don't you want to help solve this case, and try to clear your friend?"

"Yes, I do. But I know he didn't do it. He was just trying to save his...business."

Johnson leaned forward, clasping his hands. "He—who's he? How did he get involved? Doesn't he realize that it's against the law to move a dead body, not to mention tamper with a crime scene?"

Nervous, I glanced at Burton for help, but he just sat there, motionless and mute. What a pal.

"He wasn't thinking straight at the time. He was so shocked, he panicked."

"I see. And does this new friend have a name?"

When I didn't reply, Captain Johnson gestured for Burton and whispered in his ear, hand by his mouth. Then they glanced at me with concern. What now?

Burton stood up to leave when the phone rang on the captain's desk. "On the victim?" Johnson blinked a few times, listening intently. Then he slowly put down the phone, eyes wide in surprise, his cheeks red.

"Well, doesn't that beat all. That was the coroner's office. I think we may have a new motive for murder. They found something unusual during the exam."

"A weapon? A fresh wound?" Burton sat up.

"A diamond ring, like a wedding band."

"A ladies' ring?" Burton frowned. "We didn't see him wearing a ring. Where was it?"

"In his..personal effects...under his clothing." Johnson cupped his hands over his chest and shook them in front.

Seems he couldn't bring himself to say the word out loud. "You mean he was wearing a brassiere?" I piped up.

The captain's face flushed a bright pink. "Yes, a rather large one, they said. It appears he was hiding the ring...in his br-br-br...his lingerie."

"A large diamond or brassiere?" I tried to hide my smile, enjoying seeing the captain blush.

"Both, apparently. Our victim was not a small man."

Burton caught my eye. "Are you thinking the same thing?"

"Seems like a lot of theft is going around." I nodded. "Remember the purse snatcher at Mario's restaurant? Do you think the crimes may be related...?"

Burton picked up where I left off. "Perhaps Patrick was also a part-time jewel thief?"

CHAPTER TWENTY-TWO

"A jewel thief?" Captain Johnson stroked his chin. "Very possible. I understand the acting profession doesn't pay well, unless you're in the movies."

"So I hear." A sore subject. If Derek hadn't left for Hollywood, then he wouldn't be in this predicament. "By the way, did you search Derek after you arrested him?"

"Yes, we patted him down for weapons." The captain frowned. "What are you getting at, Miss Cross?"

"Why not search Derek now, while he's here? See if any jewelry turns up?" I glanced at my watch, hoping to God that Derek wasn't involved. "He's got a show tonight at seven. If he's clean, then maybe you can let him go. That way, he can work undercover and help you find the real killer."

Johnson pounded his desk. "Young lady, don't tell me how to do my job!"

Why not, if I helped solve the case? Sadly, Johnson failed to appreciate my bright ideas.

"Captain, I think she has a good point." Burton stood up, arms crossed. "We both know you can't keep him here without hard evidence. Like Jasmine says, Derek may serve as an asset in this investigation since he's on the inside."

Captain Johnson looked skeptical. "How can we be sure the killer is an actor or a musician in the troupe? May be a random killing or even an accident."

"We don't know yet, but he can help eliminate that possibility," said Burton.

"I don't want to put a civilian at risk." Johnson frowned. "May be too dangerous."

"Don't worry about Derek," I cut in. "After all, he's a good actor, as Burton knows. If anyone gets suspicious, I'm sure he can talk his way out of a jam."

"You can release Derek into my custody temporarily," Burton offered. "I'll be glad to drop him off at the Martini Theatre in time for his performance tonight."

"Thanks." I gave Burton a grateful look. "I know he'll be relieved."

Johnson stared out the window, as if waiting for a sign. "OK, Burton, make sure he's willing to cooperate. Glad we've got that settled. But now we don't have a prime suspect." Then he leaned forward, hands clasped like a preacher. "Let me ask you again, little lady. Where exactly did you find this violin string?"

Swell—now what mess had I gotten us into? If I did reveal Sammy's name, he'd likely become a second suspect—but wouldn't that help clear Derek? If I kept quiet, Burton might spill the beans. Chances were, they'd eventually find out the truth anyway. Damn, what to do?

I glanced at Burton for help, afraid to say anything.

"Young lady, do I need to remind you that if you're withholding valuable information, you're considered an accessory to murder?" The captain slapped his hand on the desk. "At the very least, you'd be guilty of aiding and abetting a killer."

"What? I'm not aiding and abetting anyone! Sammy is not a killer!" I blurted out.

Wow, those scare tactics really worked.

The captain smirked. "Sammy who?"

I heaved a sigh. "Sammy Cook. He owns the Oasis on Market Street. They stumbled across the body by accident."

"You don't say." He sat up straighter. "By accident? Are you sure?"

"If you must know, I was there."

Not only was I digging Sammy's grave, I was digging mine right next to his. All I needed was a shovel. Maybe my big mouth would fill the bill.

"And you thought to tell me this now?"

"You didn't ask." I smiled, trying hard not to look like an accomplice.

Captain Johnson stared at Burton in exasperation. "If that's true, then why did your friend move the body? Seems very suspicious."

Oh, boy. "Clearly he overreacted. He's been in trouble with the law before and wanted to avoid any problems. Sammy has no motive, no reason to kill anyone. In fact, he recently moved to Houston to get away from the gangs."

Burton finally spoke up. "Sir, I can vouch for his character. Cook is a decent man, trying to make a living. He proved instrumental in helping me get some bad hooch off the streets last summer."

"Yes, I know all about your friendship with Mr. Sammy Cook." The captain thrust his chin at Burton. "Weren't *you* instrumental in helping him escape to Houston?"

"I needed a statement from him to build a case against Johnny Jack Nounes." Burton remained calm. "I had to protect my main witness."

"Is that so? Meanwhile, Johnny Jack disappeared with several cases of rum, right? Did you have any luck in tracking him down?"

"Captain, you know how Nounes operates. He pays several influential friends in high places to protect him." Burton gave a frustrated sigh. "It's a long process."

Johnson nodded. "I know it's not your department, Agent Burton, but since you're such good friends with Sammy Cook, why don't *you* bring him downtown for questioning? The sooner we clear this up, the better."

"What? Why?" I felt like crying out for the hundredth time, *He's not guilty!*

Burton shifted in his seat. "I'd rather not, sir. He's an invaluable source of information and I don't want to lose his trust."

"Fine. Then ask Vernon to fetch him. He knows where all the bars are on Market Street."

"Yes, sir." Burton gave me an apologetic look before he left, presumably to find Vernon.

"Why don't you come with me, Miss Cross?" The captain stood up and held open the door. "You can tell the suspect—Mr. Hammond—that he's free to go for now, on one condition."

"Great." I tried to muster up some enthusiasm as Johnson led me to Derek's cell, but I felt guilty about Sammy—and mad at myself. In my efforts to help Derek, I'd inadvertently incriminated my own brother. Damn it, why'd I even give them the violin string at all?

Wild-eyed, Derek paced back and forth in his jail cell, and perked up when we approached.

"Young man, do you know anything about some stolen jewelry?" The captain wasted no time getting to the point. "Specifically a diamond ring?"

"No, why?" Derek frowned, glancing at me.

"Mind if we search your person?"

"Yes, I do. I've done nothing wrong."

"Sorry, son. We have to do it even if you do mind." Johnson unlocked the cell and signaled for an officer, instructing him to take Derek to a private room.

Derek covered his chest. "Is this really necessary?"

He nodded. "Ask your girlfriend. It was all her idea."

Girlfriend? Gee, thanks. Happy to help.

Derek scowled at me as they headed down a back hall, prodded by a burly cop.

As I waited in Burton's office, I twirled the buttons on my frock, hoping Derek wouldn't blow his top. Finally he returned and sat down, half-leaning his chair on the window sill. "Sorry about Sammy. Glad I didn't have to retrieve him myself. Sammy will think I fingered him."

"You? He'll be so mad, I doubt he'll ever forgive me." I turned to survey the half-empty police station. "I hope the cops don't razz him or get rough. What's Vernon like?"

"He's a good egg. Spends too much time in the bars, on and off-duty. I'm sure he can convince Sammy to come here peacefully."

"I hope Sammy will understand." I let out a sigh. "Now I wish I'd never found that damn violin string."

"If you and Sammy cooperate with the authorities, that will only win points with the captain." Burton grinned. "Johnson was certain we'd caught the killer and you managed to convince him otherwise. Where is Derek by the way?"

"He's undergoing a thorough body search for stolen jewelry." I grimaced. "Worse, the captain told Derek it was my brilliant idea. Now he'll think I suspect him too!"

"Derek doesn't strike me as a killer." Burton shrugged. "In fact, at first I thought he was a pretty boy. A dandy."

"Who are you calling a dandy?" Derek charged into the office, dark eyes on fire. "Hey, Jazz, thanks for offering up my body for inspection. I've never been so humiliated in my life."

I avoided his gaze. "I was only trying to help. At least you got out in time for your show."

"Well, next time don't bother," he huffed. "I'd rather be stuck in here than frisked and examined like a common criminal. In the buff, I might add."

What a picture! I suppressed a smile as I imagined a nude Derek fighting off the cops.

"Quit bickering, children." Burton seemed amused. "Time to go."

Ignoring the cops' stares, Derek kept his head down and clutched his jacket tight as we headed out of the station. Burton held the door open for me and I stopped short when I ran into Sammy, followed by a forlorn Frank, both in handcuffs.

CHAPTER TWENTY-THREE

"What are you doing here?" Sammy's eyes darted back and forth between me and Agent Burton. "Ratting me out?" The betrayed look on his face made my heart break.

"Bunk!" I replied. "I had some...evidence to turn in."

"Evidence that incriminates me, huh?" He tilted his head toward Frank. "Both of us?"

"Just the opposite. We're trying to help."

"Move along." The cop shoved Sammy ahead. "No time for chit-chat. Captain's orders."

"I'm coming with you," Burton told the cop. "Easy, Vernon. Let go of this man. He's done nothing wrong."

"Says you," Vernon taunted.

I wanted to slap his smug smile. Derek and I watched as they led Sammy and Frank to the captain's office. Stone-faced, Burton trailed behind, and pushed his way inside, telling Vernon, "Remove those handcuffs."

After Vernon obeyed, he turned to Derek. "Lucky break for you, kid."

Hoping to eavesdrop, I tried to follow Burton into the office, but Vernon blocked me, pointing at the door. "Exit's that way." What did he think I was, a rabble-rouser?

Outside, Derek looked puzzled. "What's the rumpus?"

After I explained, he said, "You found a violin string? So that's why you asked if I played a string instrument."

"May be the murder weapon." I looked around the area. "Do you think a musician in the troupe murdered Patrick? Or is the killer trying to implicate someone from the orchestra?"

"Possible on both counts. Depends on the motive." Derek's dark eyes had that far-away look, drifting off to his own private thoughts.

"Do you have any ideas? Are you sure Patrick wasn't swiping jewelry on the side?"

"He's not a thief," Derek insisted. "Say, why did the cops pat me down—again? I had to strip off to my knickers and let me tell you, in this cold weather, it wasn't a pretty sight."

It? I stifled a smile. "Sorry. I wanted to prove you were innocent—and it worked."

"Innocent of what? I had to show my goods to a couple of asshole cops in a police station? Not my idea of making whoopee."

I laughed out loud. "You're out of jail, aren't you?"

"You think it's funny?" Derek crossed his arms over his chest. "What's the gag?"

Derek sounded so agitated, I sobered up, fast. "Don't tell anyone in the troupe, promise? They found a diamond ring in Patrick's brassiere...under his frock."

"Patrick had on a brassiere? With a diamond ring?" His voice rose a few octaves. "Now I've heard everything. I can understand wearing women's clothes for a part, but a brassiere to boot?" He slapped his forehead. "What's so special about this ring? Who did it belong to?"

"Who knows? But it proves that Patrick *was* lifting baubles on the side."

"Maybe he hid it there for safekeeping."

"Obviously." I blinked. "So if he's not a jewel thief, what did he do to wind up dead in an alley?"

Derek leaned in, his face dangerously close to mine. A dark lock of hair tickled his forehead, and I resisted the urge to smooth it back into place. "I've heard rumors about the musicians...But this is just between us. No press."

"What kind of rumors?"

He clammed up when Burton burst through the door, *sans* Sammy or Frank.

"Sorry to interrupt your clambake." Burton shot Derek a cold stare as he got into his Roadster. "Come on, let's go. Don't you need a ride to the Martini Theatre?"

Ignoring his crack, I asked Burton, "What happened to Sammy and Frank?"

"The captain said it's a formality, that they have to interview everyone involved." He gave me a reassuring smile. "If anything, the violin string lets those two mugs off the hook. When was the last time you saw Sammy or Frank playing the violin?"

I smiled to myself, relieved. "Where are they?"

"The captain put them in a holding cell for a while. If the real killer thinks the suspects are in custody, he might blab to the wrong people. He's hoping Derek can provide some information." Burton nodded at Derek. "That's where you come in, sport."

"What do you mean? You expect me to get Sammy and Frank released?" Derek gulped.

"Think you're up to the task? You know how much Sammy means to Jasmine." Burton glared at Derek, then got in his car, slammed the door and gunned his engine.

"I've never had the pleasure of meeting Sammy before today." Derek tapped my shoulder from the back seat. "Are you two related?"

How did he know? Burton nudged me, warning me to keep quiet, as if I needed reminding. "He's a family friend." I gave him my standard line, not wanting to complicate matters. Derek had left town right before my father died, when I found out Sammy was my half-brother.

"I'll do my best. For both our sakes." Derek drew a dramatic breath, his head held high. "After all, the show must go on."

Corny, but true. Was he waiting for our applause?

After Burton parked at Martini Theatre, I stood with Derek by the Roadster. Burton refused to drive a simple squad car, claiming he'd blend in better with bootleggers by driving a fancy Ford. No doubt he was right. So who was picking up the tab?

"Sorry you had to go through this ordeal," I told Derek, my voice low. "I didn't know they'd force you to strip off in jail."

His face twisted. "Glad I'm out of that rat hole. How can I repay the favor?"

"Anything you can find out about this murder will be a big help. By the way, I'd like to do a proper interview with you, as soon as possible."

"I'd be honored." He bowed like a formal butler. "How about dinner, after the show?"

"Lunch tomorrow will be better. Then I can write my profile while it's still fresh in my mind." A good excuse, since I didn't want him to get the wrong idea about a late-night rendezvous. "Say, before you go inside, can you tell me about those rumors?"

Derek raised his brows like an evil villain. "We'll talk over lunch. See you tomorrow."

"Don't forget. Sammy and I are counting on you."

"Did I hear someone say lunch?" Burton asked when I got back into the car.

"Why not? Where else can we talk privately? Certainly not at the theatre, with a potential killer lurking around."

"As long as you don't make it too private." Burton winked at me. Was he really jealous or pretending? Hard to tell with Agent Burton. "So where to—the paper?"

I nodded. "Back to the grindstone for me."

"Same here. But cheer up. Maybe one of the newsboys dug up some information?"

"Better than another dead body," I cracked. When he stopped in front of the *Gazette* building, I lingered at the car window. "Please watch out for Sammy. I'd hate for the cops to charge him, especially without any proof."

"So far, it's purely circumstantial. Wrong place, wrong time, wrong suspect. Seems bad luck follows Sammy wherever he goes."

"You said it," I agreed. "He needs a break."

Burton squeezed my hand. "By the way, I hear a band is playing jazz in the Hotel Galvez lobby tonight. Thought you'd like to relax, take your mind off...things."

"Would I! That's right up my alley..." I had a sudden vision of Patrick in a dress, lying in the alley, and cringed.

"How about I pick you up at Eva's, around six?"

"Swell." I nodded. "Say, I wonder if any violinists ever play jazz?"

CHAPTER TWENTY-FOUR

After Burton dropped me off at the *Gazette*, I rushed to my desk, hoping to avoid any questions. How I wished I'd never found that stupid string and gotten Sammy in more hot water.

I sorted through the papers stacked on my desk, trying to focus, ignoring Mrs. Harper's intense gaze. Still, she was relentless. "So tell me, Jasmine. How's Derek? What scandal did you *uncover* down at the police station?"

Did she hear about his body search? Or the diamond ring in Patrick's brassiere?

"Luckily they let him go, in time for his performance." Why was she being such a Nosy Nellie? Even if I wrote it up, I knew both topics were too risqué for a family newspaper.

Her penciled brows arched higher. "A little birdie told me you helped set Derek free. Attagirl, Jazz! Did you get to ask him any questions?"

Gosh, she even had spies at the police station?

"Thanks. Fact is, they didn't have any grounds to hold him." I left out the stripping-off segment of his jail time. "I've set up an interview with him tomorrow over lunch."

"Lunch?" Her thin lips curled into a coy smile. "Business or pleasure...or both?"

"Depends if the *Gazette* is picking up the tab," I hinted, assuming Derek was broke.

"I suppose we could manage a couple of dollars from petty cash," she sighed.

Mack bustled in wearing a camel hair coat, a brown wool scarf wrapped snugly over his neck, carrying a satchel. "I heard you managed to break your boyfriend out of jail. Or did your Fed Agent fella have a hand in his escape?"

"You're daffy. The cops knew he was innocent so they released him."

"Apparently they have a new suspect." Mack pointed a finger at me. "Your old pal, Sammy Cook, is it?"

My heart stopped. "He's not a suspect. They brought him in for questioning."

"Sure looks mighty suspicious, when a body turns up behind your bar," Mack taunted. "Or is he trying to pin the blame on his manager? What's his name, Frank?"

"Says you." I froze, wondering who was his source. "They question lots of people."

"So why were they both handcuffed? They sure sound guilty to me."

Jeepers, the police department certainly boasted some big blabbermouths.

"As a journalist, you know that's pure speculation, Mack," Mrs. Harper huffed. "I thought you newsboys dealt mainly in *facts*."

For once, my boss stood up for me.

But Mack had to add, "That's right. We leave the gossip to you girls."

"Dry up, Mack," Mrs. Harper replied as we exchanged annoyed looks. Good for her, not backing down.

I only hoped Mack wouldn't turn Sammy or Frank into serious suspects on some trumped up charges—just to fill a few newspaper inches.

Flustered, I needed a break from the cigar smoke and hot air clouding the newsroom. With a smile, I sidled up to Mrs. Harper. "Mind if I take a lunch break now?"

She glanced at her watch, then at the mostly-male office, and nodded in understanding. "Go right ahead. You've earned your keep today."

Freedom at last! I felt as relieved as Derek, released from my publishing prison. Elated, I made a beeline for Nathan's, a chic new boutique on Post Office—the nice part of the street. Inside, the quaint shop retained its Art Nouveau influences with carved French walnut showcases, fresh flowers and flowing lace curtains.

A pretty young woman with long chestnut locks stood behind a carved walnut and glass counter. With her flowing wavy hair and floral velvet frock, she looked like an Alphonse Mucha painting—all she needed were a few flowers in her hair to complete the image. Did they hire help based on appearance or did she model herself to fit the shop's style?

"Are you looking for anything special?" she asked.

And how! While the selection of compacts, purses and perfumes seemed smaller than Eiband's, the quality was finer: exquisite French guilloche enameled vanity cases on chains lay next to colorful cut-steel beaded bags in geometric and figural designs with intricate long fringe.

The cut-crystal perfume bottles held jeweled and enameled stoppers, radiating mini-rainbows under the bright lights. Temptation beckoned me at every turn.

As I strolled through the store, I stopped to admire the beautiful German scenic seed beaded purses depicting castles and romantic scenes, Belgian beaded bags topped with figural celluloid frames of jesters and winged butterfly women, whimsical painted ceramic French perfume lamps shaped like harlequins and half-nude harem girls. Glittering enamel mesh bags by Mandalian and Whiting & Davis called to me like a siren's song.

So many choices, so little cash!

Longingly I fingered the fine Italian beaded purses and enameled tango compacts with finger rings and lipsticks.

A small display of French Bakelite and celluloid vanity bags caught my eye, featuring a variety of shapes and sizes, most containing powder, rouge wells and lipsticks.

Finally I settled on a beauty that took my breath away: A stunning coral-pink celluloid vanity bag decorated with dripping icicles of rhinestones outlined in gold and black paint. Embedded inside was a removable watch with black ribbon straps, finished with a thin black cord and tassel decorated with sparkly rhinestone accents. What a stunner!

Thank goodness Nathan's Boutique offered lay-away to their customers since I needed weeks to pay off this splurge. "Please take good care of my treasure." I stroked the celluloid gem as if bidding it farewell. "I hope to pick it up by Christmas." The Mucha model smiled at my delighted expression.

Afterwards, I felt giddy, refreshed and ready to go back to work. Even Mrs. Harper gave me a knowing smile when I returned to my desk. When Nathan offered me a ride home later, I gladly accepted. Not even grouchy old Mack could spoil my day or date that night with Agent Burton.

That evening, I slipped on a silk frock adorned with a red poppy print and handkerchief hem—a bit light for November, but I knew my new velvet coat with the embroidered gilt-thread collar would keep me warm.

Agent Burton arrived promptly at six, on time as usual.

"He's always so punctual!" Eva smiled with approval.

"We're going to the Hotel Galvez to hear a jazz band. Would you care to join us?" Burton asked Eva. Such a gentleman—one more reason he'd won over my aunt.

"No, you two young people go on without me. Have a good time!"

In the car, I asked Burton, "What happened with Sammy and Frank? Are they still holding them for questioning?"

Burton nodded, not meeting my gaze. "I think they want to keep them overnight."

"In jail?" I grabbed his arm, causing him to veer left. "Why? They didn't do anything!"

"Captain Johnson is sending two undercover cops to stake out the Oasis, in case the killer shows up. He may have left some evidence or an item behind at the Oasis, maybe in the alley."

"You think they're looking for the diamond ring?"

"I'd put money on it. From the size of that rock, I bet it belonged to some muckety-muck's wife or daughter."

"The killer probably wants to cash in and leave town." I let out a sigh. "Poor Sammy, stuck in a jail cell, again. Does he know the cops plan to watch his bar?"

Burton nodded. "I told him, but he didn't believe me. He thinks we're trying to set him up, plant evidence while they search the Oasis."

"What if that's the real plan? Maybe Musey made a deal with the cops."

"Bunk." Burton shook his head. "In any case, Sammy and Frank might be better off behind bars for the night."

"I'm afraid of what might happen with only Dino in charge there," I admitted.

"That muscle head can hold his own."

"True. Dino doesn't take gruff from anyone." I smiled in the dark, imagining Dino single-handedly beating up any bullies. "Why don't we check on him later?"

"May be too risky. And I don't want to blow the cops' cover. They'll probably assume I'm interfering with their investigation."

"I wouldn't mind stopping by for a friendly drink."

"Dino? Friendly?" Burton looked aghast.

After Burton pulled up at the Galvez, a valet rushed to open my door. Nice to feel like a princess for a change.

"Valet parking? You must have gotten a raise," I joked.

"Only the best for you, doll. Plus it's getting cold outside." Practical as always.

Strains of jazz filtered through the plush lobby, arched windows providing a nice view of the beach. We found a small table near the band—no ordinary trio, but a full six-piece group of musicians. Sad to say, I didn't spot a viola player or violinist in the mix, yet perked up to see a cute young fella playing an upright bass and an older cellist. String instruments! I pointed them out to Burton, but decided they looked too harmless to be murder suspects.

A perky blonde waitress with a short bob took our order, and bent over so low that we got a full view of her charms. I observed Burton's reaction, grateful that his eyes never strayed from her painted-on face. I admit, I wanted to knock the cocktail tray right out of her manicured paws, but decided that wouldn't be very ladylike, especially in public.

Instead, I faked a smile and gave her the once-over, to let her know I was onto her games. "A hot tea for me, please. Preferably *Jasmine.*" I accented my name, in case she'd read about our romance in the society pages, despite my protests. Yet I doubted the dear ever read the papers.

Burton ordered a Coca-Cola and she flashed him a suggestive smile. "What's the name? Want me to charge it to your *room*?" She acted like I was invisible. Did she want to hunt him down and wait for him upstairs?

Thank goodness he ignored her innuendo. "We're not staying overnight. Just enjoying the music."

"What a pity," she purred, licking her chops.

After she left, I hissed, "What's that floozy trying to do? Offer herself up on the menu?"

Burton grinned, obviously pleased by my jealous outburst. He drummed his knee while the band broke into two Gershwin numbers, *Fascinating Rhythm* and *Rhapsody in Blue.* The mellow jazz soothed me and I felt like drifting off, wishing I could take a nap.

Truth was, I hadn't been sleeping well lately. An ex-beau and a dead body can keep you up at night.

When a new older waitress with deep bags under her eyes delivered our drinks, I gave Burton a smug smile. No more peep shows for him tonight.

I perked up when a young brunette flapper sang *Ain't We Got Fun* and *'S Wonderful,* dancing the Charleston in a short fringed frock. Her animated performance fit the songs perfectly.

While the band played a few Cole Porter tunes, I got to study the crowd, mostly moneyed older couples, no doubt vacationers who'd escaped the cold northern climates.

Galveston never failed to attract a brisk tourist trade, even during off-season. Personally, I preferred the empty beaches and cool winter weather. To me, the gray skies and somber seascape seemed more mysterious, more romantic.

I snuggled next to Burton, enjoying the lively set. The musicians let loose, improvising on a few blues songs. The Negro saxophonist and trumpeter broke into Dixieland jazz, each playing solo for a few minutes. Burton gave me a satisfied smile, tapping his knee in time to the music. Interesting that a Yankee like Burton enjoyed Southern blues and jazz so much.

An hour later, the band leader announced a break and the musicians carefully placed their instruments in their cases. After they left, the band leader stood before the microphone and announced: "For your entertainment, ladies and gentleman, a magician will perform an array of tricks. Please stay seated and enjoy the show."

I whispered to Burton, "I wonder if he's the same magician from the vaudeville show?"

"Possible, since he's only on stage for ten minutes or so at most. He could be moonlighting on the side." He shrugged. "But these jokers all look alike to me."

During the break, I headed to the ladies' room, and made small talk with a few matrons washing their hands and powdering their noses. My silk frock paled next to their beaded gowns, glitzy jewelry and sterling mesh bags.

"I didn't think I'd enjoy jazz so much!" I heard one elderly lady in a glittering gown and long string of pearls say to a friend wearing a diamond and sapphire choker. "The music makes me want to do the fox trot! And the Charleston!"

"Absolutely. I feel so young and alive!" her friend exclaimed. "Positively giddy!"

I smiled at their excited expressions and returned to watch the magic act. The magician did a few card tricks with audience volunteers, then performed some sleight-of-hand numbers: the usual coins behind the ears, scarves pulled from his hat. Nothing as death-defying or dramatic as slicing a woman in half or making her disappear—difficult to do in a hotel lobby. This time, his pretty young assistant appeared merely decorous, flitting about the lobby, delicate hands highlighting his tricks—not as dramatic as his usual act with secret escape boxes and elaborate props.

"Must be the same vaudeville magician," I whispered to Burton, who also seemed unimpressed. "I wish the band would start playing again. I'm ready to shake a leg."

"You said it." Yawning, he stood up. "In fact, I may stretch *both* my legs a bit."

Naturally Burton was too polite to admit he needed to visit the men's room. I observed the crowd, who continued to chatter while the magician attempted to get their attention with more lackluster card tricks.

As the magician wove between the tables, I had a chance to study him more closely. He wore an elegant jacket and vest, and as he brushed by our table, I did a double-take: The jacket sported fancy enameled and marcasite buttons—except for a solid black button that didn't match the rest. Sure enough, he had to be Milo the magician from the vaudeville troupe—the "pansy" Frank described. So what was he doing with Patrick at the Oasis the night poor Patrick got stabbed? Were they *together*?

Heart pounding, I motioned for Burton to sit next to me on a loveseat closer to the front, and whispered in his ear: "Remember the marcasite button I found in the alley? Guess who's missing a button on his jacket?" I cocked my head at Milo, who was preparing to leave with his assistant. "Was he the *dandy* fighting with Patrick? Think he stabbed him or were they up to something?"

"Good question," Burton whispered back. "Still, that doesn't make him guilty of anything. Let's keep an eye on him tonight, and we'll see what happens."

"But Milo is ready to leave! Can't you do anything to stop him?" I began to panic as I watched Milo cross the lobby, no doubt to make his vaudeville act in time.

"Unfortunately I don't have any grounds to hold or question him," Burton said. "If I do, he may get suspicious and try to escape, even skip town."

"You're right." I pretended to act nonchalant while Milo walked out the exit, but I was squirming in my seat, too rattled to concentrate. Leaning against the plush cushions, I tried to enjoy the lively jazz, to no avail. While the set wound down, a few couples began to head upstairs. By now, it was nine o'clock, probably past their bedtime.

After the performance, the audience gave the band a round of applause and some patrons added a few dollars to their tip jar. The musicians were packing up their instruments when the woman wearing the fancy choker burst into the lobby, her hands fluttering around her neck.

"Help! I've been robbed!" she screeched. "Where's the hotel manager? Somebody stole my jewels—right out of my room!"

CHAPTER TWENTY-FIVE

The patrons gasped and immediately dispersed upstairs, no doubt to check on their own possessions. When a portly mustachioed man rushed to comfort the woman, Burton and I moved closer to listen.

"I'm Mr. Stillman, the manager on duty. Are you sure your jewels are missing, madam? Perhaps you misplaced them. Did you check your luggage?"

"Of course I'm sure!" The matron stomped her foot. "What do you take me for, the village idiot? I left my jewelry spread out on the dresser earlier while I changed into my evening gown. And now...now they're gone."

"Everything?" His chubby face fell.

"Well, not everything...My favorite ruby and diamond brooch has disappeared, along with a gold bracelet and earrings. I hope this hotel covers insurance for jewel theft. I'll have you know these are irreplaceable family heirlooms." Her voice quivered, her eyes misted.

My heart went out to her. Despite being rich *and* rude, she'd suffered a loss and I knew how she felt—though fortunately for me, I recovered my bag, thanks to Finn.

Burton approached the woman and identified himself as a law officer—not a Prohibition agent, thank goodness.

I'd seen quite a few flasks whisked out of jacket pockets and their contents poured into drinks tonight.

"Ma'am, if you can provide a description of the jewelry, that would be helpful."

"Yes, of course." She turned to the hotel manager. "But first I want you to search your staff, especially the Negroes and the waitresses. I saw one eyeing my necklace earlier tonight."

I perked up, hoping she meant the blonde vamp who also had her eye on Burton.

Stillman lowered his voice. "Is that really necessary? They were working in the lobby all evening."

"Your *help* could have easily seen my hotel keys on the table, and run upstairs while I was in the powder room."

"Surely your husband noticed or heard something?"

"Clarence? He's blind as a bat and half-deaf to boot."

"Very well." The manager sighed and gathered the wait staff, demanding, "Empty your pockets and purses, please. Just a preliminary precaution."

Burton rolled his eyes and gave me an exasperated look behind their backs, meaning, "Here we go again..."

Reluctantly, the staff complied, emptying their pockets of change and keys, nothing that resembled priceless gems. Too bad the blonde only had lipstick and mad money in her purse.

"There. Are you satisfied now?" Stillman crowed. "We'll look around the premises to make sure they weren't misplaced." Then he said a few words to the band leader and I thought the musicians might be forced to empty their pockets and cases as well. Aha! Did he suspect them of stealing the gems? Instead, they quickly picked up their instruments and played a soothing jazz tune.

Meanwhile, the elderly matron described her jewels to Burton in great detail while I listened. "The young Texas designer Paul Flato custom-made the ruby brooch for me. A gold and ruby horseshoe with a diamond star, worth a fortune," she wailed. "You can't miss his signature style. Signed, of course. Flato always makes such distinctive pieces...Truly works of art."

Burton stared over her head at me, as if pleading, "Help me."

I gave him a sympathetic smile, then walked over to the hotel manager, who stood by the restaurant surveying the lobby. After introducing myself, I asked, "Has this kind of theft happened before at the Galvez?"

"You're a society reporter? Tell your boss I'd prefer not to make this public." He cleared his throat. "Naturally, we've had a few incidents...the occasional stolen wallets and jewelry, mainly petty theft, not the family jewels. All luxury hotels face that problem on occasion, but we've always handled it in-house. Thankfully, the gems usually turn up without any scandal."

"What a relief. Where do you find them?"

"Most of the time they're misplaced, under the furniture or in the luggage. Unfortunately, I've had to fire a few questionable maids and bellhops." Stillman pursed his lips. "Don't forget, young lady, mum's the word."

"Of course." Nodding, I gestured toward the musicians. "Where did you find these performers? Are they locals?"

"Actually they came to me looking for work. Told me they're with the vaudeville troupe, but they can only play a few nights while they're in town. Named a price I couldn't refuse." Stillman snorted, and mopped his face with a monogrammed hanky. "Now I know why. Still, unless we find proof..."

I blinked in surprise. "You suspect the musicians?"

"Not exactly..." He glanced around the lobby. "Yet I wonder if they're providing cover for their *friends*."

"Have you checked inside their cases for the jewelry? Perfect hiding place," I suggested.

Stillman nodded, giving me a mischievous smile. "Why do you think I asked them to play just now? I'll definitely look them over before they leave."

"Good idea. What about the magician? Did you search him or his props?"

Stillman shook his head. "He left after his act, before madam's jewels were stolen."

"How convenient. Who did you originally speak to about playing here tonight?"

"As a matter of fact, it *was* the magician. He waltzed right in last night wearing his top hat, carrying a cane and satchel, as if he'd just come from a performance."

"Was it after eight o'clock? Did you get his name?"

"Orlando Como—if that's his real name." Stillman brightened. "He's supposed to stop by tomorrow to pick up the check. Perhaps that's when I can search...I mean, question, him."

"Apparently he goes by Milo for his acts. I wonder if he has other stage names? What time will he stop by? You could call Agent Burton to help."

"Burton?" The hotel manager lowered his voice, eyes shifting around nervously. "Isn't he a...Federal agent? You know...doesn't he work in a different department?"

"Yes, but since Burton was here during the burglary, I doubt he'd object."

"Object to what?" Burton placed his hands on my shoulders, towering over me.

Stillman motioned for us to follow him to a hallway, hissing, "I'd like to keep this quiet for now, do you mind?"

"Fine." Burton got the hint. "Before filing a report, you need to thoroughly search the premises after your guests have retired. Check the plants, furniture, kitchen, laundry room—the works. Examine their rooms after they've checked out, using only your most trustworthy staff."

"I'll start on it right away." The hotel manager nodded.

"I hate to bring this up, but do any of your staff members have...a past?" Burton asked. "Have your maids or employees been known to help themselves to your guests' belongings?"

"Certainly not!" Stillman huffed. "I'm not aware of any criminal wrongdoing. To be safe, I'll question the restaurant, housekeeping and maintenance managers."

Burton gave him a card. "Call the station if you need my help. Thanks for the evening."

"Thank *you*, Agent Burton." He gave us a grateful smile. "And your lovely lady, too."

As we left, Burton grinned at me. "Snooping as usual?"

"Why not? Searching for jewels is more fun than finding dead bodies. Did you notice how quickly Stillman pointed fingers at the jazz band? He must be trying to save his job, as well as the hotel's spotless reputation."

Burton nodded. "Easier to blame a bunch of traveling musicians than admit you've hired a ring of jewel thieves."

"Do you think Stillman might be in on the scam? Maybe he's in cahoots with Milo the magician." I mulled it over. "Think about it— Milo uses fake stage names and left before the woman discovered her jewels were stolen. Very convenient. And he's always making things disappear. I'll bet he has a few more tricks up his sleeve."

Burton cracked a smile. "Let's just hope he doesn't vanish into thin air."

CHAPTER TWENTY-SIX

Tuesday

"I heard there was a little mishap at the Hotel Galvez last night." Mrs. Harper called me over to her desk the next day at work. "Has anything turned up yet?"

Her spies sure stayed busy. So much for keeping quiet about the jewelry theft.

"How did you know? The hotel manager didn't want anyone to find out."

"I'm friends with *all* the luxury hotel managers, including the new Warwick Hotel in Houston. Where do you think I get my tidbits? Now Stillman owes me a favor." Her cryptic smile spoke volumes. How many more secrets did she hide under her enormous Edwardian hats?

"Let me know if you see or hear anything new. Perhaps your Agent Burton will keep us posted?" Then she handed me a short stack of papers. "Please look these over and make any needed corrections right away."

With a sigh, I glanced at the clock and returned to my messy desk. I hoped Derek hadn't forgotten about our lunch date in two hours—not an actual *date*, just an appointment.

Not to worry. At noon on the dot, Derek showed up at the *Gazette*, standing in the doorway, taking it all in, as if waiting for applause. As I recalled, he always did like to make an entrance. Mrs. Harper crowed a bit too loudly, "Is that tall, dark and handsome man Derek Hammond?"

A cub reporter snickered, echoing, "Over here, tall, dark and handsome!"

Hoping to avoid a scene, I rushed to greet him but Mrs. Harper beat me to the door, cooing, "Why, Derek. It's been ages! How's your dear mother?"

Curious, I stayed put and listened to their small talk, while Derek winked at me behind her back.

Nathan whispered, "Does Burton know you're two-timing him with a villain?"

"You're all wet. This is a *friendly* lunch. An interview."

"Whatever you say, you heart-breaker." Nathan smiled and retreated to the darkroom.

Derek cocked his elbow. "Ready to go, toots?"

"And how!" I gave a backward glance at the news crew who wriggled their brows at me like Groucho Marx.

Outside, the weather was cool and clear, the skies a bright blue. "Sure is a pretty day. How about a picnic lunch at the park?" I said. "There's a sandwich vendor nearby."

His face fell. "I hoped we could dine at some snazzy restaurant, like Gaido's or the Galvez. For old times' sake. My treat."

So Derek wasn't as broke as I expected. "Thanks, but Burton and I were at the Galvez last night, listening to a jazz band. Do you mind if we go some place private?"

His eyes sparkled. "Private? Sandwiches it is, then."

Golliwogg trotted behind us, and I reached down to pet her black silky fur, luxurious as a sable coat.

After we ordered a ham and cheese for me, and roast beef on rye for Derek, we settled on a quiet park bench—in fact, the same one where Burton interrogated me just a few months earlier. Naturally I kept my distance, and again used my leather handbag as a barrier, hoping he got the message.

"So you and Burton are thick as thieves." Derek studied me as he bit into his sandwich.

"Funny you should say that..." I smiled. "Speaking of, do the vaudeville musicians moonlight on the side? The jazz band at the Galvez last night claimed to be part of the troupe. How do they have time to do both jobs?"

"We welcome extra gigs. The director always keeps new performers on hand, just in case. Draper likes to rotate people and acts, keep them off-balance, so you never know if or when you'll be on. He claims he wants to try new acts, new players, to keep the show fresh, exciting."

Derek had confirmed the bassist's story. "Seems harsh to me. Isn't that unsettling for the troupe?"

"I'll say. If we've had a bad week or ticket sales are slow, he blames the troupe rather than himself. Between us, I think he's punishing people for a poor performance."

A cool breeze bent the lone palm tree, a relic from the 1900 Storm, looking out of place on this November day.

Shivering, I pulled my jacket tight. "Draper sounds like a real miser and a bully."

"You said it." Derek nodded. "That's not all. Recently an older performer got fresh with an actress half his age. Nothing new. But when she complained to Draper, he called her a diva and fired her on the spot. Then he hired her young understudy, a pretty novice with no talent or experience."

"Who?" I asked, but he ignored my question. "So what happened with Patrick? Did you have a falling out? I heard you had a fight Friday, the night he disappeared."

"Who told you that?" He snapped to attention.

"Bella, the ballerina. She made it seem like a big knock-down, drag-out brawl." Then I had to ask: "Was the fight over her, or another gal?"

"Bella? She's such a drama queen. She *wished* we fought over her." Derek shrugged. "Sure, we had our differences, but we staged that fight on purpose. We were acting out a scene for a short skit Patrick worked on for the show. Guess it seemed convincing."

I perked up. "A play? Patrick was a writer?"

"He was a jack of all trades. Patrick wanted to do it all. Act, write, direct, produce. Draper was so jealous of his talent, he felt threatened." Derek scowled.

"I'm sorry. Seems so unfair." Golliwogg jumped on the bench by me, and I fed her bits of ham. "By the way, do you know if Patrick moonlighted between jobs?"

"We all do, if we can get extra work. The troupe gets paid a pittance and we've got to cover expenses somehow."

"What about the magician, Milo? I may have seen him last night performing tricks at the Galvez." I decided not to bring up the missing button, yet. Instead, I wanted to pick Derek's brain, find out how much he knew.

"Milo? I wouldn't be surprised. His stage act lasts around fifteen minutes at most."

Enough time to steal expensive jewelry or stab an ambitious actor—or both. I bit into my sandwich, wondering how to broach the subject. Finally I blurted out: "Is it possible the musicians moonlight in other ways...say, as jewel thieves?"

Derek's eyes flashed, startled. "Why do you say that?"

After I described last night's scenario with the missing jewelry, he was quiet for a while.

"Maybe the hotel manager wanted to cover for his staff or he was part of the scam," I coaxed.

Derek watched the pigeons scurrying around the park, pecking at crumbs. I knew the feeling: Mrs. Harper's assignments were like leftovers from her gossip buffet. Taking pity on the poor hungry birds, I threw them my bread crusts, watching them bob and coo.

Finally he spoke up. "This is off the record, got it? Let's just say some people have sticky fingers. But they only steal from rich tourists—those society dames own so many baubles, they don't notice any jewels missing until they're home. By then, we've moved on to the next town."

Aha! My eyes and mouth popped open like a cartoon character. "There's a whole ring of jewel thieves in the troupe?"

He gave me a sly smile. "I'd call them opportunists."

"How do they get away with it?"

"This is all hearsay, right?" Derek looked around the park as if the trees had ears. "Milo targets wealthy hotel guests—well-off men and showcase wives with their jewels on display—and pockets their room keys, usually sitting out in plain sight on their tables. During the break, the musicians steal the jewelry while Milo distracts the guests with his razzle-dazzle."

"You don't say." I marveled at the thieves audacity. "No one catches him in the act?"

"You've seen Milo's performance. He's an expert at sleight-of-hand tricks. Without his makeup and sparkly costume, he blends right in with the crowd."

Sounded like Derek knew a lot more than he'd let on. Yet if he was involved in the thefts, why would he expose the tricks of their trade—to a reporter?

"How do you know so much?" I eyed him with suspicion. "Was Patrick involved?"

"No, Patrick and I stayed away from a life of crime. We wanted to be actors, not cat burglars." Like a mime, he imitated a burglar getting caught holding a bag of jewels.

"Attaboy." I recalled the gold charm bracelet the gangsters had carelessly pawned at Cucci Jewelers—or had Colin purposely sold it to them? "So what was Patrick doing at the Oasis that night? And why was he killed?"

Derek paused, his face twisted. "Milo trusted Patrick, so he asked him to do this one favor. They were supposed to meet at the Oasis so Milo could secretly give him a bag of stolen jewelry from our last stop. Milo didn't want to get caught giving Patrick the jewels at the theatre."

"I don't blame him." I nodded, recalling Milo's missing button. "So that *was* Milo with Patrick—a billboard, as Frank called him. What did he want Patrick to do—pawn the jewels?"

"Patrick was *supposed* to turn over the jewelry to a fence or a middleman," he explained. "Milo made sure to leave before the fence showed up. He assumed Patrick had plenty of time to make the drop before his final act."

"Maybe they wanted to meet in public for an alibi, just in case," I mused. "But why the Oasis? I heard they had a fight and got kicked out. Any idea what it was about?"

Derek sighed, his shoulders slumped. "Patrick probably was trying to talk Milo out of the whole scheme. He hated the idea of stealing jewelry from our supporters, and he definitely didn't condone doing business with gangsters. 'They'll own us,' he complained to me. 'We'll be forced to do their bidding.'"

"Smart guy. Sounds like Patrick had second thoughts. What did he say after...?"

"Apparently he changed his mind and decided to hide the jewels at the Oasis."

My head was swimming. "No wonder they kept going back there. Tell me, how do they sell the stolen jewels?"

"Since we're on the road, the cops can't easily connect the jewels to the troupe. Then a fence hocks the jewelry, preferably out of town," Derek explained. "Someone they trust who can't be traced back to the troupe."

"Trust? That's funny coming from a band of jewel thieves. Does the director have any idea these shenanigans are going on behind his back?"

"Draper?" Derek stared at me a full minute before answering. "Hell, I hear the whole operation was his big idea. An easy way to pay for his over-the-top productions."

CHAPTER TWENTY-SEVEN

"Are you razzing me?" I probably looked like a googly-eyed carnival doll, my head spun around so fast. "The director is using stolen jewelry to finance his vaudeville shows?"

"I can't prove it...yet." Derek frowned. "Everyone knows vaudeville is as outdated as Confederate bills. Draper encourages the musicians to moonlight on the side, usually at luxury hotels, private parties, country clubs. The troupe is so desperate to keep their jobs, they go along with his get-rich-quick scheme. He even allows them to keep one piece of jewelry as a reward."

"Only one piece?" I pondered that a moment. "Maybe he wants to hold onto the jewelry as evidence, to lord it over their heads."

"You might be right. And stupid me thought he was being generous." He snorted. "Naturally Draper's greedy paws never get near the stolen goods. No fingerprints, no proof. If anyone ever gets caught, he can just blame them. Still, they're very careful not to leave a trail."

I shook my head in disbelief. "What will you do, now that you know?"

"Patrick and I were onto Draper's tricks, and vowed to expose him as a fraud. But I can't do much until I get evidence. I'm hoping someone will lend me a stolen gem or two to show the authorities."

"Derek, isn't that risky? What if Draper finds out what you plan to do?"

"Why do you think I was arrested? He's giving me a warning: Join us or get out. Patrick and I wanted to reveal his scheme, but we didn't know how—or whom to trust."

I mulled it over, watching Golliwogg chase pigeons across the park. "Obviously Milo must be working with Draper. Is it possible Milo got so mad, he stabbed Patrick in the alley?"

"Milo? He may be a crook and a cheat, but he's not violent," Derek said. "Besides, Patrick would have told us after he snuck out of the hospital."

"Any idea who Patrick was meeting? If we find him, we may have our killer."

Derek's eyes narrowed. "Have you heard of a gang leader called George Musey? Patrick was supposed to hand over the jewelry to Musey's middleman."

"George Musey?" I was floored. "What does he have to do with this vaudeville show?"

"Keep this hush-hush, OK?" Derek moved closer to me on the bench. "Draper was desperate for cash to open his show here. When the banks turned him down, I heard he contacted both Musey and Sam Maceo. The Maceos weren't interested, but Musey wanted to make a deal. Cash for jewelry, he insisted. The real McCoy, not costume fakes."

"Is this on the level, Derek?" I asked, skeptical. "How do you know so much?"

"Patrick filled me in, before..." He wiped off his lap, crumbs sprinkling on the grass for the eager pigeons. "Like you, I have my sources. I'd rather not reveal them for their own safety."

"Be careful, Derek. If Draper thinks you're a threat, no telling what he can do to you."

"I'm not afraid of Draper. That bastard shouldn't treat people like puppets, manipulating them to do his dirty deeds. He thinks he owns everyone and everything in the vaudeville show."

I admit, I liked this new, more mature Derek. Instead of a narcissist craving the spotlight, now I saw him as a risk-taker, a crusader—like Nellie Bly. A Robin Hood of the theatre, righting backstage wrongs.

Suddenly I began to view Derek in a different light, with renewed interest. To me, he seemed exciting, even attractive again— no longer a self-absorbed lothario waiting for his big break.

What was wrong with me? Why was I even considering the possibility of dating Derek again?

As if reading my thoughts, Derek gave me a faint smile. "Are you worried about me?"

I felt a stab of guilt, wondering why I was admiring Derek when Burton was my beau. "Why not? Your actor friend is dead, and you may be next. After all this time, can't I still worry about you? We're pals, aren't we?"

"Pals? If that's the way you want it..." Derek leapt off the bench. "I thought you wanted more out of life."

"Of course I do." My face flushed. "It's been two years. We've both changed. What did you expect?"

"Nothing." He shrugged, looking away. "I expected nothing. But I was hoping for more."

The simple, straightforward way he spoke made my heart turn over. No drama, no embellishment. What could I say? True, Burton and I weren't exactly engaged or even serious, but we'd been through so much together, and most of all, he'd gained my trust.

Even if we broke up and I decided to date Derek once more, how could I be sure he wouldn't get restless and take off again? Besides, I had my own career, my own goals, to pursue—and that didn't include following an unemployed actor around the country, looking for work.

"I'm sorry, Derek. Things are different now. Let me know if there's anything I can do to help..."

"Help? How about getting your boyfriend off my back?" He thrust out his arms. "Tell him I may play a villain on stage, but in real life, I'm one of the good guys."

Jumping up, he turned on his heel and stormed off with Golly at his heels, leaving me speechless, for once.

"There you are." Out of nowhere, Burton appeared, a white rabbit in a magician's hat. "Was that Derek? He rushed by me so fast, I didn't get a chance to say anything."

Still dazed, I looked up at him as if he were a stranger. "Derek? Oh, yes, we met for lunch today. Remember, our interview?"

"Interview? So that's what you call a lunch date."

Was he teasing or genuinely jealous?

"Have a seat." I patted the space by me on the park bench. Torn, I wanted to update him on the vaudeville troupe, then decided I'd better sift through my thoughts before I blurted anything out I'd regret later.

We needed to gather more evidence before Draper and Milo— or the musicians—could be charged with any crime. Who had the most to lose? Or for that matter, the most to gain by Patrick's death?

Burton frowned as he sat down. "There goes your left eye again. What's the big secret?"

"I need to get more facts before I incriminate anyone—yet."

"Which crime are you talking about—theft or murder?"

"Possibly both. Surely you didn't come all this way to interrogate me about my so-called lunch date?"

Burton drew a deep breath. "You won't believe who stopped by the Oasis last night. George Musey, along with his old pal, Johnny Jack Nounes."

"Johnny Jack is back in town?" My back stiffened. "What did they want?"

"Guess. Good thing Sammy and Frank were locked up." Burton shifted on the bench to face me. "Those two thugs threatened Dino, said they're looking for a bunch of valuable jewels—hot, of course. That explains why Patrick and his killer kept returning to the Oasis."

"Why did they meet at the Oasis in the first place? Why hide the stolen jewelry there?" I wondered.

"I suspect Musey wanted to set up Sammy. Johnny Jack's pride may be hurt after the booze drop, but Musey is only after money. " Burton's blue eyes flashed. "Here's the kicker. Apparently the jewels were hidden in an old musical instrument case—specifically, a viola."

CHAPTER TWENTY-EIGHT

"A viola? That's what Patrick was trying to tell me after he got stabbed." I clutched Burton's arm. "I was beginning to suspect as much. He must have hidden it at the Oasis, but he died without telling anyone the exact location. Not even Derek. At least he didn't mention it to me."

"What else did Derek say? Anything I should know?"

"Can you keep this under your hat?" I'd promised Derek I wouldn't spill the beans, but frankly, I was worried he might be in serious danger. After all, his friend Patrick had paid for his silence with his life.

While Burton and I walked over to the *Gazette* building, I filled him in on the details of my lunch with Derek. Well, most of it anyway. "You'll never believe what goes on behind the scenes at these vaudeville shows. Derek admitted that the director, Draper, expects the troupe to steal jewelry to help fund the productions."

Burton stopped in his tracks. "He supports the thefts?"

"Apparently he's deep in debt." I nodded. "Our hunch was right about the musicians. Not only do they steal jewelry from hotel guests, Milo is in on the scheme."

"The magician?" Burton blinked in surprise. "How do they pull that off?"

"I had the same question. Turns out Milo swipes the guests' hotel keys while the band plays the first set," I explained. "During the break, he distracts the customers while the musicians rob the rooms. Then he returns the keys when no one is looking. Gotta admit, it's clever."

"Clever and illegal. And I thought the gangsters were the only ones we had to watch out for...now we've got to keep an eye on musicians *and* magicians?"

"Sad but true. Derek told me that he and Patrick planned to expose Draper and the troupe. He suspects that's why he was arrested, as a warning to keep his mouth shut. Derek claims that Patrick held onto the jewels as evidence, to give to the authorities."

"Evidence—is that all?" Burton frowned. "I doubt that's the whole story. Why risk his life for someone else's jewelry? Maybe he wanted to keep the loot for himself. Don't forget, he did hide a diamond ring in his...uh..."

"Undergarment? Yes, but Derek said Patrick was an honest, decent guy. I'll bet he wanted out of the troupe—and planned to hock the ring to pave his way. Still, I don't get it. Why stash the bag of jewelry at a public bar like the Oasis? Why not hide them in a private place?" I thought it over. "I suppose when you're on the road, it's hard to keep anything hidden or private."

"True. I heard Musey and Nounes searched the bar all over, but couldn't find the jewelry or viola anywhere. Then our undercover cops came in and did the same. Unfortunately, they trashed the place for nothing. This Patrick sure was good at keeping secrets."

I nodded. "Too bad he didn't get a chance to tell anyone his hiding place before he was killed."

I considered that notion, wondering if Derek possibly knew the jewels' location, but didn't want to blab—for my own protection or his safety?

Changing the subject, I asked, "How's Sammy? Frank? Did the cops release them yet?"

"Luckily, they let them both go first thing this morning. Poor guy has his plate full cleaning up. Those two-bit goons did a good job of tearing up the place. I think it was partly for show."

"Hate to admit, but maybe locking him up for the night was a good idea." I could only imagine the mess they'd made at the Oasis. "I'll go by with Amanda later and help him clean up."

"Be careful," Burton warned. "What if Musey stops by again? He might recognize you from the other night."

"Don't worry, I doubt he'll come by twice in a row. We'll be safe with Sammy and Dino there."

Slowing to a stop, I waved to Finn, hawking his papers in front of the *Gazette* building. "Better keep quiet for now. Say, what are you doing Thursday night? Feel like seeing the vaudeville show?"

"Again?" Burton groaned. "What have you got in mind?"

"Let's watch these performers in action, see if we notice anything the second time around. Maybe we'll recognize someone from last night?"

"I'll be sure to clear my calendar," he said dryly. "Good luck tonight at the Oasis. I'll call you later, make sure you got home OK."

I stopped to talk to Finn, who sat on a stack of newspapers petting Golliwogg, as if she'd never left his side.

"There's my favorite stray. How are you and Golly doing?" The black cat rubbed my ankles in greeting. I leaned over to scratch under her silky chin, and felt her purring. "I'm trying to fatten her up."

"She's OK," the tyke sighed. "But I'm not doing so hot. Folks saving up for Christmas, not spending much dough on papers now."

Feeling generous, I handed him a dollar, half a day's pay. "Go ahead and buy a treat for yourself and Golly. I'll keep an eye on your newspapers."

"Gee, thanks, Jazz! Can I get some jawbreakers too?"

"Try not to break your jaw," I joked. "Make sure you both get enough hot food to eat."

When I settled in at my desk, Mrs. Harper beamed at me and asked, "How was your date with Derek?"

"It wasn't a date, just an interview."

"Anything newsworthy?" she pried.

"I'll look over my notes. But don't you think we're overdoing the Derek stories for now?"

Sure, I wanted to write an investigative article and expose the director, but not at the risk of harming Derek. Besides, we still needed the hot jewels as evidence.

"Well, perhaps you can try a different angle. Did he give you any behind-the-scenes gossip?"

And how!

After work, I rushed home and spilled the beans to Amanda. When I told her Musey and Nounes had trashed the Oasis, she leapt to her feet. "Oh, no! Let's go help Sammy clean up."

"I hoped you'd say that." I knew he might forgive me for turning in the violin wire if I brought Amanda along.

"First, I need to change into something pretty..." She surveyed her triple armoire, filled with sheer frocks.

"Amanda, you look swell. Do you really want to wear a frilly frock to clean up a bar?"

"OK, let me throw on a nice wrap." While I changed, she reapplied her lipstick, fluffed up her hair, spritzed on some gardenia perfume and carefully draped a floral embroidered piano shawl with long silky fringe over her shoulders. A nice wrap? It was stunning!

"Where in the world did you get that beauty?" I asked her, fingering the long fringe.

"I got it at Eiband's on sale," Amanda said with pride. "I spied it last summer, then hid it in the racks until the fall. By then it was marked down almost half price!"

"I've got to hand it to you, you know how to sniff out the best deals," I teased her.

The night air felt chilly as we walked to the trolley stop, a refreshing change after the hot summers. By the time we reached the Oasis, we were shivering in our thin frocks and wraps. Frank greeted us at the door—actually, more of a grunt—and we descended the stairs into sheer and utter chaos.

Sadly, the Oasis looked like overzealous Prohibition agents had raided the place: tables turned over, chairs broken, bottles smashed. Even some of Sammy's prized model schooners and ships in a bottle lay broken on the floor. This, after a few hours of cleaning?

Amanda and I stared in shock at the disarray. Most heartbreaking of all was Sammy's helpless and hopeless expression. "What are you gals doing here? Come to celebrate my release?" He gave me a pointed look, trying to suppress his anger.

"I'm so sorry!" Amanda reached out to hug Sammy.

"Who did this—Musey and Johnny Jack? Or the police?" I flung out my hands in exasperation.

"You name it. Those bastards went crazy looking for the jewels," Dino said. "Then the coppers finished the job."

Sammy's eyes looked haunted. "Nounes and Musey warned that if I don't find the gems, they'll tell the cops that *I* stole them. Worse, they threatened to demolish the Oasis if I come up empty-handed."

I inhaled sharply, wishing I'd brought Burton along. He always remained calm while I felt like screaming and kicking those good-for-nothing goons.

"What can we do to help?" Amanda wrung her hands. In her colorful coat, she resembled a bright desert flower pushing through a barren wasteland.

"Help me find the jewels," Sammy said solemnly. "It's the only way I can pay back Musey and Nounes. They still blame me for the booze bust, and lost cases of rum."

"Pay them back with stolen gems?" I frowned. "They don't own them, and neither do you."

"Musey told me he gave a big loan to that vaudeville guy, Draper or whoever, to keep his show going." His olive eyes flashed. "The hot rocks are his payment."

Sammy confirmed Derek's claims. "Since when did a brute like Musey invest in the arts?"

"Word is, Draper tried to hock some stolen jewels first to the Maceos, then to Musey. Rose threw him out on his ass, said he wanted no part of a cat burglary ring. George Musey offered him cash upfront so he'd get part of the loot—and more to boot."

"So Draper made a deal with the devil."

Sammy nodded. "Draper arranged for a go-between in the troupe to give a viola case full of jewelry to Musey's fence that night, but Musey claims he swiped the jewels—and hid them here instead."

So Derek's story checked out. "Explains why our John Doe, Patrick, returned to the Oasis disguised as a woman, to retrieve the jewels without getting caught."

"Seems Musey's men waited here round the clock for Patrick to show up, hoping he'd lead them to the jewels. No such luck. Now Musey blames me for the murder," Sammy said. "When his fence came back empty-handed, Musey lost his head. Threatened to kill him on the spot."

"Why is Musey blaming you? It's not your fault that Patrick hid the stolen jewels here." I shook my head in frustration. "Who's the middleman? Did he kill Patrick?"

"Musey's not talking." Sammy shrugged. "They promised me that if I take the jewels off their hands and sell them in Houston, I'm off the hook. Out of their debt—for good."

My heart dropped. "*You're* the fence?"

CHAPTER TWENTY-NINE

"That's the plan. But I can't very well fence anything if I don't find the jewels." Sammy scratched his throat, his five o'clock shadow looking more like midnight. "Musey only gave me a few days to sell all the jewelry."

"You knew about this scheme all along?" I flared up. "That's the real reason you came back here? Not to visit us, but to appease Johnny Jack and Musey? Obviously you care more about the Downtown Gang!"

Amanda blinked back tears. "Gosh, Sammy. I thought you couldn't wait to see me."

"You know I wanted to see you. Everything changed after Patrick got stabbed. The fence screwed up, big-time. Believe me, my trip here wasn't planned, it was last-minute. Musey means business. He's a mean son-of-a-bitch."

"Can't you find another way to pay back Johnny Jack? Aren't you making money in Houston?" I asked.

"Not fast enough. I've got to share the profits with my partner." Sammy let out a snort. "Some partner Davis turned out to be. He charges me room and board and takes out a hefty sum to cover his gambling debts. When he's not gambling, he's drinking up our stock."

That sounded familiar. "You didn't tell me business was that bad."

"I didn't want to worry you. Tell the truth, I'm ready to move back to Galveston. But I can't do anything unless I'm squared away with Johnny and George."

"Can't the Maceos help you out?" I suggested. "They're loaded with cash."

"If word got out that the Maceos' dough ended up in Johnny Jack's back pocket, all hell would break loose." Sammy shook his head. "I can't think of any other way out of this jam."

"I'd love for you to move back to town, but not if it's so dangerous," Amanda said, stroking his unruly dark hair.

I didn't want to consider the risks. "Why don't we start hunting for the jewelry? Have you looked in the bar? The stairwell? What about your office or kitchen?"

Sammy nodded. "We've checked everywhere."

"Even back here?" I moved behind the bar and started poking around the remaining model schooners lining the shelves, shaking out some cigarette ashes and dust.

"Hey, be careful with those. I built them myself." Sammy looked alarmed. "I doubt Patrick hid any gems there. We don't let strangers behind the bar."

"Just trying to help. What about the kitchen?" I darted in and poked around the pots and pans a while until Bernie the cook gave me a dirty look.

"No jewels here, Jazz." Luckily Bernie kept a clean house, unlike Sammy, whose office resembled a junkyard.

"You've looked top to bottom?" As I stood by the bar, surveying the room, my eyes strayed to Doria hanging above. "What about Doria? Give me a hand, will you?"

"Jazz, watch your step." Sammy held out his hands.

Behind the bar, I cautiously placed my foot on the bottom shelf and he helped hoist me up onto the counter until I was face-to-face with Doria, our wooden mascot.

"What are you doing, Jazz?" Amanda yelped. "Be careful up there!"

"Just being thorough." I stood on my tiptoes and studied Doria's cavernous curves. Then I reached in her hollow frame and felt around the perimeter—and *voila!*

I found a lumpy velvet bag hidden inside her chest cavity. Holding it up to the dim lights, I peered inside the bag and gasped when I saw the bundle of glittering baubles and stones, still sparkling and bright. Triumphant, I waved the bag like a victory flag.

"Is this what you're looking for?"

CHAPTER THIRTY

Sammy's face lit up like neon. "Jazz, you're a lifesaver! Literally. What would I do without you?" He reached out for the jewels, his palms open. Then he helped me down off the bar, holding onto my arms like I was a porcelain doll. "Now I can show Musey the jewels and prove I didn't steal them."

"Attagirl, Jazz." Frank slapped my back when I was on safe ground. "We thought Sammy was a goner. Now he can return to Houston and save our necks."

"Question is, how'd Patrick hide the jewels up there?" Sammy held up the bag, and we all looked over at Buzz, the little monkey. "Seen this before, sport?"

Buzz shrugged, his face pink. "A tall man gave me the bag to hide. I thought it was a game. He said he'd come back, but I never saw him again."

Poor Buzz had no idea what had happened. Or did he? After all, he'd discovered Patrick's body in the alley after he was stabbed—and the bloody knife.

"Say, why don't you turn over the jewels to Burton?" I suggested to Sammy.

His eyes narrowed. "Why in hell would I do that?"

"A show of good faith. The owners will be grateful."

"Grateful isn't good enough. These gems are my ticket out of hell."

"How do you know Musey will keep his word? Maybe he'll want you to continue doing his dirty work."

"George Musey is a greedy son-of-a-gun. He'd rather stick me behind the bar so he can keep taking my money."

"Behind *bars* is more like it." I gave him a pointed look. "What will you do now?"

"I'm calling Musey with the good news. Then I've got to find some way to hock these babies in Houston—and fast." Sammy studied the bag of jewelry.

"When are you going back to Houston?" Amanda wailed, on the verge of tears.

"First thing in the morning. But now I feel like celebrating." Sammy gave Amanda a peck on the cheek and wrapped his arms over our shoulders. "You gals stick around for a while. Don't worry about cleaning up this dump." He sifted through the jewels, holding up a beautiful brooch made of rubies and sapphires. "Does this toot your horn?"

"Sammy!" Amanda and I cried out in unison. "They're stolen goods!" I had to admit, the thought was tempting.

"Just kidding." He grinned. "Wish I could give these to my two favorite gals, but I can't afford the price."

I glanced at the gems and thought I recognized a few designer pieces. "Can I take a look?" I hoped the cops could return the jewelry to their rightful owners before they disappeared, one by one.

"Help yourself." Sammy shoved back his chair, a big smile on his handsome face. "Excuse me while I make my phone call."

To be honest, I was tempted to borrow a few baubles to show Agent Burton. Still, what would I tell him—if anything? Should I keep quiet while Sammy returned to Houston with the jewels? Or try to convince him to turn them over to the police? Of course I had mixed feelings about the whole dilemma—but Sammy was in a tight spot, and he came first.

When Sammy sat back down, his smile had become a scowl. "Damn that Musey. He wants to meet tomorrow to make sure all the jewelry is there. Said he memorized them by heart. Obviously he doesn't trust me."

"I doubt he trusts anyone in his line of work." I cleared my throat. "Hate to tell you, but don't be surprised if a diamond ring is missing."

"A diamond ring?" His eyes widened in alarm. "How do you know? You didn't..."

"Me? No! Patrick. Agent Burton told me it was hidden in his...her...bra." I stifled my smile.

"He was wearing a bra? Now I've heard it all." Despite his sour mood, Sammy began to laugh. "Say, can Burton help me get the ring back before Musey finds out it's missing?"

"Sammy, it's stolen property. I doubt Burton will just hand it over to you...unless...you can return the favor." Suddenly I had a brainstorm, but needed to discuss it with Burton before I got Sammy's hopes up. "Can I use your phone to call Agent Burton?"

"Be my guest." Sammy nodded. "But I won't change my mind. Be sure to tell him my hide is on the line."

Luckily, Burton was working late when I called the police station. "Guess who found the jewels Patrick hid? Doria stashed them away when no one was looking."

"Swell. You must be a mind-reader. Or did Doria tip you off?" Burton joked.

"Both. Say, I've got a favor to ask. Has anyone claimed the diamond ring yet?"

"Not yet. You won't believe who it belongs to." He paused. "Rose Maceo's wife."

I sucked in my breath. "Are you kidding? How did anyone manage to steal a wedding ring off her finger?"

"Who knows? She filed a report a few days ago." Burton exhaled into the phone. "Rather, Rose Maceo stormed into the station demanding that we locate her lost ring. We had our secretary file a formal report."

"Do you still have the ring?"

"The captain is holding onto it for now. Mrs. Maceo is supposed to come in tomorrow to ID the ring. Apparently Maceo has the papers to prove it's theirs."

"Burton, you've got to give Sammy the ring for now. He's meeting with Musey tomorrow," I pleaded. "Who knows what Musey will do to Sammy if that ring is missing. Can you stall the Maceos for a while? I have a brainstorm."

"OK, but you'd better have a damn good idea. Rose Maceo is not a patient man."

"So I've heard." I cleared my throat. "Can you stop by the Oasis right away? I may have a way to catch Musey red-handed."

"Musey? I'll be right over."

Half an hour later, Burton arrived at the Oasis, his jaw clenched.

"Got the ring?" Sammy's eyes were wild with worry.

"Not so fast, pal." Burton remained in the doorway. "Jazz has a plan to get you out of trouble. But I need to get you on board before I talk to the brass."

"Oh yeah?" Sammy seemed skeptical. "Pull up a chair."

Amanda waited at the bar while we moved to a back table. Briefly, I outlined my plan: "It needs to appear as if you and Musey are working *together* to fence the jewels. The cops must see him holding the jewels or it may seem like you're working alone."

Burton cut in, adding, "When you show Musey the jewelry, make sure he handles a few pieces so we can get his fingerprints for our records."

"You want to catch *Musey* holding the bag," Sammy cracked. "What happens to me?"

"We'll have to arrest you both on the spot so Musey doesn't become suspicious," Burton explained. "After he's booked and charged, we'll return you to Houston later."

Silently, Sammy stared at Doria above the bar, puffing on a Camel cigarette.

"What do you think?" I asked.

Sammy eyes darted back and forth warily. "Let's hope Musey doesn't get wise. I don't want to be a stool pigeon."

"Why would he suspect anything? After all, the meeting was *his* idea," I pointed out.

"Worth a shot." Sammy looked hopeful. "I'll try anything to get Musey locked up."

CHAPTER THIRTY-ONE

"You and me both," Burton told Sammy.

"Good luck." I gave Sammy a hug. "It's in the bag."

"You're a riot." Sammy forced a smile.

After we said our good-byes, Burton drove me home while Amanda stayed behind at the Oasis. I felt guilty for not telling her our plans, but it was best to keep quiet for now. Amanda worked at the biggest rumor mill in town—Star Diner—and if she said one word to anyone, that could be curtains for Sammy.

"You think Musey will get suspicious?" I asked Burton as we rode in his Roadster.

"Depends on Sammy. If he starts acting nervous or gets cold feet, he'll give it away."

"Sammy, nervous? You've seen him in action. He's cool as a popsicle."

"True. He wasn't fazed a bit when I raided his place last summer." Burton gave me a sly smile. "As I recall, neither were you."

"Sure I was." I poked him in the ribs. "I just didn't want you to know."

"I figured as much. I wonder if I should follow Sammy to his meet, in case he needs back-up, just to be safe."

"Now you sound like me. I wish you could, but Musey's men are bound to spot you."

"Don't worry, Jazz. We've all got a lot at stake."

After Burton walked me to the door, I told him, "Thanks for going along with my idea. I wasn't sure Sammy could be convinced."

"Beats any other option. I'll ask Johnson to put his best men on the job." He tapped his watch. "I'd better scram. Need to set the wheels in motion if this is going to work."

"We're counting on you." I gave Burton a quick kiss before Eva came out on the porch to spy. Now that her Sheriff Sanders was living in Houston, she had more time to fret over me.

He smiled. "Tell me if your newsboys hear anything."

"You got it. By the way, don't forget about the vaudeville show," I reminded him. "Derek promised us front-row seats. We can keep an eye on the orchestra *and* Milo."

"Can't wait," Burton said dryly as he turned to go.

I waited until midnight for Amanda to come home, reading an old copy of *Collier's Weekly*, but she still was late. Did she spend the night with Sammy?

At 22, Amanda could do as she pleased, but I knew Aunt Eva wouldn't approve if she ever found out. Like a typical bluenose, Eva liked to lecture, living by the adage: *Why buy the cow if you can get the milk for free?*

All night, I tossed and turned, worried about my plan to catch Musey with the jewels. Was it so smart to use Sammy as bait to lure Musey into our trap?

Wednesday

The next day, I showed up at the *Gazette*, red-eyed and exhausted, hoping to avoid Mrs. Harper's scrutiny. "How's your profile on Derek coming along?" Mrs. Harper called out. "What have you written so far?"

Profile? Oh no—I'd completely forgotten my deadline. "I'll surprise you," I squeaked out as I slumped in my banker's chair. "It'll be worth the wait." Why did I have to promise her a piece I couldn't deliver? Not yet anyway.

I tried to rack my brain for inspiration, a new story angle. How could I report on the stolen jewelry without actual proof? Sure, I'd found the bag of jewels, but that only incriminated Sammy—not the vaudeville director and his treasure-stealing troupe.

Instead, I decided to put a positive spin on the piece, adding that the director mixed up the acts and performers to keep the show fresh and exciting—not to cover up a murder. No one needed to know that, to make ends meet, the musicians moonlighted as cat burglars.

Derek became a minor sidebar, a toned-down version of the 'Hometown hero does good' piece of fluff the public loved to read. Should I mention his false arrest and accusations? Dare I rattle the troupe without actually pointing fingers? I'd have to run it by Mrs. Harper first since she clearly liked to fiddle with my copy.

But before I finished, I got an urgent call from Burton. "There's been a change of plans."

"What do you mean?" I kept my face expressionless since I was sitting at Mrs. Harper's desk right in the middle of the bullpen. Thank goodness she'd left for an early luncheon and wasn't around to eavesdrop.

"Guess who came by the police station this morning? Rose Maceo and his wife, demanding the ring. She was hysterical, making a big scene, ready to raise holy hell."

"So you gave it to her." I kept my voice flat, knowing Musey probably had men killed for losing a bet, much less a valuable diamond ring.

The newsroom had suddenly gone quiet, ears pricked up in anticipation. "I had no other choice." Burton waited for my reaction. "But there's good news. Meet me outside in ten minutes and I'll explain."

There went my deadline—again. Ten minutes later, I rushed out the door, ignoring the reporters. "What's the hurry, toots? Got an urgent manicure? Or a hot date with a villain?"

"You slay me." I rolled my eyes to shut them up.

Burton was prompt as usual, parked outside in his Roadster. The street noise of newsies, trolleys, cars and sidewalk vendors drowned out our chatter. An old man in a brown felt derby paraded back and forth, wearing a crude sandwich board advertising hot deli lunches for 25 cents.

"First, tell me the good news." I faced him, glum.

"You'll never believe this." He grinned from ear to ear. "Have you seen Rose Maceo's wife? She's quite a looker."

I shook my head. "Mobsters tend to keep a low profile, except for Sam Maceo. He's not exactly camera-shy."

"No doubt about it, Big Sam likes the spotlight. Speaking of, remember the rich dame at Mario's, the vamp whose purse was stolen? Guess who she's married to?" Burton paused for effect. "Rose Maceo."

"You don't say!" I almost popped out of the Roadster. Too bad we couldn't print this tasty tidbit in the society section—but we'd all have to do a lot of explaining. "Obviously her handsome escort was not Rose Maceo. She must have hidden her ring in the purse before she met her beau for dinner. Did she recognize you?"

"She almost fainted on the spot. I was a gentleman and pretended I'd never seen her before. I figured she gave me a phony name and number that night." Burton grinned.

"No wonder she wanted to dine at Mario's, away from the Beach Gang's turf—so she wouldn't be spotted. Think she's dating a member of the Downtown Gang?"

"I wouldn't be surprised. Get this: Mrs. Maceo gave us a five-hundred dollar reward for finding her ring. I think it's hush money to shut me up. Small price to pay for her life."

I couldn't stop smiling. "Did Rose Maceo notice anything was fishy?"

"Let's just say I wouldn't want to be in her fancy French shoes."

"So how did the ring end up with Patrick?" I wondered, thinking out loud. "The purse snatcher must have given it to Musey's middleman—or he *was* the fence. What if Patrick robbed him the night he got killed? Do you think anyone knew she was Rose Maceo's wife?"

"If they did, she wouldn't still be alive." Burton's eyes narrowed. "Who knows? Maybe she's a liaison between the Beach and Downtown gangs."

"Either way, she's playing a dangerous game. At least her ring is back on her finger."

"For now," he cracked. "Fortunately for Sammy, we're willing to give him the reward money for his meeting, if he returns the cash to the police. He can use it to stall Musey, pretend he sold the diamond ring to a rich tourist."

I heaved a sigh of relief. "How will he get the cash in time before Musey shows up?"

Burton started the Roadster. "I hope you'll help us out. Musey's goons are likely watching the Oasis and they'd spot a cop a mile away. But they won't suspect a pretty young gal like you."

"Me?" I gulped. "When? Now?"

"The sooner, the better. I can't very well waltz in there myself to deliver the cash. To be safe, I'll drop you off a block away."

"Does Sammy know I'm coming?"

"Not yet. I'm afraid you'll have to break the news about Mrs. Maceo's ring, too. But I'm positive Musey prefers dough over diamonds," Burton reassured me. "He's supposed to call Sammy right before the meet. Naturally he wants control over the time and place."

"So how will you find them?"

Burton gave me a sly smile. "We have our ways. Ever hear of wire-tapping?"

"Sure," I nodded, surprised that they'd go to such lengths. "Whose phone did they tap?"

"Both. That's all I can say. I'll wait for you at the end of Market, and give you a ride back to the *Gazette*."

"Too risky. I'll walk back to work and grab a bite on the way, pretend I went to lunch."

"Thanks, Jazz." Burton handed me an envelope filled with cash, his hand lingering on mine. "Feel free to back out now if you think it's too dangerous."

"What do you take me for—a coward?" I forced a smile to cover my nerves. "You know I'd do anything to help Sammy."

Heart pounding, I stuffed the envelope into my leather handbag, straining at the seams. Ironic that Sammy was about to hand over Rose Maceo's money to the Beach Gang's biggest rival.

CHAPTER THIRTY-TWO

At the Oasis, Dino swung open the door with a frown. "Jazz, what are you doing here now?"

"Good day to you, too." I began to panic. "Where's Sammy? He's still here, isn't he?"

"Downstairs." He pointed with his stubby thumb like a hitchhiker. "Make it snappy. He's got some place to go."

Where? I wanted to ask, but stayed mum.

Sammy sat at the bar with Frank, counting cash, both men clamming up when I approached.

"Jazz? Is anything wrong?" Sammy glanced at his watch. "I'm waiting for a call."

After I told him about the diamond ring, he looked stricken. "So what am I supposed to tell Musey? That some fairy actor stole the ring and stuck it in his bra? He'll get a big laugh before he puts a gun to my head."

"Tell him you found an out-of-town buyer right here. Give him the cash to prove it." I opened my purse and his eyes bulged at the bundle of bills.

"Jazz, where in hell did you get that jack? Put it away before anyone sees you."

"Here, take it all. Burton gave it to me in good faith. Call it reward money from the Maceos. Rose Maceo and his wife."

"The ring belonged to his wife? No shit?" Sammy rubbed his chin. "I wonder if Musey was behind this robbery. Most of the jewels are supposed to be from out of town, not locals."

"Good question. Aren't the Maceos sworn enemies with Musey and Nounes?"

"I'll say." Sammy nodded. "You get those hot-headed gangsters in a room and I swear it could start another Great War. No wonder they wanted me to hock the jewels in Houston."

"Then he'll be glad it's gone." I patted his back. "Be careful, Sammy. Just do your part and you'll be fine." Who was I trying to convince?

"Thanks, Jazz." Sammy faked a smile as he looked up at his favorite figurehead. "Hope Doria will be watching over me..."

After I left the Oasis, I kept looking over my shoulder, shivering as I rushed back to the *Gazette*. Was I being followed? Every time a car honked or slowed down, I stopped to stare, afraid they were chasing me. After a few recent close calls, I had the heebie jeebies—and how!

I stopped at a sandwich vendor and bought my ham and cheese on wheat to go with a bottle of frosty Dr. Pepper, gulping it down while I walked. Outside the *Gazette* building, I winked at Finn, who belted out today's headlines: "*Charles Lindbergh back from U.S. Tour! Plans to visit Latin America!*" I suspected he'd been coached. If so, I'd make it my mission to teach him to read.

Entering the newsroom, I noticed how quiet it seemed. The smart-aleck reporters had left and only a handful of staff remained.

Great—that gave me time to read about our newest American hero, Charles Lindbergh, who made headlines wherever he went. After I finished, I spotted Nathan rushing out of the dark room, his camera equipment hanging off his shoulder.

"Where is everyone?" I asked. "Where's the fire?"

"Haven't you heard the latest?" He stopped, breathing hard under the weight of his equipment. "They found another dead body down by the Martini Theatre."

My heart skipped a beat. Surely it wasn't Derek... I'd just had lunch with him yesterday. "Who was it? When did this happen?"

"We don't know all the details yet. Mack and the fellas are already down there, waiting for me."

"Let me give you a hand." I grabbed onto his tripod, as if holding it for ransom. "I'm coming with you."

"Be my guest." Nathan gave me a grin. "Seems you're getting used to the routine by now."

While he drove in his crazy, bat-out-of-hell way, I peppered him with questions: "Tell me everything. Is it a performer or musician? Who found the body? When? How was he or she killed?"

"All I know is Mack got a call about half an hour ago. Someone found the body behind the Martini Theatre this morning," Nathan said. "Seems he'd been there since last night but no one spotted him because he'd been hidden under some old stage sets."

"You don't say. They're positive he's a performer? A member of the vaudeville troupe?"

"Probably. Why else leave the body behind the theatre—and pretend to cover it up?"

"Someone must be giving the troupe a warning. Or deliberately trying to jinx the show."

"Jinx it?" He raised his brows. "Seems to me the killer wants to drive them out of town."

"Do they think it's the same killer?" I wondered.

Nathan shrugged. "Looks that way. We'll see for ourselves soon enough."

At the crime scene, we pushed past the crowd of reporters, performers and cops encircling the body. I held my breath, hoping that Derek was OK, that his prediction hadn't come true. Thank goodness I spotted him in the crowd, next to the saddest-looking harlequin I'd ever seen. The sword swallower paced around the perimeter, followed by the farmer in overalls and a straw hat. Were they friends of the victim or just curious troupe members?

Gingerly I eased into the tight band of onlookers and spied the victim in the alley behind the theatre—the same spot Sammy had left Patrick. Merely a coincidence or purposely planned?

The coroner knelt by the man's side, examining the victim— who was dressed like a genie straight out of *Arabian Nights*. He wore a sparkling vest and harem pants, his face made up with brown paint and kohl-rimmed eyes—even a moustache with a fake beard.

I didn't remember him from the opening night performance— was he a new act and recent hire as Derek mentioned? Or was he in hiding, wearing an outlandish disguise, like Patrick?

Nathan sprung into action, taking pictures of the corpse from different angles, puffs of smoke appearing from his flash.

A couple of cops grabbed his arms and shoved him out of the way, but Nathan managed to wriggle out of their grasp, wily as usual.

The M.E. studied the victim's neck and jotted down a few notes. Moving closer, I noticed the man had several lacerations on his throat, similar to the red marks on Patrick's neck. Was it the same killer, or perhaps a copycat? Were they trying to frame the viola player? I spied Mack across the parking lot with his cronies, busy taking notes. Of course, I was tempted to find out what he knew, but wasn't in any mood for his arrogant attitude.

Instead, I circled the area and entered the alley from the opposite side, away from the crowd. A few set displays leaned against the building, rotting away, and I noticed an object tucked behind a cut-out tree display.

That's when I spotted the open viola case, its lining ripped out, the interior sliced to shreds.

CHAPTER THIRTY-THREE

Looking over my shoulder, I squatted down by the viola case, using a hanky to hold it by the neck, careful not to touch the worn leather or damaged interior. Seems someone was searching for the jewels when they sliced out the lining. Who had abandoned the case—the victim or the killer—and when?

The genie didn't look familiar to me, but then again he'd be hard to recognize with all that grease paint on his face. There had to be a connection between Patrick and the victim, especially since it appeared they were both strangled with a viola string, probably by the same killer.

Glancing around, I didn't see any cops nearby so decided to leave the case alone for now. I wanted to talk to Derek, find out what he knew. For once, he was wearing street clothes, not in costume or stage make-up, looking like a clean-cut College Joe—reminding me of the old Derek.

I rushed over to him, placing my hand on his arm. "So glad to see you, Derek. When I heard the news...I thought the worst."

He smiled and gave me a quick squeeze, seemingly touched. "Thanks, Jazz. I appreciate your concern."

Face flushed, I pulled away, trying to act nonchalant. "So who is the victim? Any idea what happened?"

"I don't recognize him, but his costume looks familiar. He must be a new act, a snake charmer or Oriental mystic? Maybe he's an unfortunate fortune teller."

How could he joke? "You've never seen him? Has the troupe used the costume before?"

"For a few months, we featured a scene from *The Sheik*, but that was canceled after Valentino died. Too many weeping women. Guess who played the sheik?" Derek struck a dashing pose.

"What a heartbreaker," I teased. "Does the troupe often share costumes?"

"Sure, if it's not already used in another skit or act." He gave the victim the once-over. "I bet this guy was hired to replace the pig routine. Their act only went over well in farm towns."

"Too bad. I enjoyed the talking pig. Say, Derek, I've got something to show you." I led him toward the back alley, away from the crowd, and pointed to the battered viola case. "Could this be the viola case Patrick had mentioned? Looks empty, but we'd better not touch it."

Derek's dark eyes widened as he bent down to examine the case. "I heard Milo carried the jewels in a viola case to avoid suspicion. Then Patrick must have hidden the jewelry and handed the fence an empty case."

"Makes sense. No wonder poor Patrick got stabbed."

I paused, wondering how much to say. Sure, I trusted Derek, but would he accidentally spill the beans to the wrong person?

We walked back toward the crime scene, still talking, observing the crowd. "By the way, I wanted you to know we found the jewelry—Patrick hid the bag at the Oasis."

Derek's olive skin turned pale. "What? How'd you find them? Where are they now?"

"Let's just say they're in safe hands." For all I knew, they could be in Musey's hands by now. "I'm sure there's a connection between Patrick and this victim."

"Probably." He shrugged. "We'll wait to see what the cops and your *boyfriend* dig up."

His sarcastic tone made me mad. "Burton's a Prohibition agent, not a cop," I huffed. "He helps out on various cases when he has time. Say, do me a favor and don't tell anyone we found the jewelry. Between us, we have a plan to recover the jewels and catch the thieves."

"That's swell." His face brightened. "You have no idea what it's like to sit by and watch my *friends* rob innocent people blind and not be able to do anything. All I can do is bide my time and keep my mouth shut."

"I'm sure they'll catch them before the troupe leaves town." For now, I had to find out: "What do you plan to do then?"

Derek gave me a sheepish look. "Who knows? I might decide to stick around Galveston for a while."

"How nice." I forced a smile, wondering how his presence would affect my life, his life, if he remained in town. Would things change between me and Agent Burton? As if on cue, Burton walked up then and glared at Derek, meaning: "Leave her alone."

He took my arm, a bit too possessive for my taste. Derek's dark eyes flashed and he backed away, melting into the crowd. There went my chance to ask him more questions. "Thought I'd find you here. What were you and Derek talking about?" Burton raised his brows.

"The victim. Turns out he was strangled the same way as Patrick, with a viola string."

Burton nodded. "That narrows it down. Seems likely it was a musician or a performer."

"Would they be that obvious, using instrument strings? I wonder if it's a copycat or a frame-up."

"Killers aren't always the brightest bulbs," Burton pointed out. "Lucky for us."

"You said it. Do the cops know the victim's name yet?"

"Until we get him out of his costume and face paint, we can't properly ID him. I'll wait for the coroner's report. Wonder if we'll find any more *surprises* under that get-up?"

"Hope not." I made a face. "Say, I've got good news. Guess what I found? A viola case with its lining ripped out in the alley. Want to see it?" I failed to mention that I'd just shown it to Derek.

"*The* viola case? Sure—it might be the evidence we need. Forensics can try to dust it for fingerprints. Did you touch it?"

"I know better than that." Once out of earshot, I asked him, "What's happening with Sammy? Is everything OK?"

"Our men are on their way. Musey wanted to meet at our old spot, Mario's restaurant. No doubt he'll be surrounded by his Downtown Gang goons."

"So he'll be covered while Sammy will be left alone to fend for himself."

"Don't forget, our men will be in hiding nearby."

"How close—a hundred yards away?" I sighed. "Sammy will be a sitting duck."

CHAPTER THIRTY-FOUR

Luckily, the viola case remained half-hidden behind the set in the alley. "Good eye, Jazz." Burton pulled out a linen handkerchief and picked up the case by the neck. "Sure there aren't any gems tucked away?"

"I was afraid to touch it. Be careful—you don't want to drop the Crown jewels," I cracked. " On second thought, it might be nice to own a diamond tiara or two..."

"Just a tiara? Not a ring?"

"Who said anything about a diamond ring?" I rolled my eyes, annoyed. Why did men assume that all women wanted to do was get married—right away?

Frowning, he shook the case and found a small brooch stuck inside. "Take a look."

I studied the brass pin—a sunflower with a few paste stones forming the petals. "Looks like the cheap costume jewelry you'd find at Woolworth's, no better than a Cracker Jack charm." I mulled it over. "What if Patrick stuffed the viola case with a bunch of junk and tried to pass off the fakes as real gems? I doubt these trinkets fooled anyone, not even a two-bit thug."

"At least these fakes weighed down the case, making the killer think it was loaded with loot," Burton said. "Maybe the middleman didn't notice the difference in the dark at first. After he realized he'd been conned, he demanded Patrick turn over the real jewels or else."

I nodded, adding, "When Patrick refused, he got so mad that he stabbed him in the gut—not enough to kill him, but to show he meant business. Seems Patrick planned to retrieve the jewels later since he returned to the Oasis in disguise. Too bad he didn't fool anyone for long."

"Notice he only kept the diamond ring—the most valuable item in the bunch," Burton pointed out. "What if the fence found out it belonged to Rose Maceo's wife and wanted to blackmail her? Or tried to frame Patrick? Until we find the killer, we may never know the truth."

After discussing all these theories and scenarios, I felt as dizzy as a bobble-headed doll. By now, the crowd seemed to be dispersing, and I scanned the area, wondering if Nathan had already left.

"Say, I'd better take the case to forensics now," Burton said. "Need a lift back to work?"

"I think I'll stick around here, ask a few more questions. Keep me posted on Sammy." I took a deep breath. "Fingers crossed everything turns out OK."

"Don't worry. Just be prepared for the aftermath. Remember, we need to arrest them both for the sting to look convincing."

How could I forget? "Good luck." I sighed and gave Burton's arm a slight squeeze. Naturally I wanted to nose around and find out more about the murder, but I couldn't stop worrying about Sammy's meeting with Musey.

My mind raced: What if he got suspicious and turned on Sammy? Worse, what if the cops started shooting?

A trolley jostled by, interrupting my train of thought, the clanging noise matching the ringing in my head.

Making my way through the crowd, I stopped a few performers still in costume—a fire-eater, a juggler, and a hoofer—and asked routine questions about the victim's murder. After a series of "Who are you?" reactions, they told me the same static I'd heard from Derek—nothing. Was this a conspiracy? Did the guy appear out of thin air? Were they all told to keep quiet?

I wanted to ask the director a few questions, but he was being interviewed by the police. Draper seemed to be an average Joe, the kind you wouldn't look at twice, a mild-mannered milquetoast with balding hair and glasses.

Hard to believe he was a devious mastermind controlling a band of thieves. Edging closer, I stood by, trying to eavesdrop.

"I recently got rid of an act and needed some new talent," Draper was saying, "and this guy showed up just in time. He was supposed to be a mystic, a mind-reader. We were in a jam so I hired him on the spot. I figured I'd try him out and get the troupe's reaction during rehearsals. When he never showed, we got worried. Later we found the body behind the alley."

"What's his name?" a detective in a trench coat asked.

"Nick Turner," Draper said.

"Name doesn't ring a bell. Who discovered the body?"

"The clown. Part of his set was missing and he started searching the premises, as well as the grounds. That's when he found the body, underneath the set."

"Does the clown have a name?" the cop asked.

"He's Bonkers, the happy clown."

The cop glared at Draper, probably thinking *he* was bonkers. "A real name?"

"Of course." The director wiped his face with a hanky, though it was a cool 50 degrees outside. "It's Peter Peterson. He should be around here. He's hard to miss."

"I'll bet." The officer raised his brows at two other cops flanking his side, and looked around the area. "Got that, boys? We're looking for Bonkers, the *happy* clown."

"Funny, he seems to have disappeared." Draper frowned. "He was here a minute ago."

"Until we can talk to your clown and troupe, I'm afraid we'll have to close your show tonight," the cop snapped.

"Close down my show?" The director bristled. "You can't do that. Everyone depends on me. Trust me, officers, I'll round up my troupe and bring them to your station within the hour."

"You'd better keep your word, pal, or we'll padlock these doors and put your whole troupe in jail." The cop glared at Draper, then turned and left, his men following behind. Strange how Sammy and Draper seemed to be in the same boat, with the police on their heels.

I scanned the crowd, keeping my eyes open for a suspicious clown. With a name like Bonkers and a clown outfit, how dangerous could he be? Or had he changed into street clothes and run away? I watched the medics put the victim inside an ambulance, assuming they planned to do an autopsy. The whole scene seemed surreal, almost comical, because of the genie's outlandish costume.

Inching forward, I took a quick look at the group of gawkers, wondering if the killer was among them, watching and waiting. A face looked familiar and I did a double-take: Were my eyes playing tricks or was that really Rose Maceo in the background—and what was he doing at this murder scene?

CHAPTER THIRTY-FIVE

Determined to follow the mystery man—Rose Maceo?—I tried to find the short, stout gangster in the dwindling crowd but, like Bonkers, the now-suspicious clown, he had disappeared. Was it possible Maceo knew the victim? Did he have him killed—if so, why?

Out of breath, Nathan suddenly showed up, smiling like a Chesire cat. "You gotta admit, dead genies make for some colorful photos. I couldn't take close-ups of his neck wounds because of his damn beard. Still got some good shots that'll make the boss happy."

I shuddered. "Hope Mr. Thomas doesn't put the photos on the front page. A dead genie will give kids nightmares for months."

"This story *belongs* on the front page with my pics!" Nathan argued. "Mack's stories always get top billing."

Mack again. If only the editors would give the rest of us a chance. "What did Mack find out? Anything besides the obvious?"

"Not much. The victim seemed to appear out of nowhere—like a genie." He grinned. "Hey, maybe I should start writing news stories myself. Can't be that hard."

"Says you. Good luck sharing the spotlight with Mack. Say, did you overhear Draper talking to the cops? Sounds like he hired the victim without an audition. Doesn't that sound dicey?"

"Seems risky. What if he stinks on stage? They throw tomatoes, shoes and all sorts of stuff. Then they'll pull you offstage by the neck with a huge hook. Tough job."

"I've seen a few duds yanked off the stage." True, I felt a bit sorry for the troupe, sympathizing with their plight. Still, that didn't give them the right to steal strangers' jewelry, no matter how rich and privileged. "Say, did Mack get to interview the troupe? Or Draper?"

"He tried, but they avoided answering his questions, like they were hiding something."

"I got that feeling too." I nodded. "Strange that this genie popped up out of nowhere."

"Maybe he'd escaped from his bottle?" Nathan cracked. "Let's see what the cops and newsboys dig up."

Newsboys? What about news women?

On the way back to work, I kept mum about Musey and Sammy's plan to fence the stolen jewels. Had the cops shown up at their meet yet? How I wished I could be a fly on the wall...

At the *Gazette*, the newshawks hadn't gotten back yet, so I sat at my desk, trying to piece together details about the victim. Were they at the morgue, waiting for a report?

Mrs. Harper frowned at me from across the room. "That was a nice long *lunch*, Jasmine. Where were you?"

"I was helping the fellas at a crime scene," I fibbed, glad that Mack hadn't yet returned. "Didn't you hear about the murder at Martini Theatre?"

"Yes, of course, but why is that your concern?"

Trying to think fast, I brought up the one subject that I knew would melt her frosty heart. "When I heard the news, I was so worried it might be Derek. I wanted to make sure he was OK."

Only then did her stony face soften. "Did you get to see him?"

"Yes, thank goodness." I fluttered my hand over my chest for emphasis. "I even got to ask him a few questions—for Mack, naturally."

Speak of the devil. Mack burst in with his entourage of eager cub reporters, Chuck and Pete, his broad face flushed with excitement. "Have I got a scoop for tomorrow's paper! A real humdinger. You'll never guess who this so-called swami or genie was in real life!"

Mr. Thomas peeked out of his office door. "Who?"

"His real name is Nico Turturo, a con artist with a rap sheet ten miles long." Mack paused as the staff gathered round to hear his latest news. "They call him the Turtle 'cause he likes to wear different disguises. I recognized him the minute they removed his face paint."

I figured Nick Turner was an alias. "Did he work for one of the gangs?" I piped up.

Mack studied me for a long minute. "What makes you say that?"

"Just a hunch."

Mack glared at me before he continued. "Get this: His last job was a bank heist. Turturo freelanced as a jewel thief and part-time fence. He just got out on parole about two weeks ago from Huntsville prison. Under that corny costume, he's got the prison tattoos to prove it."

I knew it! Then a thought hit me: Did the genie work for Maceo—or was it Musey? After hearing Draper's answers, I began to wonder if Musey forced him to hire the genie or mystic to keep his eye on Draper and his band.

The genie costume and even his act may have been merely a cover, a way to infiltrate the troupe. Maybe Musey wanted to make sure he got back his investment—either in jewelry or cash.

The staff crowded around Mack, asking questions, but he shooed them away. "Beat it, boys. You'll just have to wait till you read tomorrow's paper. I gotta make this deadline." When Mack thought no one was looking, he motioned me over, his voice low. "You think the Turtle was working for a local gang?"

"Makes sense to me." I shrugged. "Or else he was freelancing."

"I saw you talking to your two beaux at the crime scene. What did they tell you?"

I ignored his crack. "Not much. I heard the director say that Bonkers, the clown, found the body under a circus set in the alley."

Why mention the viola case to Mack? Let him do his own detective work.

"They're still looking for him. Peter Peterson. Sounds like a bogus name to me." Mack glanced around the room. "Keep me posted."

I nodded. "I'll let you know if they find out anything." Feeling smug, I sat at my desk, wondering if Mack was playing dumb or playing me.

Half an hour later, I jumped when the phone rang on Mrs. Harper's desk.

"For you, Jazz," the secretary, Mrs. Page, called out. "That dreamy Fed agent."

Swell. Did she have to blurt it out now? Was she planning to eavesdrop on all our calls?

"Jazz, I've got some bad news." Burton's voice sounded urgent.

"What happened?" My heart banged in my chest. "Is Sammy OK?"

"Sammy's been taken into custody. Damn it, Musey never showed up. I think some snitch tipped off Musey about our sting."

CHAPTER THIRTY-SIX

"What?" I cried out, trying to lower my voice so the nosy news hawks couldn't overhear. "Who spilled the beans? I thought everything was all set."

"I thought so, too." Burton sounded worried. "Let's just say things didn't go as planned. Don't know what to tell the brass. Only a handful of cops knew about our sting to set up Musey. Instead they caught Sammy with the jewels and the cash. Sorry to say, he looked guilty as hell."

"So Sammy was framed instead." My breath caught in my throat. "Do you need me to testify? I can tell them where I found..." I noticed the newsroom grew silent... "the stuff."

"Thanks, Jazz, but you'd be safer staying quiet. We don't want Musey to know you're connected in any way."

"I want to help. After all, it was my dumb idea."

"Your idea was fine. Trouble is, these wiseguys have shadows everywhere." Burton snorted. "Why don't you type up a formal statement and I'll pick you up after work. Say, by five or six? We can talk more then—in private."

Dazed, I hung up the phone. My nice neat plan to set up Musey and take the heat off Sammy had completely backfired. Now Sammy was in jail for a crime he didn't commit and Musey was free as a bird.

Who'd blabbed to Musey?

"What was that all about?" Mack poked his head over his typewriter.

"Nothing. Just a personal matter."

Upset, I paced around the newsroom, pretending to be filing, trying to avoid the reporters' curious stares. Couldn't a gal have any privacy at work?

All I wanted to do was help give Sammy a chance to escape from Johnny Jack and George Musey, to break away from the Downtown Gang forever. Burton had promised me that Sammy's arrest was only for show, that he'd be released soon after they'd taken Musey into custody.

Defeated and deflated, I sat down to write my statement, wondering how much to reveal without incriminating Sammy—or myself. Less is more, I decided, and began typing a short, professional-sounding statement that said I'd stumbled onto the jewelry by accident. No reason to admit that Sammy was my half-brother, or that Doria, our wooden figurehead and mascot, was the secret hiding place. What would the cops do—arrest her and force her to talk?

Nathan peered over my shoulder, and I covered my typewriter with my hands, shielding the paper. "Why the long face, Jazz? What's eating you?"

"Just working on a short item, trying to concentrate." Twirling around, I blocked his view. How could I tell him the truth with a nosy bunch of reporters a few feet away?

Fortunately, Mack's phone rang and as he listened, he waved Nathan over with his free hand. "You don't say? He's in custody now? I'm on my way."

Mack stood up, hiking up his khaki pants and puffing out his barrel chest. "Today's my lucky day, fellas."

Mack nodded at me and Mrs. Harper. "And gals. Now I've got not one, but two hot potatoes dropped right in my lap." He glanced over at me, giving me a condescending look, and I knew what was coming.

"Now I understand why you're so down in the mouth, Jazz. Your pal Sammy was caught red-handed, trying to fence a stash of stolen jewels."

The staff gasped and looked over at me with pity, waiting for my reaction. I raised my head, meeting his steely gaze. "You've got it all wrong, buster."

"How can I be wrong? Got a hot tip from my good source." Mack flung his arm toward the door. "Go down to the police station and see for yourself."

"No, thanks. Trust me, Sammy didn't steal any jewelry. It's all a big misunderstanding."

"Oh yeah? How do you know? Where's your proof?"

"That's all I can say for now." I stood closer, eyes narrowed. "Why don't you get your facts straight before you make false accusations?"

"False? I hope to God you're right. Look what happened to their last fence."

Gee, thanks. Did he have to rub it in my face?

Mack slapped on his hat, threw a scarf around his neck and grabbed his satchel. "While I'm waiting on the coroner's report for Turturo, I may as well investigate this new case myself. Care to join me, Jasmine?"

I crossed my arms, fuming, wondering if the same snitch who tipped off Musey was also Mack's personal spy. "Who's your source? Some dirty cop?"

"My source? Which dirty cop?" Mack's face reddened and he drew in a heavy breath, looking like he wanted to slug me.

"You tell me. What's his name?"

"I'm too much of a gentleman to tell you what I really think." Mack gritted his teeth, his dark eyes blazing. The staff's heads collectively swiveled back and forth, enjoying our verbal tennis match. I bit my tongue, aware all eyes were watching us feud.

In a flash, Nathan jumped between us, blocking me with his camera equipment, his expression like a red flag. The reporters circled around, egging us on with stupid grins. What did they expect—a duel? A fistfight? Right—as if I'd take on a seasoned soldier like Mack, more than twice my size and age.

Mack scowled as he turned to go. "Coming, Nathan?"

Nathan gave me a sheepish smile and trailed behind Mack like a servant—that traitor.

Still shaking with anger, I started to follow them out the door, then remembered my police statement, still fresh in my typewriter.

Mrs. Harper waddled over to my desk just as I snatched the paper right out from under her nose. Quickly I folded the sheet in half, and tucked it into my handbag, heart thumping. Close call.

"Jasmine, I need to talk to you," she scolded. "You know that's not proper behavior for a society reporter, especially in public. Why, you were asking for a fight!"

My face flaming, I heard a few reporters snicker, feeling like a kid getting chewed out by an old school marm. "Sorry I lost my temper. But Mack deserved every word." I shrugged on my coat, grabbed my bag and knit scarf. "Excuse me, I've got some place to be. It's urgent."

Before she could stop me, I rushed out the door and almost ran right into Agent Burton walking toward the *Gazette*. "You got here just in time." I took a few deep breaths to calm down. "Hurry, let's go down to the police station before they crucify Sammy."

CHAPTER THIRTY-SEVEN

"Blame the police." Burton worked his jaw. "Musey was a no-show 'cause of some dirty cop. I thought Sheriff Sanders helped us clean house last summer." He held open the car door for me, parked in front of the *Gazette* building. Police privileges.

"Sammy has provided enough fodder for Mack's sensational stories. All he needs is another front-page spread of his latest arrest." I sighed. "But if Sammy admits he was helping the cops set up Musey, he'll have to worry about a lot more than a night in jail. Musey and Johnny Jack will waste no time getting revenge."

"Maybe Mack *should* write a story on Sammy to get Musey off his back," Burton said. "Think about it, Jazz. He may be safer in jail than at the Oasis."

"You mean incriminate him in print?" I considered his words. "Musey may buy it, but the last thing Sammy needs is to be labeled a fence or a jewel thief."

"As I recall, didn't he agree to go along with Musey's idea to fence the jewels in Houston?"

I glared at Burton. "Did he have any choice? If the cops had done their jobs, Musey would be locked up by now—instead of Sammy."

"Obviously we need a new plan." Burton sounded apologetic. "Let's stop by the station and drop off your statement, so you can talk to Sammy."

"What am I supposed to say?" I knotted my hands. "I feel terrible—this was all my fault."

"Gosh, you sound so guilty, you may as well be locked up next to Sammy."

"Gee, thanks," I pouted, wondering how to apologize to him behind bars. 'I'm sorry' wasn't enough. How many times would Sammy have to go in and out of jail before he was free of the Downtown Gang? "Mack and Nathan will have a field day with this story. If they publish it, there's no doubt Draper and the vaudeville troupe will pack up and leave town without warning. The cops can't let them get away."

Burton nodded. "Frankly, it'll be hard to accuse Draper unless we catch them in the act, or with the stolen jewelry. Or a victim needs to press charges and prove ownership. To do that, first we have to find out who the jewels belonged to and where they were stolen. What we need is a confession, someone who's willing to testify on record."

"You mean one of the performers? Good luck getting them to cooperate."

"Can you talk to Derek? Maybe he can convince one of his friends to testify."

"His friends? From what I hear, he's a persona non grata with the troupe. Maybe we can ask him before the performance tomorrow night—if they're still in town."

"Believe it or not, now I'm actually looking forward to the show," Burton said. "These musicians have got to slip up one way or another."

At the police station, Burton and I arrived in time to see Mack and Nathan leaving, frowns on their faces.

"What's wrong? Sammy wasn't willing to spill his guts or pose for you?" I couldn't help but taunt them—not very mature, I know.

Mack scowled at me and kept walking to his car.

Nathan shrugged. "The cops already released him, said he wasn't guilty."

"What? When?" I was relieved, yet surprised.

"We just missed him," Nathan said. "Guess we'll go over to the morgue now, see what they found out about the Turtle."

"Keep me posted, will you? By the way, sorry about my outburst. Mack really got my goat."

"I noticed." Nathan stared at me in mock-terror. "Jazz, I had no idea you could be such a firebrand. So what caused the ruckus?"

Burton flashed me an amused grin. "Sorry I missed all the excitement."

"Musey was supposed to get caught with the jewels, but he never showed up to meet Sammy," I explained to Nathan. "So Sammy's arrest was faked to throw off Musey's gang."

"I suspect a dirty cop tipped off Musey before the meet," Burton grimaced.

"If Mack wants a real story, I suggest he find out who's the snitch," I told Nathan.

"Only one?" He raised his brows. "Good luck."

Inside the station, Burton knocked on the captain's door, then walked inside, motioning for me to follow. "Here's Miss Cross's statement," Burton told Captain Johnson. "I know it's a bit late. Say, I heard you released Sammy Cook. Why so soon, if you don't mind me asking?"

"Why not?" Johnson shrugged. "Cook has no prior history of stealing or fencing jewels, unlike Musey and his gang. We hope Cook can lead us to Musey, eventually."

"So you're using Sammy as bait?" I flared up.

"Mr. Cook agreed to our terms." The captain rearranged himself in his chair, eyes narrowed.

Burton gave me a warning look, that meant, "Keep your trap shut."

I hung my head, pretending to act apologetic for Burton's sake. "Sorry, I didn't mean..." Then I noticed the crime scene photos and mug shots spread out on the captain's desk. "Is that the victim?"

"Yes, you could say they're his before and after photos. Why?" Johnson said, frowning. "We've already ID'd him as Nick Turturo, the Turtle."

"He looks familiar..." With a start, I picked up the photos and showed them to Burton. "Don't you recognize him? From the other night at Mario's?"

Burton shrugged and shook his head. "Looks like your typical ten-cent hood to me."

"You know when Musey bumped our table, accidentally on purpose at the restaurant? And soon after, Mrs. Maceo's purse was stolen off the table?"

"How could I forget? He practically challenged me to a boxing match on the spot."

"Do you remember there was a young violinist playing that night?" I tapped the photo. "If I'm not mistaken, he's the same violinist from Mario's. Or rather, a viola player?"

Burton's eyes widened in surprise. "You don't say. They all must be working for Musey, and Mario's is their meeting place."

The captain sat up, alert. "The victim is one of Musey's men? Not a performer?"

"Makes sense." I pointed to the photo. "Musey must have planted him in the troupe to find out where Patrick stashed the jewels. Too much of a coincidence."

"Or he wanted to help himself to a fresh batch of gems, like the jewels stolen from the Hotel Galvez," Burton added. "I wonder if he ever found the Galvez gems?"

"We searched his person but no jewelry was recovered," Johnson told us.

"How in the world did a thug like the Turtle learn to play the viola?" I wondered out loud.

Johnson leaned forward. "The prison system provides various educational tools to help non-violent prisoners learn different skills before their release. I assume he took lessons in prison since they do have a musical program for non-death row inmates."

"Apparently he learned how to kill in prison as well," I pointed out. "I wonder if Draper went along with Musey's plan or he was in the dark? I suspect he had no idea—and that's why the Turtle wore such an elaborate costume as a cover."

Burton nodded. "Question is, if he killed Patrick, who strangled *him*—and was it with his own viola string? Seems the second killer made it look like a copycat murder to mislead the police and cover his own tracks."

"Possibly Musey had his man murdered for failing his assignment," Johnson said. "That's their usual punishment."

"I wouldn't doubt it a bit." Burton nodded.

I tugged on Burton's arm. "Let's shake a leg. Musey may be looking for Sammy."

"Keep me informed," Chief Johnson called out as we left. "Good luck."

"Will do, Chief." After we exited the station, Burton said, "Jazz, you really need to learn to control your temper. It's in your best interest to keep the police chief on your side." How many times did I need to be reprimanded in one day?

"I can't help myself. You know I have a soft spot for Sammy. He's my only brother."

Burton patted my hand. "I know. Just be careful." He veered around the corner and headed to the Oasis, driving like a fireman to a burning building. After all, cops never got speeding tickets.

"Any idea who might have blown Sammy's cover?"

"I might, but it'll be hard to prove. I'll have to catch him in the act and show a pattern of behavior. Better yet, find another cop or witness willing to tell me the truth. I'll have to do this on my own time. We can't keep letting these lawbreakers get away, scot-free."

"Especially hard-boiled hoods like Musey."

At the Oasis, Burton pounded on the door and when no one answered, he burst inside. Shouts and scuffling noises sounded in the bar below. A bar brawl?

Heart pounding, I exchanged worried looks with Burton as we crept downstairs, then stopped on the steps: Musey and Sammy were fighting in the middle of the bar room, chairs and tables pushed back like ringside seats.

My worst fears had come true. Watching the surrealistic scene unfold, I clamped a hand over my mouth, trying not to cry out, a bad habit. Dino and Frank stood by, gaping, flanked by two of Musey's men. I clutched Burton's arm, squeezing so tight my nails dug into his flesh.

"You set me up, you son-of-a-bitch!" Musey yelled at Sammy between blows.

"Bullshit! I had nothing to do with it." Sammy took a swing at his jaw, but Musey ducked out of the way.

"So why did they let you go?" Musey demanded, bringing his fist down on Sammy's skull.

Sammy reeled backward, clutching his head with both hands, moaning in pain.

I gasped and bit my lip, but it was too late: I let out such a screech that both Musey and Sammy stopped to glance our way.

"Get out of here, copper. This ain't your fight," Musey yelled at Burton.

"Like hell it isn't." Burton stepped out of the shadows, drawing his revolver, pointing it at Musey.

Sammy stared at us, breathing hard, his eyes widening in warning, fists still raised. My heart squeezed at the haunted look in his eyes, his bloody face, scratched and bruised arms. I'd seen Sammy fight before—and win—but he wasn't a match for this heavyweight.

"Try and stop me." Like a trained torpedo, Musey pulled out a gun and aimed it at Burton.

Surely Musey was bluffing. I held my breath. Would he really try to kill a Federal agent—in front of witnesses?

A shot rang out, then two, reverberating against the walls, echoing in my ears like drums. Terrified, I jumped and turned away instinctively, squeezing my eyes shut, covering my ears.

That's when I heard something—or someone—hit the hardwood floor with a loud thud.

CHAPTER THIRTY-EIGHT

"You bastard!" I heard George Musey yell. "You almost shot my goddamn arm off!"

Slowly I opened my eyes, peering out between my fingers at Musey writhing on the floor in pain, clutching his limp arm. Dark blood seeped into the wood floor and he started jerking all over while we stood by, staring open-mouthed.

Musey seemed to be going into shock, but we continued to gape, as wooden and motionless as totem poles. My stomach lurched and I tried not to upchuck at the sight of his bloody arm, ragged bone jutting out of his skin, snapped in half like a tree branch. Sure, he was a killer and a heartless hood, but I couldn't stand to see anyone suffer, even if I couldn't help.

"So glad you're OK." I sighed to Burton. "I thought..."

"His bullet whizzed right by my head," he said, dazed. "My ears are still ringing."

"Thank God he missed." Spots floated before my eyes and my knees began to buckle. I clutched Burton's arm, my body swaying back and forth. "Go help Musey. I'm sure he needs a tourniquet."

My lack of medical training and queasy stomach made me utterly useless in a crisis. All I could do was grab a clean tablecloth and carefully lay it over Musey like a big bib, for his sake as well as mine. His coal eyes flickered in gratitude. "Thanks, toots."

Mechanically Burton knelt down by Musey, and rolled up his shirt sleeve, soaked with blood.

"Stay away from me!" Musey grabbed his shattered arm. "You'll just put me in the pen. Might as well call a hearse."

"I may be a good shot, but I'm no cold-blooded killer. Not like you and your gangsters. I won't leave you here to die." Burton ripped off the tablecloth's edge and wrapped Musey's arm with a make-shift bandage, pulling it tight right above the protruding bone.

Gingerly I took Sammy's arm. "How about you? Are you OK?"

"I'll live." Sammy grimaced, and stumbled over to a nearby chair. I got a glass of water and handed it to him, sitting down. "Glad you two showed up," he said as Burton walked over to the table. "One more minute and Musey would've put a bullet in my head."

"You looked like you were holding him off all on your own," Burton replied.

Sammy shrugged. "I did my best."

Musey's two men hovered over him, shuffling their feet. "Are you OK, boss?"

He groaned in pain. "I'm bleeding to death. Don't just stand there. Whack this guy."

I froze, watching their reaction. The goons stared at each other, and shook their heads. "A Fed?"

"I'll call an ambulance." Burton walked behind the bar, and gave Musey a tight smile as he dialed John Sealy Hospital. "Please send an ambulance to the Oasis Grill on Market Street. And make it snappy. This man has lost a lot of blood."

"You said it, Fed. And it'll be your fault if I lose my arm too," Musey snapped before his eyes closed.

"He's out cold. Let's scram!" Musey's two thugs bolted up the stairs without looking back.

After Burton hung up, he sat down at Sammy's table.

I turned to examine Sammy. "How are you feeling?"

"Nothing serious." He tried to shrug, but his face twisted in pain, beads of sweat on his forehead.

"I'll be glad to take you to Big Red," Burton offered. "You've got some shiner there, sport." Indeed, Sammy's right eye socket was turning various shades of purple, framed by a cut and imprint where Musey hit him above his right brow.

"Hell, no. Musey's goons will be waiting for me there. I'd better head back to Houston before Nounes finds out about his right-hand man. Too bad Musey won't be using his right hand *or* his right arm for a while," Sammy cracked.

Glad he hadn't lost his wits. Sammy attempted to stand, then collapsed into a chair.

"You're in no shape to drive to Houston or anywhere tonight," I scolded. "Why don't you come over to the boarding house and let Eva fix you right up. She used to volunteer down at Big Red."

"I can vouch for her nursing skills," Burton said. "She took care of me when I had my lights punched out a few months ago. Plus it's a lot safer there than staying here."

"Sure?" Sammy frowned. "I thought Eva didn't want a barkeep in her hoity-toity home."

"Believe it or not, she's mellowed since she met Sheriff Sanders," I reassured him. "And you need a good hot meal. Wait till you've sampled her delicious home-cooking. You'll be on your feet in no time."

Sammy looked sheepish. "I don't want you gals to go to any trouble."

"We've got plenty of spare rooms upstairs. Besides, it'll give you a chance to see Amanda before you leave."

Eva had a strict policy about keeping male and female guests on separate floors. Luckily a few male boarders had left recently, vacating their rooms before the holidays.

Sammy's face brightened, and he slowly stood up, wincing in pain. "OK, you talked me into it, Jazz. Frank, you and Dino hold down the fort while I get some shut-eye." As he hobbled out the door, he gave Musey a hard kick in the leg. "Two-bit bastard. He and his brother Freddie. Got too greedy, too fast."

Burton pulled Sammy away, saying, "Hey, you had your turn. Good thing you two didn't kill each other."

"We might have if you didn't come along. We could've taken him, too, without your help."

"Sure, Sammy." I helped him up the stairs. "I saw what a big help Frank and Dino were, watching on the sidelines, letting you take a pounding."

When the ambulance arrived, the medics gave Burton a questioning look as they placed Musey on the gurney. "What happened here?" a heavyset medic asked. "Shoot-out at the OK Corral? You'd better call the cops, buster."

"I am the cops." Burton scowled, and flashed his badge. "How about you take care of this man and mind your own business."

"Yes, sir," the medic stammered, backing away.

We suppressed a smile while he lumbered up the stairs.

"Would you rather go with them or hitch a ride with me?" Burton asked, helping Sammy stand up. This time, Sammy didn't balk at Burton's offer for a ride. In the Roadster, he stretched out on the back seat, his head propped up against the door, and promptly fell asleep. No wonder, after the past few days. I took Burton's hand and squeezed it hard. With that one shot, he'd quite possibly saved Sammy's life—and his own.

After we arrived at the boarding house, Eva's face broke into a smile, then a frown when she saw Sammy. "Are you hurt? What happened? Come in, let me get you cleaned up."

Amanda rushed in from the parlor. "Oh no! You poor thing. Who did this—that thug?"

Burton and I exchanged smiles, knowing Sammy was in safe hands. While the gals were tending to Sammy, we stepped out onto the front porch and sat on the old wooden swing.

"Thanks for helping Sammy today," I told him. "We're all so grateful."

"Some good I did. Musey's goons saw me shoot their boss trying to protect Sammy. No doubt they'll report to Johnny Jack with the news. They'll think we're in cahoots."

"It was self-defense!" I pointed out. "For all they know, you planned to arrest both men. And they saw you administer first-aid and call the hospital. Nounes can't blame you for protecting yourself, all of us, from Musey."

"Hope you're right." He shook his head. "Why in hell they released Sammy early, I don't know. Sammy cooperated with the cops, and turned in all the cash and jewelry as promised."

"They may as well put a bull's-eye on his chest," I said. "Musey must be paying that snitch a pretty penny."

"You said it. To be honest, I'm glad I shot that bastard where it counts."

"I'll say." Burton put on a brave face, but I saw his hands trembling. "Sure you don't want some supper?"

"I'll let Sammy enjoy all this attention. He'd better leave town before Nounes hears the news."

"You saved his life." I gave him a grateful smile. "And you certainly took care of Musey. I doubt he'll be the sharpest shooter with only one arm."

He tried to show remorse. "That wasn't my intention. I only use violence as a last resort." He looped his arms around my neck. "So we're still on for Thursday night?"

"Sure—as long as Sammy is fine. I'm hoping to go backstage and search for some stolen Galveston gems."

"Attagirl. Hate to admit, that's where your friend Derek comes in handy. Backstage access."

After Burton left, I joined Amanda and Sammy, who were chatting and snuggling in the parlor. They both looked so content and relaxed, you'd never know George Musey almost snuffed out Sammy two hours earlier.

"Glad you're feeling better," I said with a grin. "Burton and I suspect some dirty cop blew your cover."

Sammy reddened and leaned forward, clearly embarrassed at being caught with Amanda smooching all over him. Amanda had no such qualms and continued to stroke his back and arm in a playful and possessive way.

"I'll bet. Does Burton have any idea who it might be?"

"I think so, but he needs proof first. Meanwhile, why don't you rest up a few days until you're ready to travel back to Houston."

"Houston?" Sammy scowled. "I'm no safer there than here. Fact is, I've had a change of heart." He and Amanda traded furtive glances. "I may stay put after all."

My heart flip-flopped, delighted that Sammy might remain in Galveston, yet fearful for his security. "That's swell. But what about Musey and Nounes?"

"I have a feeling their days are numbered. I hear my buddies, Sam and Rose, are kings of the Island."

Sammy was right: Word around town hinted that the Beach Gang could soon take over the Downtown Gang. Evidently the Maceos had gained favor with the right crowd while Johnny Jack continued his downward descent. Not to mention the fact that now Musey wasn't quite so intimidating with only one arm.

Before I went upstairs to bed, Eva stuck her head in the room. She waved a finger at Amanda and Sammy, who quickly moved apart on the loveseat. "No hanky-panky, you two. I've got standards to uphold, even if we are kin."

"Yes, ma'am." Sammy saluted Eva, his eyes wide in surprise. For once, Eva acknowledged Sammy as family.

CHAPTER THIRTY-NINE

Thursday

After Burton's confrontation with Musey, I steeled myself for a barrage of questions the next day in the newsroom. Instead the reporters seemed hard at work, especially Mack who snuck peeks at me over his not-very-noiseless typewriter. Suspicious, I stared right back at him, wondering what he was up to.

Finally Mack approached my desk, dangling some papers before my nose like a feed bucket. "Thought you might like to take a look before it goes to press."

"What's that?" I feigned indifference, wondering who he wanted to torture in print.

"See for yourself. Make it snappy. Wanna make the evening edition." With a smirk, he dropped the papers on my desk, pulled out a cigar and stepped outside.

Skimming the pages, I felt my face grow hot as I read Mack's *article*, full of innuendos and implications about Sammy. His diatribe claimed the cops released Sammy not only because he'd paid them off, but implied that he served as a go-between with the gangs—he all but called Sammy a snitch. Mack may as well have signed Sammy's death warrant. Talk about libel!

"The question remains: How has Sammy Cook, who's been in and out of prison for the past year, managed to escape the law's wrath? Could it be that he plays both sides, as friend and foe to both the local gangs and police force? Perhaps his alliance with Prohibition Agent James Burton explains away his luck with the law. Other than his ramshackle bar on Market Street, Cook doesn't seem to have been born with a silver or even silver-plated spoon in his double-dealing mouth."

Livid, I clutched the papers, my hands shaking, trying to control my breathing. How dare he! Mack still stood outside, yakking it up with a few newsboys who lingered on the steps, taking a smoke.

Surely Mr. Thomas would object to such a flagrant piece of sensationalism without any hard evidence. No use confronting the enemy directly, so I decided to take Mack's tripe to the top—and walked into Mr. Thomas' office without knocking.

"Have you seen this yet?" I sputtered. "Mack's latest handiwork."

I bit my lip, tempted to say "hatchet job" since he'd chopped Sammy to pieces in print, but didn't need to editorialize. Fortunately the editor-in-chief was a decent, fair man with a good reputation to uphold. His friendship with my father had landed me this job, and I trusted his judgement.

While waiting for his reaction, I glared at Mack through Mr. Thomas' window. By now, Mack had figured out what I was doing and he stormed back inside the office, also without knocking.

His eyes shifted back and forth between us. "What's going on?" he demanded. "A conspiracy?"

Mr. Thomas slowly placed the paper on his desk, his fingers laced. "Why don't you answer that question, Mack? What was your motive in writing this piece of yellow journalism? Are you trying to provoke a gang war? Why are you trying to tarnish this man's name, and possibly get him killed in the bargain? Have you gotten an official statement from Chief Johnson saying Sammy Cook is a police informant, or is this simply sensationalism based on mere observation and opinion?"

Mack looked dumbfounded. "From what I've seen, all evidence points to..."

"What evidence? I don't see one bit of evidence to support your theory. We don't publish libelous statements that might implicate a man in print. You can't serve as both judge and jury." Furious, Mr. Thomas gathered up the pages and threw them in the trash.

"That's my only copy!" Mack protested, starting to pull the papers from the trash bin.

Mr. Thomas stuck his leg out and pushed the bin away. "Leave it there—where it belongs. We're not a yellow rag. I'd advise you to work on stories with more merit, backed up by fact, not fiction."

By now, I couldn't hide my smile and turned to Mack with glee—and yes, to gloat. Mack gave me such an indignant glare that I pretended to shiver with fright. Mack stormed out of the office, slamming the door behind him.

"Thank you," I told Mr. Thomas.

"You're welcome. But I didn't do it only for you and your friend Sammy. I wanted to avoid a libel lawsuit—and to keep the peace between the gangs and local law enforcement."

"Whatever the reason, you saved the day—and probably Sammy's life."

Mr. Thomas gave me a wink. "It's the least I can do for you and your father. After all, I made him a promise—to look out for his children, both of them."

I stared at him in surprise. So Mr. Thomas knew about Sammy all along. I opened my mouth to speak, but he only nodded at me as a reply. Without a word, I left his office and returned to my desk, too rattled to work.

Still now I had to face the wrath of Mack. "What in hell were you doing, going behind my back? Who said you could give Mr. Thomas my article?" His chubby face looked like an overripe tomato, ready to burst. "I should have known better than to show my work to a ditzy dame."

"Who are you calling a ditzy dame?" I gave him the once-over, hands on my hips. "At least I don't use snitches for sources and pass off rumors as facts just to sell papers."

A couple of guys jeered, and Mack moved closer to me, fisting his right hand. "My stories pay for your wages."

"Oh yeah? Maybe you should take up fiction and start writing serials for the penny dreadfuls!" I shot back, emboldened by Mr. Thomas' support.

"Mind your own beeswax. If you weren't a dame, I'd slug you," Mack threatened, inching forward.

"What a gentleman." Eyes blazing, I stood my ground, all five-feet-five inches, knowing I wouldn't be so brave once we left the office. So much more I could say, but name-calling never accomplished anything.

"Lay off, Mack." Nathan stood between us, hands out like a referee. "Men aren't supposed to hit girls." I knew he was thinking of Holly, who'd survived her boyfriend's brutal attack.

"Tell that to the wife-beaters who kill their spouses and get away with murder." I glared at Mack. "Sammy may own a speakeasy, but at least he knows how to treat women with courtesy and respect."

Mack seemed to deflate before my eyes. "If Sammy's such a hero, maybe he should run for mayor. Better yet, governor of Texas."

"Thanks for the suggestion." Still fuming, I let my breath out slowly, trying not to provoke him any longer. From now on, I knew I'd have to learn the world of journalism on my own, without Mack's guidance. Not that he'd offered much help in the past.

If my heroine—famed female journalist Nellie Bly—could travel the world in seventy-two days all alone, couldn't I navigate a small-potatoes town like Galveston on my own?

Mr. Thomas stuck his head out of his office. "What's the ruckus out here? Why don't you reporters go cool your heels? We've got a deadline at noon." He gave Mack a warning look. "Work on something we can actually print."

Mack looked like he'd been struck by a firing squad as he skulked off to his desk. Glad Mrs. Harper wasn't around to hear our latest row, and lecture me on "unladylike behavior."

To cool off, I headed to the broom closet that doubled as the ladies' room, and stopped Nathan on his way to develop photos. "Thanks for sticking up for me. I can't believe Mack was such a bully today. What's wrong—are the gangs threatening him again?"

Nathan pulled me inside the darkroom. "We need to talk." Inside, the room glowed an eerie red. Photos hung from wires strung across the ceiling like a clothes line.

"I've never seen Mack so volatile, so out of control before, have you?" I shook my head. "What was he thinking, writing those ridiculous lies? The paper could be sued for libel!"

Nathan nodded in understanding. "Between us, I think Mack's been hitting the bottle a little too hard. To go off half-cocked that way, in the middle of the newsroom?"

"Mack should dry out before he comes to work and takes out his frustrations on us. Prohibition was passed because of drunks like him. I doubt Mr. Thomas will put up with his antics for long."

"You said it," Nathan agreed. "Mack's on thin ice. One of these days, I'm afraid he may go too far."

CHAPTER FORTY

That evening when the door bell rang, I opened the door expecting to see Agent Burton, but jerked back in surprise when I spied Sam Maceo standing on the porch. After all, it's not every day that a notorious gangster shows up at your door.

"Well, hello, Mr. Maceo," I stammered, trying to regain my composure. "I didn't know you made house calls."

"Call me Sam." Maceo flashed me a smooth smile and held out a hand. "I remember you—from the paper, right? I'm here to pick up our pal, Sammy Cook." He didn't seem the least fazed that we all appeared to be staying at the same boarding house—no doubt he had a no-questions-asked policy that kept him out of more trouble.

Sammy appeared next to me with a devilish grin. "Ready to go, Big Sam."

I gave Sammy a questioning look, but he only winked.

"Keep up the good work," Maceo called out to me as they left. What did that mean? Did he have my editors in his back pocket or did he actually read the society pages?

"What in the world is Sammy doing with Sam Maceo?" I said to Amanda. "I know they're friends, but if Johnny Jack or any of his men catch Sammy with the Maceos...."

"I wouldn't worry. Did you see the muscle he brought along?"

Indeed, two armed thugs leaned against Sam Maceo's fancy black Cadillac, parked not-so-discreetly across the street. I only hoped the neighbors wouldn't notice—fortunately, it was getting dark. Wouldn't that have been a spectacle if Agent Burton also appeared at that moment?

After they left, Eva stuck her head out of the kitchen. "Who was that, Agent Burton? Why didn't he come inside for a bit?"

"Just a friend of Sammy's. He'll be back later," I said quickly.

Close call! What would Eva say if she knew Sam Maceo and his goons had shown up at her boarding house?

For once, Burton was running late so I checked my new frock and matching wool cloche in the hallway mirror. No, it wasn't the fanciest shindig in town, but I wanted an excuse to wear my latest finds from Eiband's.

By the time Burton picked me up, we only had fifteen minutes until curtain. In his Roadster, I asked, "What was the hold-up?"

"We got back our reports from the M.E. on Nick Turturo's murder. Turns out he wasn't only strangled, he'd been stabbed."

"Stabbed? You mean like Patrick?" I was stunned. "Do you think it was the same person who killed Patrick?"

"We don't know yet. The captain suspects it may have been a revenge killing—to even the score for Patrick's death. Or we go back to our theory that perhaps it's a copycat, to throw off the police."

"Who had ties to both Musey and the vaudeville troupe—and the most to lose?" I wondered.

Burton and I traded looks, both voicing our suspicions. "The director, Draper?"

"I thought he didn't want to get his hands dirty. At least that's what Derek told me," I reasoned. "Besides, wouldn't he ask someone else to do the deed?"

"Let's keep our eyes on Draper tonight," Burton said, parking in front of Martini Theatre. When the valet came out to object, Burton simply flashed his badge and the young man retreated, hands up in apology.

Inside the theatre, the lights were dim and the M.C. had just started introducing the new acts. As we settled in our seats by the aisle, I glanced at the program, noting quite a few changes in the line-up, to cover for the actors who had dropped out or "disappeared."

The first few acts remained the same, save for Bella, the ballerina, who did a short routine from the Nutcracker, probably to promote the show starting two weeks before Christmas.

A cute Pierrot and Columbine sketch was next—with a handsome harlequin added who was vying for her affections—a sort of modern-day love triangle. Naturally, Pierrot won her heart in the end. Was there ever any doubt?

I glanced over at Burton, wondering if he considered Derek a rival at all? Perhaps he was a bit too sure of himself to feel threatened by an old beau. Speaking of, Derek appeared on stage next, twirling his handlebar moustache and swishing his cape around, acting more dastardly than ever. No chance that a hometown actor would be cut from the routine since he was so popular with the audience. Mrs. Harper and his mother made sure of that with their fawning "reports."

Burton kept his eyes glued to the stage, waiting and watching the director, who doubled as the MC and appeared to introduce or explain a new act. So far, nothing seemed amiss or out of order. I nudged Burton, whispering, "See anything unusual tonight?"

"Nothing." He shook his head. "That's what worries me. It's running like clockwork."

After someone shushed us, I slid down in my seat, staring at Derek from my safe distance. I had to admit, he'd turned into a handsome man, almost the polar opposite of Burton with his dark hair and eyes and pale skin. Even his wanderlust spirit seemed appealing since I'd definitely felt restless lately.

The orchestra broke into a crescendo during the fight between the sheriff and the villain, with the cowboy circling Derek in a menacing way. Tonight Derek was ultra dramatic, waving his arms around and rubbing his hands together in a most evil fashion. Was he overdoing the theatrics a bit for my sake?

When the cowboy finally pulled out his pistol and took a shot at Derek—I mean, the villain—his eyes widened and he dropped convincingly in a heap onto the stage floor.

He had outdone himself this time—was it for my benefit? When the curtain fell, the audience leapt to its feet, shouting out "Bravo!" Whether it was for Derek's dramatic demise or the overall production, I couldn't tell, but the applause was long and appreciative.

Soon the curtain calls came and the acts appeared one by one to take their bows, the applause growing louder each time. When the final act came onstage, the sheriff appeared alone, without Derek. Strange.

Was Derek taking a separate bow? Had he hurt himself when he tumbled down? If I knew Derek, he basked in the limelight—so why wasn't he there?

"I didn't see anything suspicious tonight, did you?" Burton said as he reluctantly stood up to applaud a second and third curtain call. Still no Derek.

"Something's wrong," I told him after the final curtain. "Derek's not onstage."

"Probably too busy helping the girls out of their costumes," Burton cracked.

I ignored his jab. "I'll go backstage, see where he is."

"Want me to come?"

"No need. I'll return in a jiffy."

I snuck past the stage and climbed up the side steps behind the curtain, surrounded by a flurry of excited performers, speaking in loud, exaggerated voices.

"Did you see the crowd? They loved us!" the sword-swallower exclaimed.

"We were the bee's knees tonight!" an acrobat agreed.

I smiled at their enthusiastic expressions. Looking around for a familiar face, I spied Bella the ballerina, who'd already changed into a smart wool suit, yet she was easy to recognize from the tiara still attached to her head, her long blonde hair in a bun. Always a prima donna.

When I approached, she frowned and turned in the other direction. Frantic, I poked my head down a few halls but couldn't find Derek. I saw Milo rush past followed by his assistant, still in their sparkly costumes topped with capes. Her long black velvet cape fanned out as she hurried by, and I held out my arm to stop her.

"You're Millie, right? Have you seen Derek? I didn't see him onstage after the show."

"Oh, I'm sure he's around here somewhere." She threw out her hands and kept walking. "You know how crazy things get after a performance."

Trying to stall, my eyes focused on a striking jeweled brooch shaped like a horseshoe pinned on her velvet lapel.

"What a pretty pin!" I reached out to touch the gleaming gem, realizing it was the same one the wealthy woman described at the Galvez. "Very chic." And expensive, I thought.

Her face brightened and she placed her hand over the pin, possessively. "It's a gift from a fella. I couldn't possibly afford such a luxury on my pauper's salary."

"Lucky you. Who's the generous guy?" I smiled.

Was Millie having an affair with Milo, twice her age? Perhaps it was an actor or musician—or did she steal the jewelry herself?

"Oh, he works with the troupe." Millie shrugged, looking around nervously.

"So unusual. Looks like a Flato design." I watched her reaction.

"Flato?" Her blue eyes flashed and her sweet face turned stony when she realized that I knew. "Thanks. Say, I think Derek may be in his dressing room."

She led me by the elbow down a side hall to a room in the back, away from the gaiety and the noise. I noticed her fingers felt sticky, waxy—rosin?

"I don't need an escort." I yanked away from her grasp, but her talons dug deeper as she shoved me inside. Various props covered the room, a rack of costumes stood to one side, and a row of make-up mirrors lined one wall. At least she told the truth about the dressing room.

"What do you want?" she hissed, twisting my arm.

Ouch! I had no idea such a tiny gal could be so strong. "Jewelry, is that it? Did Derek send you here?"

"Jewelry?" I tried to remain calm, so she wouldn't overreact. "Horsefeathers!" I forced a laugh. "I got worried when Derek didn't make his curtain call, that's all."

Her eyes narrowed. "How much did he tell you?"

My heart began a slow thud. "Enough to know the troupe is in trouble. Maybe I can help you?"

"How?" Millie's sweet face twisted. "By ratting us out to the cops? Your Fed fella? The papers?"

"I'm here as a friend, not as a reporter. Derek said Draper was behind all these thefts, that you were all victims, forced to steal on demand."

She let out a sigh. "Now you understand the pressure we're under, trying to keep this stupid show going. They expect us to perform round the clock, onstage and off."

"You mean Milo and Draper? Did they force Patrick to steal the jewels?"

She shook her head no, blinking back tears. "Poor Patrick. He only wanted to help."

"Patrick stole the jewels for you?"

When she didn't reply, I tried a different approach. Playing on a hunch, I said, "Derek told me Patrick was in love with you. I'm sure you were devastated when you found out he was murdered."

"I wanted to die myself." Her eyes misted. "But we kept our romance a secret, because of the owner. He forbade anyone in the troupe to date or...have relations. Dumb rules. Patrick wanted to get away so we could start over, just the two of us. He promised to give me a diamond ring to show our bond."

Suddenly his actions made sense. Is that why he stole the diamond ring from the Turtle?

"What about the second victim? Nick, the Turtle? Was he connected?"

"I'll say! He was the middleman—the bastard who killed Patrick. We shut him up but good." Her face froze and she clamped a dainty hand over her mouth.

"We?" I held my breath. "Who—you and Derek?"

Ignoring my question, Millie stuck her head out the door, turning right and left. "I think your fella is looking for you."

"Agent Burton?" I peeked outside the door, but I only saw half-dressed performers, clutching their costumes and running around, packing up, carrying boxes and trunks.

That's when I heard her say, "Sorry, sister, but you know too much."

I twirled around to see Millie grab a silver candlestick, and that's when the world went black.

CHAPTER FORTY-ONE

A jolt shook me awake and I felt dizzy, disoriented, as if I'd been asleep for a month. I tried to stretch but my legs and hands hit the sides of a wooden box. My head throbbed and I felt a knot on top starting to swell. Luckily my thick wool cloche helped shield the blow from the heavy silver candlestick.

Where was I? What happened? With a start, I realized they must have crammed me into the "vanishing act" box. Were they going to make me disappear, permanently? My heart seized and I took a few deep breaths to calm down. The small decorative cut-outs in the box provided just enough ventilation and visibility.

Faint images came to me as I retraced my last steps. Burton and I had gone to see the vaudeville show. Derek...Millie, the magician's assistant. She must be working with Milo—and they'd knocked me out, and trapped me inside his trick box. I knew there had to be a latch or some sort of opening inside the box for the trick to work. Frantic, I felt along the rough wooden walls for a hidden panel, a lock, some sort of internal opening.

Loud voices surrounded me, a jumble of words, street noise. I strained to listen but the voices seemed to meld together, not making sense. Without warning, one side of the box lifted, then the other, knocking my head against the end. God, as if I didn't already have a blinding headache.

A male voice I didn't recognize: "What should we do with her?"

"I'll drop her off somewhere and take my box. Just leave her over here for now."

Milo? Where were they taking me? Whoever the culprit was, he wasn't thinking clearly. What threat was I to a traveling vaudeville show and a group of jewel thieves?

Then just as suddenly, the box dropped with a thud. Damn, that hurt my back and head all over again. At least now I could see some light filtering down through the cut-outs. They must be closer to the street, ready to escape.

Where was Burton? How could he ever find me, hidden inside this box? If I screamed, they might knock me out again—or worse. I had to find a way out. Surely there was a way out. Despite the cool fall air, my face started to sweat and I felt hot and sticky all over. I never knew how claustrophobic I was until I got stuck in this coffin.

"Got the jewels?" I heard a woman say, but I didn't recognize her voice. Vera, the burlesque dancer?

"They're right here," Milo said in his soothing tone. "They'll have to kill me before they ever find them."

"Don't say that, love," she pleaded. So Milo had another partner in crime besides Millie.

Slowly the voices faded, and I realized I had to move fast. Luckily the box shifted slightly when it was dropped, just enough to loosen a section on one wall. I peered out the side and saw that they'd dropped me—the box—outside by the parking lot.

Through the cut-outs, I saw a flurry of activity behind Martini Theatre: Apparently Milo and his crooked pals were packing up his props and boxes. Was he going to leave me here? Desperate to escape, I tugged on the panel, hoping to pry it loose, but it remained in place. As I patted the walls, my hands caught on rough patches of wood and splinters stabbed my fingers.

My elbow hit a metal hinge and I turned sideways until I felt a latch on the edge of a lower panel. An opening? Squinting in the dark, I fumbled with the locked trap door, pushing with my shoulder until I forced open the panel. Trouble was, the box sat on its side but I twisted my back, and managed to squeeze out the door. Hooray!

Crawling on my hands and knees, I inched out of the box and ended up in the parking lot, my skin scraped till it was bloody. Finally, I was free!

My head reeling, I stumbled forward, trying to get my bearings. Since the area was dark, I tiptoed toward Martini Theatre until I was out of view. When the voices got louder, I darted behind the theatre, my heart beating so hard and fast, I felt as if my chest might explode.

When I thought the coast was clear, I turned to go inside, to find James. Instead a man yanked me up by my arm and I recognized him at once by his glittering costume: the master of ceremonies and owner, Dan Draper.

"Who have we here?" Draper said, jerking me to my feet. "Say, you're that nosy reporter from the paper. What are you doing snooping around the back lot?"

"I'm not snooping. They locked me up in that stupid magic box." I struggled to get loose and pointed to the coffin-like container.

He frowned, alarmed. "Who's they? What did you do?"

"Nothing. I was looking for Derek." I tried to squirm out of his grasp, but he clamped my arms like iron bands.

"You're a friend of Derek's? What do you want?"

"He didn't show up during the curtain call and I got worried." I'd had enough chit-chat. "Did you know Milo and his friends are loading up his truck, ready to get-away?"

Draper gave me the once-over. "Says you. I have a good mind to stick you back in this box myself."

"See for yourself." I pointed down the alley. "Milo and Millie are making a run for it, as we speak."

Draper stole a backwards glance as he raced down the alley to the truck. I headed toward the commotion, and heard Milo and Draper battling it out, yelling insults, while the troupe crowded around to watch. With their flamboyant costumes and exaggerated mannerisms, the spectacle seemed like a melodramatic fight scene in a play.

"How long did you think this charade would last?" Milo faced Draper head-on, waving his arms.

"You planned this all along, you back-stabbing bastard!" Draper moved forward, clenching his fist. "Do you know what those gangsters might do to me, to all of us, if we don't turn over the jewelry?"

"Hell, yes. Why do you think I'm leaving town? Now it's your problem, not mine."

With that, Milo attempted to jump into his truck, with Vera, the burlesque dancer, gunning the engine. Draper lunged at Milo, yanking on his arm, almost pulling off his sparkly jacket. Milo tried to shove Draper back with the door, and succeeded in knocking him to the ground.

"Step on it, Vera!" he yelled. The truck jerked forward while Millie held on for dear life in the back, sandwiched in between the boxes. I suppose my box was useless, especially after I'd clawed and mangled it to death.

Draper got up and chased the truck until it was out of sight. Wheezing and panting, he paused to catch his breath, then got into a new Ford, and drove off after them.

Still dizzy, my head aching, I bolted toward the theatre, and ran right into Agent Burton. He enveloped me in a warm hug. "What happened to you? Are you hurt?"

"They stuck me in a trick box." I gulped, breathing hard. "Hurry, Draper's getting away!" I pointed down the alley. "Milo's escaped with Millie, his assistant. Vera, the dancer, is driving his truck. I still can't find Derek. Can you catch them in time?"

"Don't worry, a truck full of vaudeville performers in costume is hard to miss." He grinned. "Besides, there's only one way out of Galveston."

CHAPTER FORTY-TWO

"I think Milo and Millie killed the Turtle," I gasped, my ribs still sore. "And I'm positive the Turtle killed Patrick."

"Did Milo or Millie confess?" Burton's eyes widened.

"Not exactly." I leaned against him for support, his arm propping me up. "We need to find Derek. He may be locked in a box, like me. Got any back-up?"

Burton nodded. "Soon as you disappeared, I called the station for help. They're searching the lobby."

As Burton and I raced into the theatre, I briefly filled him in on my ordeal. Burton commanded the cops: "Head the truck off at Broadway. You can't miss them—they're still in costume. But be careful of the boxes in back. An actor may be trapped inside, dead or alive."

Dead or alive? My heart sank at the thought.

Impatient, I tugged on his arm. "What are we waiting for? Let's go! Where's your car?"

"Sure you're up to a police chase? Possible shooting? Could get messy." Burton eyed me. "Don't forget, they're cold-blooded killers."

"They're desperate vaudevillians, not real villains. We need to catch them before they reach the causeway."

The causeway bridge opened at random day and night to allow large ships and freighters across the bay. If Milo's truck made it across the bridge first, then they could easily disappear in the traffic going to Houston.

"Good point. OK, I'm game if you are." He grabbed my hand and we rushed to his Roadster, parked in front. "Hang on to your hat, what's left of it."

While Burton raced after the caravan, I held onto the car straps, my heart thudding like a thunderstorm. Was Derek still alive? Would we catch them in time? The night breeze felt refreshing and cool, a welcome change after being locked in that vault of a box.

Burton turned onto Broadway, gunning his engine. A half-moon illuminated the boulevard, the only road leading to the causeway, lighting up the Texas Heroes monument at 25th Street. His Roadster easily overtook the cops' old cars and as we raced by, I spied dim tail lights in the distance. A trolley clanged past, heading out of town.

"We've almost caught up," I said, breathing hard. "Why don't you get in front, try to block their way?"

"Too risky." Burton shook his head. "I thought of shooting their tires but it's dangerous to do in the dark."

"You're right. We don't want anyone to get hurt."

"You mean Derek?" Burton raised his brows. "I have an idea. There's a flashlight in my glove box. I'll pull alongside them and you flash the light off and on, signal them to stop."

"Sure, if you think they'll pay attention." As we overtook the truck, I waved my arms wildly, then flashed the light off and on, but they ignored our warning. Figured.

Behind us, the cop cars gained momentum, their sirens blaring. He groaned, "Now the truck will really speed up."

I looked in the back seat, hoping to find an object, anything to slow them down. On the floor, I felt a long wooden stick: A baseball bat? Was it for protection or for raids? I held it up for his approval. "How about this?"

"You want me to beat them up with a baseball bat?" Burton frowned. "What happened to no one getting hurt?"

"No, I meant throw a bat at their tires. It may slow the truck down long enough for us to stop them."

He grinned. "Worth a try. You can steer while I try to get a good shot. Ever driven a car before?"

"My dad let me drive around his parking lot for fun."

"Here, take the wheel. I trust you."

"You do?" I felt the steering wheel vibrate in my grip, the car shake momentarily as his foot slipped on the pedal. "How fast does this go?"

"Fast enough. Fifty or sixty if I floor it. Let's get on their right side so I can get a good shot."

With all my strength, I pulled the car around the truck to the right, feeling his body, taut and muscular, as I leaned over. My eyes darted back and forth, trying to watch the road while Burton took aim. With a grunt, he tossed the bat in front of the old truck—just in time for the wheels to hit. The brakes squealed, then I heard a snap as the tires ground down on the bat, hard. A piece flew out, almost hitting the cops in the car behind us. Did it pop a tire?

Vera swerved toward Burton's Roadster, the truck weaving all over the road, then ramming into a palm tree. A squad car arrived on the scene first and a young cop rushed up, yanking Milo out of the passenger seat.

"Looks like Rusty beat me to the punch." Burton seemed angry. "Wait here, make sure no one gets away."

Sit by and miss all the action? No, thanks.

Burton pulled Vera out of the truck, grabbed her keys and clasped her arm tight. "Well, hello, tall, blond and handsome," she purred, still half-dressed in her burlesque outfit. He turned her over to a cop, then looked for Milo—who was running down Broadway to catch the trolley.

"What the hell?" he asked the red-headed cop. "Why didn't you arrest him? He's getting away!"

Rusty held up his arms, his wrists handcuffed. "He hypnotized me! Before I knew it, he took my handcuffs. Get me out of these damn things!" I suppressed a smile as Burton shook his head in disbelief, unlocking the cuffs.

"Don't just stand there. Go get him!" He pointed toward the trolley, directing two cops who were standing around, laughing at Rusty, jabbing elbows. Surprised by Burton's tone, they chased after Milo, who by now had boarded the trolley heading to Houston.

"Where's Draper?" Burton asked a senior cop.

"I lost him," he stammered, wiping his face.

"Damn it!" Burton exploded. "Let's set up a roadblock. Spread out and canvas the area. He could be hiding anywhere by now. Try to retrace our route, see if you can find him down the road."

I noticed a movement by the truck and moved closer, just in time to see Millie jump off the truck bed, onto the easement. "Where do you think you're going?" I hissed, grabbing her wrist tight. She stared at me in alarm, as if she'd seen a ghost. "That wasn't very nice of you, knocking me out and locking me in that trick box."

"I'm sorry..." She began to cry. "I just panicked."

I didn't fall for her crocodile tears. "Tell me, where's Derek? Did you lock him up in a coffin too? Is he alive?"

"He's fine. Milo just wanted to scare him, drop him off on the road. No one was supposed to get hurt."

"Tell that to poor Patrick. He and Derek were onto your scheme. So he was killed for a few baubles?"

Her face was pale as the moonlight. "Don't you understand? I did it for Patrick, the whole troupe." She gestured to a painted Egyptian-style sarcophagus on the truck bed that I recognized from Milo's act. "Derek's in that pharaoh coffin thing. Take a look."

As I turned, I felt a hard metal object shoved into my back. "Let go of her. Now."

A familiar voice. I whirled around to face my assailant, my body starting to shake. Draper grabbed my neck, the gun pressed deeper into my spine. "What are you going to do? Shoot me over a few gems? Strangle me to death?"

"Don't do it, Daddy," I heard Millie say. "We're already in enough hot water."

Daddy? Draper was her father? I squirmed under his tight grasp, trying to pry free from his chokehold.

"Did you know this bitch found the jewels, our jewels, at that goddamn dive? No one was supposed to know. Then she gave them to the cops, like a goody two-shoes."

How did he find out? The dirty cop? "That's not exactly what happened..." I gasped. His grip tightened on my windpipe, and I clawed at his fingers, trying to breathe.

A semi-circle of cops moved toward us, with Burton in the lead. "Drop the gun, Draper. She's no threat to you."

"Wanna bet? This busybody was nosing around the theatre, asking lots of questions, getting in the way." Draper hid behind me, using my body as a shield.

"You've already got two murders on your hands." Burton leveled his gun. "Don't make it worse. Let her go."

Despite the chilly breeze, I started to sweat, watching the men face-off. Of all my close calls, this was the worst.

"I didn't kill anyone." Draper waved the gun around, one hand clutching my neck. "I only wanted to save my vaudeville show. I'm providing family entertainment for you people, and jobs for my performers. Is that so wrong?"

Behind me, I heard a voice: "Stop, you're hurting me!"

We turned around to see Derek, holding Millie's arms behind her back, a knife to her throat. Still in costume, he looked like a real-life villain gone rogue. I felt so relieved, my body went limp.

"Let go of her, Draper," Derek threatened. "Drop the gun. Then I'll release Millie."

While Draper hesitated, frozen, I stomped on his foot, jumping back while he howled in pain. Burton knocked the gun out of his hand, and it fell onto the street with a clatter. Quickly Burton picked up the pistol, examining the chamber. "This isn't even a real gun. One of your props?"

"I fooled *you*, didn't I?" Draper scowled.

"Not for long. Looks like this will be your final act, Draper. 'Cuff him, men." The cops rushed toward us, handcuffing both Millie and Draper.

I smiled at Burton, admiring his strength, his resolve.

"I did it for you, Daddy," Millie told Draper.

Daddy? Draper was her father? "I know, baby." His sour expression softened. "I did this all for you, too. Don't worry, we'll find a way out of this mess. We always do."

The two cops showed up holding Milo, who grinned from ear to ear. "How'd you like my trick?" he asked Rusty, whose face turned as red as his hair.

"I'll show you a trick," Burton said, handcuffing Milo to both cops. "Take him downtown, boys. While you're in custody, maybe you can teach these rookies a few tricks."

"It's all smoke and mirrors and a little luck." Milo acted smug. "What do I get in return—a reduced sentence?"

"I'll see what I can do, but I'm no magician," he joked.

I smiled at Burton's jab as he and Derek flanked me on both sides. "Thanks for rescuing me." I patted their backs, too grateful to feel awkward. "Both of you."

Amused, Burton shook Derek's hand, studying his villain costume. "Appreciate your help, kid. We'd better take you to Big Red to get checked out."

"I'm fine," Derek protested. "Can we stop by the police station first? I heard an earful while those palookas thought I was unconscious."

"Sure. Wait here a minute." Burton gave the cops instructions while Derek and I piled into his Roadster.

"You make a great villain." I squeezed his hand. "But have you ever considered playing the hero for a change?"

Derek winked. "You're a heroine worth saving."

"Thanks. Glad you're OK." Blushing, I changed the subject. "Say, did you know Millie was Draper's daughter? Explains a lot."

"I had no idea," he admitted. "They fooled us all."

CHAPTER FORTY-THREE

Saturday

Saturday morning, I sat at my desk, compiling my notes for my first official news article. When Mr. Thomas and Mrs. Harper balked earlier, telling me it was too dangerous, I tried to sell them on the idea. Frankly, I was tired of always being the understudy, never the lead, at the *Gazette*.

"The *Gazette* could be the first paper to expose Draper and his band of jewel thieves," I pointed out. "Derek Hammond promised to give me an exclusive interview and inside information—access no other reporter has, including Mack. If you're not interested, I can try to sell my story in Houston, and other towns where the troupe has appeared."

I couldn't resist adding that last zinger, though I saw from their resigned expressions that they'd already agreed to give me a shot.

"Are you sure that hard news is the path you want to take, Jasmine?" Mr. Thomas asked, his craggy features downcast. "You'll be exposed to the unpleasant, seamy side of society. You may see some things you wished you'd never seen, and hope to forget."

"That's reality," I nodded with a shrug. "I wouldn't mind writing a few features and profiles. But I've had enough cotton candy fluff to last me a while."

My boss sighed, disappointed. "It's fine if Mr. Thomas wants to assign you a few news stories on the side, but I'll still need help with my column, plus proofing and editing."

"Thanks for giving me a chance. You won't be sorry."

Captain Johnson allowed me to conduct my interviews inside the "interrogation room," a glorified description of a plain back office without windows. On Friday, I got to interview Millie, the not-so-innocent magician's assistant, and boy, did I get an earful! Fortunately, she confirmed most of our theories and hypothetical scenarios in an emotional, tearful confession.

Without her make-up and flamboyant costume, she looked like a sweet school girl, no more than seventeen or eighteen. "This was all my fault. I got Patrick involved with this stupid scheme. God, the last thing I wanted was to get him killed. He was kind, a true gentleman. How did Nick recognize him, dressed as a woman? That murderer!"

"Hard to pass for a dame when you're six-feet-two in heels," I pointed out.

"You're right. I wasn't thinking." She'd covered her face and sobbed a few minutes, then wiped her eyes.

"Are you sure Nick murdered him?"

"After Nick joined the troupe, he told me he had a goldmine coming to him. Then he flat-out admitted he killed Patrick, called him a dandy, a fairy, a daffodil. I got so damn angry that the next time he came to my trailer, wanting a midnight favor, I was waiting with a steak knife."

Trying to give her the benefit of the doubt, I had to ask: "Was your dad behind this or was it self-defense?"

"Neither. I could lie and say it was an accident, but it was all my idea. I had it planned out in advance—like those gals on Murderers' Row in Chicago." Her eyes flashed, cold and unblinking, like a street light changing colors.

"What about the cuts on his neck, like Patrick's?"

"That was Milo's idea, to make it look like a copycat."

"Sounds like a crime of passion," I added, recalling Burton's description. "An isolated incident."

"Passion? More like hate. So what will happen to me?"

"Since it's your only crime, the courts may be lenient, given your age and situation." I hated to think the worst.

"Hope you're right." She blinked back tears.

I patted her hand in sympathy. "Before I go, did you know Patrick hid a diamond ring under his clothes?"

No reason to mention that the ring actually belonged to Mrs. Rose Maceo and spoil her surprise.

"A diamond ring?" Millie's face lit up and she clapped her hands like a child. "So Patrick kept his promise after all." She gave me a grateful smile as a cop cuffed her wrists with shiny steel bracelets. "Time to face the music."

Luckily, Derek suffered only a mild concussion and spent one night at Big Red. He revived long enough to give me the exclusive interview he'd promised.

"Break a leg!" he told me with a smile.

I even asked Draper and Milo a few questions, but they weren't much help, always changing their story. Later, Sammy told me that Rose Maceo was indeed at Turturo's crime scene. A snitch told Rose that the Turtle had stolen his wife's purse (with the ring) at Mario's. Rose threatened to kill him—and his wife's lover—and wanted to see his body in person. That tidbit never made it into my article.

Finally, I started writing my lead, leaving the sordid details of both murders to the crime reporters:

"A traveling vaudeville troupe recently offered thrills to Galveston audiences, but the real chills came from behind the scenes. Turns out the qualifications needed to work in Director Dan Draper's show include the ability to act, sing or dance, juggle or swallow swords, play a musical instrument—and oh, yes, the willingness to steal pricey jewelry in between gigs.

Apparently the costs of running these lavish vaudeville productions escalated over the years, and owners like Draper struggled to keep up with the times by adding more popular acts, more outlandish costumes, more elaborate sets—more money. Unfortunately for a few local belles—victims of the troupe's get-rich-quick schemes—they'll attend this season's holiday balls and festivities without their favorite jewelry and heirloom gems.

In order to earn their keep, and afford their top-billed acts, Draper anointed the orchestra as the saviors of his colorful productions—the replaceable musicians whom he forced to steal on the side so the show could go on...."

CHAPTER FORTY-FOUR

Sunday

When my article came out on Sunday, I felt a rush of pride at seeing my first byline on the front page of the *Gazette*, with the headline above the fold: VIXENS, VICTIMS AND VIOLINS with a subhead: Behind-the-Scenes Secrets of a Treasure-Stealing Vaudeville Troupe. Seemed the whole town was interested in a traveling vaudeville troupe that moonlighted as cat burglars.

Had to admit, I was delighted to hear Finn belting out the headline—my headline—up and down the street all day. Soon he'd work for us as a copy boy in the afternoons, after school—giving me a chance to teach him to read.

So what should I do for an encore?

That night, Agent Burton picked me up to celebrate at our favorite Beach Gang night spot, the Hollywood Dinner Club. Dressed in my new rose beaded gown, matching headband and velvet coat with gold brocade cuffs and shawl collar, we arrived fashionably late, just in time to hear the jazz band play: *"Yes, sir, That's My Baby."*

I did a double-take when my brother Sammy greeted us at the door, looking snazzy in his black tux and tie, like he was dressed for his own wedding.

"Sammy, what are you doing here? You look like the peacock's plume! Did Sam Maceo invite you tonight?"

He nodded. "Tonight and every night. He asked me to be the manager here, full-time."

"Attaboy!"   I patted his back, surprised and delighted. "What about the Oasis?"

"Frank and Dino will keep it open for now, but we plan to relocate to the Seawall as soon as possible." He gave me a big smile. "From now on, we're officially part of the Beach Gang."

"Congratulations." I hugged my only brother, sincerely happy for him and overjoyed that he was remaining in Galveston. "This is what you've always wanted."

He grinned as he escorted us to our table, a nice plush booth near the dance floor.

"Let me know if you need anything," Sammy bowed, enjoying his new role. "A bottle of Champagne?"

"Fancy French Champagne, if you please." I nodded. "We've got a lot to celebrate, including your new job. Maybe you can join us later?"

"Thanks for the offer. Sure, I'd enjoy a break. I doubt Big Sam would mind. Enjoy your evening, sis."

Sis? How nice! After he left, I told Burton, "Sammy's a natural. This position fits him like a glove. And as long as he's working here, he's safe from the Downtown Gang."

"Better to be on the winning team, than a losing one." Burton smiled. "Speaking of, don't you think *we* make a great team? Fighting crime, solving mysteries?"

What was he getting at? "Of course we do. Why?"

He reached for my hand. "Just wondering if we should make it exclusive. You and me. Official."

"Official?" Did he mean engaged...? What brought this on—Derek? Caught off guard, I tried to lighten the mood. "I'm flattered, but...I'm not ready to get handcuffed yet."

"Too bad. I've got handcuffs in my car," he cracked.

I hope he didn't expect me to jump for joy and rush into his arms like a giddy film star. Frankly, I had serious concerns and doubts about his job, our future.

"Don't you want to travel the world first, experience different cultures? London, Paris, Rome, Cairo..." I stalled, logic battling my feelings. "To be honest, I'm not ready to settle down...or even think about getting engaged yet."

"Who said anything about settling down? Why don't we have our own exciting adventures—together?"

"Sounds swell, James, but..." How could I explain? "Tell the truth, your job frightens me to death. I'm terrified that you could be killed on the job—either by gangsters or your own unscrupulous men. I can't live with that constant fear hanging over my head. How can you?"

"Is that why you're holding back?" He frowned. "You know Prohibition is on the way out. Even our government realizes no one pays attention to the Volstead Act."

"I didn't know Prohibition agents went after jewel thieves and murderers," I added. "I noticed how the men followed your lead when you caught Milo and Millie."

"As a Federal agent, I got involved since the troupe was operating across state lines. Besides, Johnson asked me to help after we first found Patrick." Burton leaned forward. "To be honest, all these murder investigations are making me consider a career as a Homicide detective."

"But that's not any safer!" I sighed, all balled up, wary. "Face it, police work is dangerous, unpredictable."

"Who wants to be predictable?" Burton stroked my hand, lacing his fingers with mine. "Danger doesn't seem to deter you, chasing after all these crime stories. Don't you want to ditch this one-horse town, move to a big city?"

"At last count, I saw two horses and a donkey cart." I grinned, trying to lighten the mood. All this discussion of the future made my head spin. Who knew what could happen tomorrow, let alone a year or two from now? "Yes, I want to leave Galveston, but I need to get a few articles under my hat before I make that leap."

"Good idea," he nodded. "By the way, I hear Sheriff Sanders may be coming back to Galveston, so I could ask if there's an opening in Houston."

"You don't say!" I perked up. "Aunt Eva will be thrilled. But you told me Houston was a cesspool—and besides, Sammy just moved back to town."

"True. What about New York? I've got a job waiting for me in Manhattan. Wouldn't you like to follow in the footsteps of your idol, Nellie Bly?"

Tempting. I'd always wanted to live in New York City, try my luck in the Big Apple. "There's only one Nellie Bly."

"There's only one Jasmine Cross." Burton gave me a cryptic smile. "Don't worry, we'll figure it out. Together."

Then I had a brainstorm: "What about becoming a private eye? Maybe I could help you with a few cases."

"That's a thought. I'll need more experience, but it's a possibility for the future."

In the background, the jazz band played a favorite new tune, *Star Dust,* and I watched a few couples sway to the music, arms linked, bodies pressed close.

Burton held out his hand. "Care to dance?"

"I'd love to, James." I flashed a smile, our eyes locking, my heart humming. "Takes two to tango."

1920s JAZZ AGE SLANG

All wet - Wrong, incorrect ("You're all wet!" "That's nuts!")

And how! - I strongly agree!

Applesauce! – Nonsense, Bullshit (e.g. "That's ridiculous!")

Attaboy! - Well done! Bravo! Also: Attagirl!

Baby grand - A heavily-built man

Balled up - Confused, Unsure

Baloney - Nonsense, Hogwash, Bullshit

Bathtub Booze - Home-brewed liquor, Hooch (often in tubs)

Bearcat - A hot-blooded or fiery girl

"Beat it!" - Scram, Get lost

Bee's Knees - An extraordinary person, thing or idea

Berries - Attractive or pleasing; Swell ("It's the berries!")

Big Cheese - Big shot, an important or influential person

Blotto - Very drunk, Smashed

Blow - (a) A wild, crazy party (b) To leave

Bluenose - A prim, puritanical person; a prude, a killjoy

Bootleg - Illegal liquor, Hooch, Booze

Breezer (1925) - A convertible car

Bruno - Tough guy, enforcer

Bug-eyed Betty - An unattractive girl or student

Bum's rush - Ejection by force from an establishment

Bump Off - To murder, to kill

Bunk – Bullshit, Hooey, Wrong as in : "That's Bunk!"

Cake-eater - A lady's man, a gigolo; an effeminate male

Carry a Torch - To have a crush on someone

Cat's Meow/Whiskers - Splendid, Stylish, Swell

Cat's Pajamas - Terrific, Wonderful, Great

Clams - Money, Dollars, Bucks

Coffin varnish - Bootleg liquor, Hooch (often poisonous)

Copacetic - Excellent, all in order

Dame/Doll - A female, woman, girl (usually attractive)

Dolled up - Dressed up in "glad rags"

Don't know from nothing - Don't have any information

Don't take any wooden nickels - Don't do anything stupid

Dough - Money, Cash

Drugstore Cowboy - A guy who picks up girls in public places

Dry up - Shut up; Get lost

Ducky - Fine, very good, swell (Also: Peachy)
Dumb Dora - An idiot, a dumbbell; a stupid female
Egg - Nice person, One who likes the big life
Fall Guy - Victim of a frame
Fella - Fellow, man, guy (very common in the 1920s)
Fire extinguisher - A chaperone, a fifth wheel
Flat Tire - A dull, boring date (Also: Pill, Pickle, Oilcan)
Flour lover - A gal wearing too much powder and make-up
Frame - To give false evidence, to set up someone
Gate Crasher - A party crasher, an uninvited guest
Giggle Water - Liquor, Hooch, Booze, Alcohol
Gin Joint/Gin Mill - A bar, a speakeasy
Glad rags - "Going out on the town" clothes, Fancy dress attire
Go chase yourself - "Get lost, beat it, scram"
Hard-Boiled - A tough, strong guy (e.g. "He sure is hard-boiled!")
Hayburner - (a) A gas-guzzling car (b) A losing racehorse
Heebie-jeebies (1926) - The shakes, the jitters, (from a hit song)
High-hat - Snobby, snooty
Holding the bag - To be cheated or blamed for something
Hooch - Bootleg liquor, illegal alcohol
Hooey - Bullshit, Nonsense, Baloney (1925 to 1930)
Hoofer - Dancer, Chorus girl
Horsefeathers – Ridiculous, Silly, Bunk, Nonsense, Wrong
Hotsy-Totsy - Attractive, Pleasing
(I'll be a) Monkey's uncle – Expression of amazement, disbelief
    (re: Scopes' 1925 trial challenging Darwin's theory of evolution)
Jack - Cash, Money
Jake - Great, Fine, OK (i.e. "Everything's jake.")
Jeepers creepers – Exclamation of surprise ("Jesus Christ!")
Joe Brooks - A well-groomed man, natty dresser, student
Juice Joint - A speakeasy, bar
Keen - Attractive or appealing
Killjoy - Dud, a dull, boring person, a party pooper, a spoilsport
Lollygagger - (a) A flirtatious male (b) A lazy or idle person
Lounge Lizard - A gigolo; a flirtatious, sexually-active male
Mick - A derogatory term for an Irishman
Milquetoast (1924) - A very timid person; a hen-pecked male
    (from the comic book character Casper Milquetoast)
Moll - (Gun Moll) A gangster's girlfriend
Neck - Make-out, kiss with passion

"Oh yeah?" - Expression of doubt ("Is that so?")

On a toot – On a drinking binge, Bar-hopping

On the lam - Fleeing from police

On the level - Legitimate, Honest

On the trolley – In the know, Savvy ("You're on the trolley!")

On the up and up - Trustworthy, Honest

Ossified – Drunk, Plastered

Palooka - A derogatory term for a low-class or dumb person
  (Re: Comic strip character Joe Palooka, a poor immigrant)

Piker - (a) Cheapskate (b) Coward

Pitch a little woo - To flirt, try to charm and attract the opposite sex

Rag-a-muffin - An unkempt, dirty and disheveled person/child

Razz - To tease, to insult or make fun of

Rhatz or Ratz! - "Too bad!" or "Darn it!"

Ritzy - Elegant, High-class, "Putting on the Ritz" (Re: Ritz Hotel)

Rotgut - Cheap hooch, inferior alcohol, poisonous bootleg liquor

Rummy - A drunken bum, an intoxicated man, a wino

Sap - A fool, an idiot; very common term in the 1920s

"Says you!" - A reaction of disbelief or doubt (also "Hogwash!")

Screaming meemies - The shakes, the jitters, to be afraid

Screwy - Crazy, Nuts ("You're screwy!")

Sheba - An attractive and sexy woman; girlfriend
  (popularized by the film "Queen of Sheba")

Sheik - A handsome man with sex appeal
  (from Rudolph Valentino's film "The Sheik")

Scram – "Get out," "Beat it"; to leave immediately

Speakeasy - An illicit bar selling bootleg liquor

Spiffy - An elegant appearance, well-dressed, fine

Stuck On - Having a crush on, attracted to

Sugar Daddy - A rich, older gentleman (usually married)

Swanky - Elegant, Ritzy

Swell - Wonderful, Great, Fine, A-OK

Take for a Ride -To try to kill someone (bump them off)

Torpedo - A hired gun, a hit man

Upchuck - To vomit, especially after drinking too much

Wet Blanket - A dud, a dull date or person, a party pooper

Whoopee - (Make whoopee) To have fun/a good time, to party

"You don't say!" – i.e. "Is that so?" "Oh, really? I didn't know"

"You slay me!" -"You're hilarious!" or "That's funny!"

Zozzled - Drunk, intoxicated, (Also: Plastered, Smashed)

BIOGRAPHY

Ellen Mansoor Collier is a Houston-based freelance writer and editor whose articles and essays have been published in several national magazines including: BIOGRAPHY, FAMILY CIRCLE, MODERN BRIDE, NATION'S BUSINESS, FIRST, GLAMOUR, COSMOPOLITAN, COUNTRY ACCENTS, THE WRITER, PLAYGIRL, etc. Several of her short stories have appeared in WOMAN'S WORLD.

A flapper at heart, she loves all things Deco and runs MODERNEMILLIE on Etsy, specializing in vintage accessories.

Formerly she worked as a magazine editor and freelance writer, and in advertising/marketing and public relations. Collier graduated from the University of Texas at Austin with a degree in Magazine Journalism, where she lived in a 1926 dorm her freshman year. She served as an editor on UTmost magazine and was active in Women in Communications (W.I.C.I.), acting as President her senior year. During college summers, she worked as a reporter on a community newspaper and once as a cocktail waitress, both jobs providing background experience for her Jazz Age mystery series.

FLAPPERS, FLASKS AND FOUL PLAY is the first novel in her Jazz Age Mystery series, first released in 2012. BATHING BEAUTIES, BOOZE AND BULLETS, the sequel, was published in 2013. GOLD DIGGERS, GAMBLERS AND GUNS was released in 2014, followed by VAMPS, VILLAINS AND VAUDEVILLE in 2015, all set in 1920s Galveston.

"When you grow up in Houston, Galveston is like a second home. I had no idea this sleepy beach town had such a wild and colorful past until we visited a former speakeasy-turned-diner and heard some colorful gangster stories. Curious, I began doing research and became fascinated by the real-life legends and landmarks of 1920s Galveston. In my series, I tried to recreate that exciting era from an ambitious, adventurous young reporter's point of view."

DEDICATION

Thanks to Gary E. Collier, my supportive husband, who has helped me from day one and read several drafts of this novel.

To my mother, May Mansoor Munn, also a writer, who inspired me to write at a young age and often offered words of wisdom, and especially to my late father, Isa Mansoor, who enjoyed our family trips to Galveston as much as we did.

ACKNOWLEDGEMENTS

Many thanks to my wonderful beta readers and editors, including Amy Metz, who was there from page one, as well as Rana Copeland, Gary E. Collier and Karen Muller, whose suggestions and feedback helped shape the story. A special thank you to Dr. Dick Elam, whose meticulous editing sharpened the manuscript. I greatly appreciate your enthusiasm and encouragement!

I owe a debt of gratitude to *Texas Monthly* contributor Gary Cartwright, author of *Galveston: A History of the Island*, whose painstaking research made Galveston's past come alive.

For my cover art, I'm delighted to credit George Barbier, the fabulous French Deco artist (1882-1932) of the Pantomime Stage illustration (c. 1924). The alternate cover features period photographs of a Hollywood starlet and a beautiful Austin theatre, the Paramount. My talented husband, Gary, designed and formatted the interior.

I'm grateful to the friends and family members who offered support and words of wisdom, especially Summer Lane and Noreen Marcus, and of course my family, Mom, Albert, my brother, Jeff and my late dad, Isa Mansoor, and my aunt Sina Mansur Hutchison, forever young.

I especially want to thank my swell husband Gary, who not only read several drafts and formatted the print versions of each novel, he always offered his help, ideas and encouragement.